hausfrau

random house / new york

hausfrau

[a novel]

jill alexander essbaum

Hausfrau is a work of fiction. Names, characters, places, and incidents are the product of the author's imagination or are used fictitiously. Any resemblance to actual events or persons, living or dead, is entirely coincidental.

A Random House International Edition

Published by Random House, an imprint and division of Random House LLC, a Penguin Random House Company, New York.

Published in the United States in hardcover by Random House, an imprint and division of Random House LLC.

LIBRARY OF CONGRESS CATALOGING-IN-PUBLICATION DATA
Essbaum, Jill Alexander.
Hausfrau: a novel / Jill Alexander Essbaum.
pages cm
ISBN 978-0-8129-9918-1
eBook ISBN 978-0-8129-9754-5
1. Married women—Fiction. 2. Adultery—Fiction. 3. Self-realization in women—Fiction. 4. Domestic fiction. 5. Psychological fiction. I. Title.
PS3555.S66H38 2015
813'.54—dc23 2014026118

Printed in the United States of America on acid-free paper

www.atrandom.com

246897531

Book design by Susan Turner

for my father, Jim Schulz

1942–1999

When the morning skies grow red
And o'er us their radiance shed,
Thou, O Lord, appeareth in their light.
When the Alps glow bright with splendor,
Pray to God, to Him surrender,
For you feel and understand,
For you feel and understand,
That he dwelleth in this land.
That he dwelleth in this land.

—First verse of the "Schweizerpsalm," the Swiss national anthem

Like everything metaphysical the harmony between thought and reality is to be found in the grammar of the language.

—Ludwig Wittgenstein

A man who has not passed through the inferno of his passions has never overcome them.

—Carl Jung

Love is a fire. But whether it is going to warm your hearth or burn down your house, you can never tell.

—Joan Crawford

september

1

ANNA WAS A GOOD WIFE, MOSTLY.

It was mid-afternoon, and the train she rode first wrenched then eased around a bend in the track before it pulled into Bahnhof Dietlikon at thirty-four past the hour, as ever. It's not just an adage, it's an absolute fact: Swiss trains run on time. The S8 originated in Pfäffikon, a small town thirty kilometers away. From Pfäffikon, its route sliced upward along the shores of the Zürichsee, through Horgen on the lake's west bank, through Thalwil, through Kilchberg. Tiny towns in which tiny lives were led. From Pfäffikon, the train made sixteen stops before it reached Dietlikon, the tiny town in which Anna's own tiny life was led. Thus the ordinary fact of a train schedule modulated Anna's daily plans. Dietlikon's bus didn't run into the city. Taxicabs were expensive and impractical. And while the Benz family owned a car, Anna didn't drive. She did not have a license.

So her world was tightly circumscribed by the comings and goings of locomotives, by the willingness of Bruno, Anna's husband, or Ursula, Bruno's mother, to drive her places unreachable by bus, and by the engine of her own legs and what distance they could carry her, which was rarely as far as she'd have liked to go.

But Swiss trains really do run on time and Anna managed with minimal hassle. And she liked riding the trains; she found a lulling comfort in the way they rocked side to side as they moved forward.

Edith Hammer, another expatriate, once told Anna that there was only one reason the Swiss trains ever ran late.

"When someone jumps in front of one."

Frau Doktor Messerli asked Anna if she had ever considered or attempted suicide. "Yes," Anna admitted to the first question. And to the second, "Define 'attempt.' "

Doktor Messerli was blond, small-bodied, and of an ambiguous but late middle age. She saw clients in an office on Trittligasse, a cobbled, lightly trafficked street just west of Zürich's art museum. She'd studied medical psychiatry in America but had received her analytic training at the Jung Institute in Küsnacht, a Zürich municipality not less than seven kilometers away. Swiss by birth, Doktor Messerli nonetheless spoke an impeccable, if heavily accented, English. Her *w*'s masqueraded as *v*'s and her vowels were as open and elongated as parabolic arches: *Vhat dooo yooo sink, Anna?* she'd often ask (usually when Anna was least likely to give an honest answer).

There was a television commercial that promoted a well-known language school. In the ad, a novice naval radio operator is shown to his post by his commanding officer. Seconds into his watch the receiver pings. "Mayday! Mayday!" a markedly American voice grates through the speaker. "Can you hear us? We are sinking! We are sinking!" The operator pauses then leans toward his transmitter and replies, quite graciously, "Dis is dee Germ-ahn Coast Guard." And then: "Vhat are yooo *sinking* about?"

Anna would invariably shrug a sluggard's shrug and speak the only words that seemed worth speaking. "I don't know."

Except, of course, Anna most always did.

It was a drizzly afternoon. Swiss weather is mutable, though rarely extreme in Kanton Zürich, and typically not in September. It *was* September, for Anna's sons had already returned to school. From the station Anna walked slowly the culpable half kilometer up Dietlikon's center street, lingering over shop windows, biding small bits of time. All postcoital euphorics had evaporated, and she was left with the reins of ennui, slack in her hand. This wasn't a feeling she was new to. It was often like this, a languor that dragged and jaded. The optometrist's on-sale eyeglass display dulled her. She yawned at the *Apotheke*'s pyramid of homeopathic remedies. The bin of discount dishtowels by the SPAR bored her nearly beyond repair.

Boredom, like the trains, carried Anna through her days.

Is that true? Anna thought. *That can't be entirely true.* It wasn't. An hour earlier Anna lay naked, wet and open atop a stranger's bed in an apartment in Zürich's Niederdorf district, four stories above the old town's wending alleys and mortared stone streets upon which kiosks vended doner kebabs and bistros served communal pots of melted Emmental.

What little shame I had before is gone, she thought.

"Is there a difference between shame and guilt?" Anna asked.

"Shame is psychic extortion," Doktor Messerli answered. "Shame lies. Shame a woman and she will believe she is fundamentally wrong, organically delinquent. The only confidence she will have will be in her failures. You will never convince her otherwise."

IT WAS ALMOST 3:00 P.M. when Anna reached her sons' school. Primarschule Dorf was positioned next to the town square between the library and a three-hundred-year-old house. A month earlier on the Swiss national holiday, the square was thick with citizens eating sausages and swaying like drunkards to the live music of a folk band under a sky made bright with fireworks. During army maneuvers, soldiers parked supply trucks in sloppy diagonals next to the square's central fountain, which on summer days would be filled with splashing, naked children whose mothers sat on nearby benches reading books and eating yogurt. Bruno had finished his reserve duty years earlier. All that was left of the experience was an assault rifle in the basement. As for Anna, she didn't care for paperbacks and when her sons wanted to swim she took them to the city pool.

That day, the traffic in the square was thin. A trio of women chatted in front of the library. One pushed a stroller, another held a leash at the end of which panted a German shepherd, and a final one simply stood with empty hands. They were mothers waiting on their children and they were younger than Anna by a factor of ten years. They were milky and buoyant in places where Anna felt curdled and sunken. They wore upon their faces, Anna thought, a luminous ease of being, a relaxed comportment, a native glow.

Anna rarely felt at ease inside her skin. *I am tight-faced and thirty-seven years,* Anna thought. *I am the sum of all my twitches.* One mother tossed her a wave and a genuine, if obligatory, smile.

SHE'D MET THIS STRANGER in her German class. *But Anna—his cock's been in your mouth,* she reminded herself. *He's not really a stranger anymore.* And he wasn't. He was Archie Sutherland, Scotsman, expatriate, and, like Anna, language student. *Anna Benz, Language Student.* It was Doktor Messerli who had encouraged her to take the German course (and, by a backspin of redoubtable irony, it was Bruno who'd insisted she see a psychotherapist: *I've had enough of your fucking misery, Anna. Go fix yourself,* is what he'd said to her). Doktor Messerli then handed Anna a schedule of classes and said, "It's time you steer yourself into a trajectory that will force you into participating more fully with the world around you." The Doktor's affected speech, while condescending, was correct. It was time. It was past time.

By the end of that appointment and with some more pointed cajoling, Anna conceded and agreed to enroll in a beginner's German class at the Migros Klubschule, the very class she should have taken when, nine years prior, she arrived in Switzerland, tongue-tied, friendless, and already despairing of her lot.

An hour earlier Archie had called to Anna from his kitchen: *Would she take a coffee? A tea? Something to eat? Was there anything she needed? Anything? Anything at all?* Anna dressed cautiously, as if thorns had been sewn into the seams of her clothes.

From the street below, she heard the rising cries of children returning to school post-lunch and the voices of American sightseers who grumped about the pitch of the hill atop which Zürich's Grossmünster was built. The cathedral is a heavy building, medieval gray and inimitable, with two symmetric towers that rise flush against the church's façade and jut high above its vaulted roof like hare's ears at attention.

Or cuckold's horns.

"WHAT'S THE DIFFERENCE BETWEEN a need and a want?"

"A want is desirable, though not essential. A need is something without which you cannot survive." The Doktor added, "If you cannot live without something, you won't."

ANYTHING AT ALL? LIKE Doktor Messerli, Archie spoke a magnificently accented English intoned not by the shape-shifting consonants of High Alemannic, but by words that both roiled and wrenched open. Here an undulant *r*, there a queue of vowels rammed into one another like a smithy's bellows pressed hotly closed. Anna drew herself to men who spoke with accents. It was the lilt of Bruno's nonnative English that she let slide its thumb, its tongue into the waistband of her panties on their very first date (that, and the Williamsbirnen Schnaps, the pear tinctured eau-de-vie they drank themselves stupid with). In her youth Anna dreamed soft, damp dreams of the men she imagined she would one day love, men who would one day love her. She gave them proper names but indistinct, foreign faces: Michel, the French sculptor with long, clay-caked fingers; Dmitri, the verger of an Orthodox church whose skin smelled of camphor, of rockrose, of sandalwood resin and myrrh; Guillermo, her lover with matador hands. They were phantom men, girlhood ideations. But she mounted an entire international army of them.

It was the Swiss one she married.

If you cannot live without something, you won't.

Despite Doktor Messerli's suggestion that she enroll in these classes, Anna *did* know an elementary level of German. She got around. But hers was a German remarkable only in how badly it was cultivated and by the herculean effort she had to summon in order to speak it. For nine years, though, she'd managed with rudimentary competence. Anna had purchased stamps from the woman at the post office, consulted in semi-specifics with pediatricians and pharmacists, described the haircuts she desired to stylists, haggled prices at flea markets, made brief chitchat with neighbors, and indulged a pair of affable though persistent Zeugen Jehovas who, each month, arrived on her doorstep with a German-language copy of *The Watchtower.* Anna had also, though with less frequency, given directions to strangers, adapted recipes from cooking programs, taken notes when the chimney sweep detailed structural hazards of loose mortar joints and blocked flues, and extracted herself from citations when, upon the conductor's request, she could not produce her rail pass for validation.

But Anna's grasp of grammar and vocabulary was weak, her fluency was choked, and idioms and proper syntax escaped her completely. Occurring monthly, at least, were dozens of instances in which she commended a task into Bruno's hands. It was he who dealt with local bureaucracy, he who paid the insurance, the taxes, the house note. It was he who filed the paperwork for Anna's residency permit. And it was Bruno who handled the family's finances, for he was employed as a mid-level management banker at Credit Suisse. Anna didn't even have a bank account.

Doktor Messerli encouraged Anna to take a more active role in family matters.

"I should," Anna said. "I really should." She wasn't even sure she knew what Bruno did at work.

There was no reason Anna couldn't join the mothers chatting in the square, no rule forbidding it, nothing that prevented her from sharing in their small talk. Two of them she knew by sight and one by name, Claudia Zwygart. Her daughter Marlies was in Charles's class at school.

Anna didn't join them.

By way of explanation, Anna offered the following self-summary: *I am shy and cannot talk to strangers.*

Doktor Messerli sympathized. "It is difficult for foreigners to make Swiss friends." The problem runs deeper than a lack of command of German, itself problem enough. Switzerland is an insular country, sealed at its boundaries and neutral by choice for two centuries. With its left hand it reaches out to refugees and seekers of asylum. With its right, it snatches freshly laundered monies and Nazi gold. (Unfair? Perhaps. But when Anna was lonely she lashed out.) And like the landscape upon which they've settled, the Swiss themselves are closed at their edges. They tend naturally toward isolation, conspiring to keep outsiders at a distance by appointing not one, two, or three, but four whole national languages. Switzerland's official name is in yet a fifth: *Confoederatio Helvetica.* Most Swiss speak German however, and it is German that's spoken in Zürich.

But it's not precisely German.

Written German in Switzerland is standard schoolbook Hochdeutsch. But the Swiss speak Schwiizerdütsch, which isn't standard at all. There is no set orthography. There is no pronunciation key. There is no agreed-upon vocabulary. It varies from canton to canton. And the language itself leaps from the back of the throat like an infected tonsil trying to escape. This is only a minor exaggeration. To the non-Swiss ear it sounds as if the speaker is construing made-up words from the oddest rhythms and the queerest clipped consonants and the most perturbing arrangement of gaping, rangy vowels. It is impervious to all outside attempts to learn it, for every word is shibboleth.

Anna spoke the barest minimum of Schwiizerdütsch.

ANNA DIDN'T JOIN THE other mothers. Instead, she scuffed the sole of a brown clog against the sidewalk's curb. She fiddled with her hair and pretended to watch an invisible bird flying overhead.

It is hard to love a man outside his native tongue. And yet, it was the Swiss one Anna married.

The school bell rang and children spilled from the building and into the courtyard. Anna noticed Victor first, roughhousing with two friends. Charles followed close behind, caught in a throng of jabbering children. He ran to Anna when he spotted her, hugged her, and began prattling about his day without Anna's prompting. Victor lingered with his pals and dragged his feet. This was Victor being Victor—standoffish and moderately aloof. Anna indulged his reticence and settled on just mussing his hair. Victor grimaced.

Anna experienced her first pinpricks of guilt as they walked toward the house (she couldn't really call them pangs). They were scattershot and nondebilitating. This level of indifference was fairly new to her pathology. It rendered her queerly self-satisfied.

The Benzes lived no more than a hundred meters away from Primarschule Dorf. Their house would be visible from the schoolyard but for the *Kirchgemeindehaus*, the nineteenth-century timber-framed parish hall of the village church, which stood exactly between the two. Anna did not usually walk her children home. But it was an hour after the fact and she still felt Archie's hands on her breasts; a moderate remorse was in order.

They moved to Switzerland in June of ninety-eight. Anna, pregnant and exhausted, had no wherewithal for debate. She telegraphed her compliance in long, silent sighs and hid her many anxieties inside one of her heart's thousand chambers. She looked for a bright side, a glass half full. Who, after all, wouldn't snatch the chance to live in Europe were it offered? In high school Anna locked herself in her room most nights and obsessed over the many *elsewheres* her men would one day take her. In those limp, submissive dreams she gave her men entire charge. Bruno had worked for Credit Suisse for years. They wondered, Would he take a Zürich post? Anna was married and pregnant and more or less in love. That was enough. *This will be enough*, she thought.

And so they moved to Dietlikon. It was close enough to Zürich to be serviced by two city trains. It was near a large shopping center. Its roads were safe and its houses were well kept and the town's motto held great promise. It was printed on the website and on pamphlets. It was posted on the sign in front of the *Gemeinde,* and noted on the first page of the *Kurier,* Dietlikon's small weekly newspaper: *Menschlich, offen, modern.* Personal. Open. Modern. Anna poured all optimism into those three words.

Dietlikon was also Bruno's hometown. His *Heimatort.* The place to which the prodigal returned. Anna was twenty-eight. Bruno at thirty-four strode effortlessly back into his native space. Easy enough to do—Ursula lived just a short walk away on Klotenerstrasse in the house in which she raised Bruno and his sister Daniela. Oskar, Bruno's father, was over a decade dead.

Bruno argued a good case. Living in Dietlikon would merit their children (*We're having more? Are you sure?* They hadn't even really deliberated the first) a wholesome, unbounded childhood, safe and stable. Once she settled into the idea of it (and after Bruno swore that all future children would be discussed prior to their conception), Anna was able to concede the move's virtues. So when it did happen, rarely in those first months, that she grew lonesome or wistful for people, things, or places she never dreamed she would miss, she consoled herself by imagining the baby's face. *Will I have a ruddish-cheeked Heinz to call me Mueti? A Heidi of my own with blond and braided hair?* And Bruno and Anna were, more or less, in love.

THE QUALIFICATION "MORE OR less" troubled Doktor Messerli.

Anna explained. "Is that not always the case? Given any two people in a relationship, one will always love more, the other less. Right?"

* * *

At eight, Victor was Anna's eldest child. Charles was six. They were indeed the ruddish-toned, milk-fed children Anna had imagined. They were ash blond and hazel eyed. They were all boy, rowdy, absolutely brothers, and without a doubt the sons of the man Anna had married.

"But you had more children, yes? It must not have been entirely terrible."

Of course not. It hadn't been terrible at all. Not always. Not everything had not always been terrible. Anna doubled her negatives, tripled them. Ten months earlier Anna had given birth to a black-haired, bisque-skinned daughter whom she named Polly Jean.

And so they were the Benz family and they lived in the town of Dietlikon, in the district of Bülach, in the canton of Zürich. The Benzes: *Bruno, Victor, Charles, Polly, Anna.* A plain and mostly temperate household who lived on a street called Rosenweg—Rose Way—a private road that cul-de-sacked directly in front of their house, which itself lay at the foot of a slow, sloping hill that crested a half kilometer behind their property and leveled off at the base of the Dietlikon woods.

Anna lived on a dead end, last exit road.

But the house was nice and their yard was larger than nearly all the other ones around them. There were farmhouses to their immediate south, whose properties abutted fields of corn, sunflower, and rapeseed. Eight fully mature *Apfelbäume* grew in their side yard and in August when the trees were pregnant with ripe, heavy apples, fruit tumbled from the branches to the ground in a *thump-tha-thump-thump* rhythm that was nearly consistent with light rainfall. They had raspberry bushes and a strawberry patch and red currants and black currants both. And while the vegetable garden in the side yard was generally left untended, the Benzes enjoyed, behind a thigh-high picket fence in front of their property, a spate of rosebushes, blooms of every shade. *Everything comes up roses on Rosenweg.* Sometimes Anna thought this to herself.

Victor and Charles barreled through the front door. They were greeted before they passed through the boot room by a dour-faced Ursula pressing her finger to her lips. *Your sister's asleep!*

Anna was grateful for Ursula—really she was. But Ursula, who was usually never blatantly unkind to Anna, still treated her as a foreign object, a means to the end of her son's happiness (if indeed "happy" was the word for what Bruno was, and Anna was almost sure it wasn't) and the vessel by which her grandchildren—whom she deeply loved—were carried into the world. The help that Ursula offered was for the children's sake, not Anna's. She had been a high school English teacher for thirty years. Her English was stilted but fluent and she conceded to speak it whenever Anna was in the room, which sometimes Bruno didn't even do. Ursula shooed her grandsons into the kitchen for a snack.

"I'm taking a shower," Anna said. Ursula raised an eyebrow but then lowered it as she followed Victor and Charles into the kitchen. It was no concern of hers. Anna took a towel from the linen closet and locked the bathroom door behind her.

She needed the shower. She smelled like sex.

2

"WHAT CAN'T YOU LIVE WITHOUT?"

This, Anna asked Archie as they shared, incautiously, a cigarette in bed. Anna didn't smoke. She was wrapped in a top sheet. It was Friday.

"Whiskey and women," Archie said. "In that order."

Archie was a whiskey man. Literally. He stocked it, stacked it, and sold it in a shop he owned with his brother, Glenn.

He laughed in an up-for-interpretation way. Archie and Anna were new lovers, green lovers, *ganz neue Geliebte*. Nearly virgin to each other, they still had reason to touch. Archie was ten years older than Anna, but his brown-red curls had not yet begun to thin and his body was taut. Anna responded to his laughter with laughter of her own: the sad, empty laughter of knowing that the newness, nice as it was, wouldn't last. Novelty's a cloth that wears thin at an alarming rate. So Anna would enjoy it prior to its tattering. Because tatter it surely would.

* * *

"If," Doktor Messerli asked, "you are miserable, then why not leave?"

Anna spoke without reflection. "I have Swiss children. They belong to their father as much as to me. We are married. I'm not really miserable." Then she added, "He wouldn't accept a divorce."

"You have asked him." This wasn't a question.

Anna had not asked Bruno for a divorce. Not directly. She had, however, in her most affected and despondent moments, hinted around the possibility. *What would you do if I went away?* she'd ask. *What if I went away and never came back?* She would pose these questions in a hypothetical, parenthetically cheerful voice.

Bruno would smirk. *I know you'll never leave because you need me.*

Anna couldn't deny this. She absolutely needed him. It was true. And honestly Anna had no plans to leave. *How would we split the children?* she wondered, as if the children were a cord of wood and the divorce an axe.

"Anna," Doktor Messerli asked, "is there someone else? Has there ever been anyone else?"

The lunch hour folded into early afternoon. Archie and Anna shared a plate of cheese, some greengage plums, a bottle of mineral water. Then they set everything aside and fucked again. Archie came in her mouth. It tasted like school paste, starchy and thick. *This is a good thing I am doing,* Anna said inside herself, though "good" was hardly the right word. Anna knew this. What she meant was *expedient.* What she meant was *convenient.* What she meant was *wrong in nearly every way but justifiable as it makes me feel better, and for so very long I have felt so very, very bad.* Most accurately it was a shuffled combination of all those meanings trussed into one unsayable something that gave Anna an illicit though undeniable hope.

But all things move toward an end.

That night, after she had put the children to bed and washed the dinner plates and scoured the sink to the unimpeachable shine that Bruno demanded (Doktor Messerli asked "Is he truly that much an ogre?" to which Anna responded *no,* which translated as *sometimes*), Anna spread her notebooks on the table and began her German exercises. She'd fallen behind. Bruno was locked in his office. Separate solitudes were not an unusual arrangement between them, and Bruno retreated to his office most nights. Left alone, Anna would either read or watch television or put on a jacket and take an evening walk up the hill behind the house.

The house, when Anna was alone inside it, often assumed a pall of unbearable, catatonic stillness. *Has it always been like this?* Anna would be lying if she'd said it had. They'd shared good times, Bruno and she. It would be unfair to deny it. And even if he barely tolerated what he called her "melancholic huffs" or her "sullen temperaments," Bruno too, if pressed, would have admitted a love and fondness for Anna that, while often displaced by frustration, held an irrefutable honor in his heart.

It was just the previous Monday that Anna steeled and sent herself to school for the first time since college. The class at the Migros Klubschule was called German for Advanced Beginners. This was the course intended for anyone pre-equipped with a minor to moderate knowledge of the language but who lacked a rigorous understanding of grammar and a nuanced usage of syntax.

Migros is the name of the largest chain of supermarkets in Switzerland and Switzerland's biggest employer. More people work for Migros than any Swiss bank worldwide. But Migros is bigger than supermarkets alone. There are Migros-owned bookshops, Migros-owned gas stations, Migros-owned electronics outlets, sports stores, furniture dealers, menswear shops, public golf courses, and currency exchanges. Migros also governs a franchise of adult education centers. There isn't a Swiss city of significant population where at least one Migros Klubschule doesn't exist. And it's not just language classes they offer. You can study most anything at the Migros Klubschule: *cooking, sewing, knitting, drawing, singing.* You can learn to play an instrument or how to read the future with tarot cards. You can even learn how to interpret dreams.

DOKTOR MESSERLI, AT THE onset of Anna's analysis, asked Anna to pay attention to her dreams. "Write them down," the Doktor instructed. "I want you to write them down and bring them to our meetings and we will discuss them."

Anna protested. "I don't dream."

The Doktor was undeterred. "Nonsense. Everyone dreams. Even you."

Anna brought a dream to her next appointment: *I am sick. I beg Bruno for help but he won't give it. Someone films a movie in another room. I am not in it. A dozen teenage girls kill themselves for the camera. I don't know what to do so I do nothing.*

Doktor Messerli arrived at an immediate interpretation. "It's a sign of stagnancy. The movie's being made and you're not in it. This is why the girls do not survive. The girls are you.

You are the girls. You do not survive. You are ill with inaction, a patron sitting passively in a dark theater."

Anna's passivity. The hub from which the greater part of her psychology radiated. Everything came down to a nod, an acquiescence, a *Yes, dear.* Anna was aware of this. It was a trait she'd never bothered to question or revise, which, through the lens of a certain desiccated poignancy, seemed to be its proof. Anna was a swinging door, a body gone limp in the arms of another body carrying it. An oarless ocean rowboat. *Am I as assailable as that?* Yes, it sometimes seemed. *I have no knack for volition. My backbone's in a brace. It's the story of my life.* And it was. The very view from her kitchen window looked out upon it. Triangulated by the street and the apple trees and the path that led up the hill an invisible marquee flashed over a secret door that led into that same dark theater she dreamed of. Anna didn't need to see it to know it was there. The titles changed but the films were all of a sort. One week it was *You Could Speak Up, Have Your Say!,* the next it was *You're No Victim, You're an Accomplice.* And *Not Choosing Is Still a Choice* was held over for years.

Then there were the children. Anna hadn't longed to be a mother. She didn't yearn for it that way other women do. It terrified her. *I'm to be responsible for another person? A tiny, helpless, needy person?* Still, Anna got pregnant. And then again and then again. It seemed to just happen. She never said *Let's do this* and she never said *Let's not.* Anna didn't say anything at all. (Nor in this case, did Bruno. That discussion regarding future progeny? *It never happened.*)

But it wasn't as terrible as she'd feared and for the most part and for most of the time, Anna was glad to be someone's mother. Anna loved her children. She loved all her children.

Those beautiful Swiss children that a firmer-footed Anna would never have known. So Anna's passivity had merit. It was useful. It made for relative peace at the house on Rosenweg. Allowing Bruno to make decisions on her behalf absolved her of responsibility. She didn't need to think. She followed along. She rode a bus that someone else drove. And Bruno liked driving it. Order upon order. Rule upon rule. Where the wind blew, she went. This was Anna's natural inclination. And like playing tennis or dancing a foxtrot, or speaking a foreign language, it grew even easier with practice. If Anna suspected there was more to her pathology, then that was a secret she kept very close.

"WHAT'S THE DIFFERENCE BETWEEN passivity and neutrality?"

"Passivity is deference. To be passive is to relinquish your will. Neutrality is nonpartisan. The Swiss are neutral, not passive. We do not choose a side. We are scales in perfect balance." Doktor Messerli spoke with something that might have been pride in her voice.

"Not choosing. Is that still a choice?"

Doktor Messerli opened her mouth to speak, then changed her mind.

ANNA SAT AT THE dining table for almost a half hour fumbling through homework before Bruno emerged from his office like a marmot from a burrow. He came to the table, yawned, and rubbed his eyes. Anna saw their sons in that gesture. "How's the class?" Bruno asked. Anna couldn't recall the last time Bruno asked after her. She surged with a momentary affection for him and reached around his waist with her arms and tried to draw him closer into her. But Bruno—impervious or obstinate—did not respond in kind. He reached down and rifled through her papers. Anna dropped her arms.

Bruno picked up a page of exercises and gleaned it for accuracy. *"Du hast hier einen Fehler,"* he said in a voice he intended to be helpful, but one that Anna interpreted as condescending. She had made a mistake. "This verb goes at the end," Bruno said. He was right. In both the future and the past tense, the action comes at the end. It is only in the present tense that the verb is joined to the noun that enacts it. Bruno returned her work absently. "I'm going to bed." He didn't bend to kiss her. Bruno shut the bedroom door behind him and went to sleep.

Anna lost all interest in her exercises.

She checked the wall clock. It was after eleven but she wasn't tired.

"A DREAM IS A psychic statement," Doktor Messerli explained. "The more frightening the dream, the more pressing the need to look at that part of yourself. Its purpose is not to destroy you. It simply fulfills its compulsory task in a highly unpleasant manner." And then she added, "The less attention you pay, the more terrifying the nightmares become."

"And if you ignore them?"

Doktor Messerli's face took on a cast of gravity. "Psyche will be heard. She demands it. And there are other, more threatening ways of capturing your attention."

Anna didn't ask what those were.

* * *

That late in the evening, most of the houses on Rosenweg were entirely dark, their inhabitants already asleep. It took years for Anna to become habituated to this, how Switzerland, machine that it is, powered down at night. Shops closed. People slept when they were meant to. In the States if you couldn't or didn't want to sleep, you could always shop at a twenty-four-hour supermarket, wash clothes at a twenty-four-hour Laundromat, eat pie and drink coffee at a twenty-four-hour diner. The television networks ran viewable programming the entire night. So much never shut off. Lights always burned somewhere. It was an insomniac's solace.

Doktor Messerli asked about Anna's insomnia. How long had she suffered, how it presented. How she curbed it. Anna had no real answer and instead replied, "Sleep won't solve my situation." Even to Anna's ears it sounded canned.

When Anna stepped outside, the porch lamp, sensitive to motion, flickered on. The front steps led to the driveway. The driveway opened up to the street. The playground in the yard of the *Kirchgemeindehaus* was across the way. Anna crossed the street and stepped over a small wooden fence and took a seat on a wooden swing intended for very young children. She was uneasy and perturbed and the night air was just damp enough to be cruel.

Even Anna would admit she prowled Dietlikon's streets too often in the dark hours. In her second month in the country, Bruno woke in the middle of the night and Anna was gone. She wasn't in the house or the attic or the yard. He ran outside and called for her. When she didn't answer, he called the *Polizei. My wife is gone! My wife is pregnant!* The officers came to the house and asked insinuating questions and swapped readable looks. Had they fought recently? Did she take anything with her? What was their marriage like? Did he know if she'd been seeing anyone? Bruno screwed his face into a question mark and forced his fists into his pockets. *She is pregnant and it's two A.M.!* By the time he steered them from that line of questioning Anna had come home. She'd barely crossed the threshold when Bruno threw himself around her as if she were a soldier back from battle. One policeman said something low and curt in Schwiizerdütsch that Anna didn't understand. Bruno answered with a grunt. The officers left.

When they were alone and out of earshot, Bruno dug his fingers into Anna's shoulders and shook her. *Who are you fucking? Who were you with?* She'd embarrassed him in front of the policemen. *No one, Bruno—never! I swear!* Bruno cursed at her and called her a whore and a cunt. *Who did you suck off? Whose cock was in your mouth? Nobody's, Bruno, I swear!* That was the truth. Anna and Bruno were in a version of love and Anna had gone for a walk because she couldn't sleep. *It was just a walk! That's it!* And whose cock would it have been, in any case? This she thought but did not say. It took almost an hour, but Bruno finally came to believe her. Or said he did.

A neighbor's cat hissed and sputtered at what was likely a hedgehog. Three minutes later, the quarter-hour toll of the church bell rang.

WHEN SHE PRESENTED HERSELF for the first of her German classes, Anna was empty of expectation. She was not fully indifferent to first-day-of-school jitters, even at her age. At breakfast she told her sons that she was starting school. Charles sweetly offered his pencil box. Charles was like that. Victor was silent; he had no opinion. Ursula made a show of snapping out a dishtowel.

The Deutschkurs Intensiv met mornings, five days a week. That first day, Anna arrived six minutes late and knocked into a woman with her book bag as she tried to wedge past and take the last seat at the table. It was a modest-sized class, fifteen students whose ages varied and whose nationalities and reasons for expatriation diverged. Their teacher was Roland, a tall Swiss man whose first command was that they go around the room and introduce themselves using whatever German they already knew. He pointed to a blond woman with heavy-lidded eyes and a darting gaze. Her name was Jeanne and she was French. The woman next to her, Martina, was also blond but ten years younger than Jeanne. She told the room she came from Moscow, that she loved music but hated dogs. Then a woman Anna's age introduced herself as Mary Gilbert and said she was from Canada and that she'd come here with her children and her husband, who played left wing for Zürich's hockey team. She'd only been in Switzerland two months. Mary apologized for her ham-fisted German but she'd finished the basic class and there was no place for her but here. It didn't really matter. Everyone's German was unmistakably foreign, slow and littered with mistakes.

Then the man sitting next to Mary leaned forward. His accent, even over broken German, was irrefutably Scottish. Glaswegian, Anna would come to learn. His name was Archie Sutherland. As he talked, his eyes scanned the perimeter of the table. By the time his introduction was over, he'd locked his gaze on Anna, who sat across the room at an angle from him. He ended with a small, slight wink, intended for her alone. She blushed beneath her clothes.

Something in Anna started to burn.

There was Dennis from the Philippines. Andrew and Gillian, both from Australia. Tran from Vietnam. Yuka from Japan. Ed from England. Nancy from South Africa. Alejandro from Peru, and two other women whose names Anna didn't catch. They made all together a little UN.

When Anna introduced herself, she flashed a sincere-seeming smile (a trick she'd taught herself) and spoke the words she'd practiced in her head. *Ich bin Anna. Ich bin in die Schweiz für nine years. Mein Mann ist a banker. Ich habe three children. Ich bin from America. Ich bin, ich bin, ich bin.* When she couldn't lay her tongue to the German word, she substituted an English one. Anna hated introducing herself. It was like opening a door.

Anna looked to Archie. She was compelled by how strong his hands seemed, even from across the table. A man's hands always did her in. *A cock wants a hole. There are only so many. But a man can put his hands anywhere he wants, anyplace I ask him to.*

While standing in line in the cafeteria during their first coffee break, Archie leaned toward Anna and spoke in a low, purling voice rarely heard outside of chapels or alcoves in museums.

"Anna, is it?"

"It is."

"I'm Archie."

"So I heard." Anna was tentative, but kittenish. *Volley and lob. He wants a game of ping-pong. Sure,* she thought, *I'll play.*

Archie took a chocolate croissant from a line of plated pastries and put it on his tray. "You want one?"

Anna shook her head. "Not a big pastry fan." The line moved forward at an even clip. The *Kantine* was crowded, but the Swiss cashier was efficient.

"So what do you nosh on when you fancy a bite?"

Oh, this man's good, Anna thought. "A bite? Or a bite to eat?"

Archie put on an act of impatience. It was husky and hot. "What do you eat, woman?" Anna responded with a blushing, sidelong glance and a half-cocked smirk. They moved forward again. Archie grinned. "Banker husband, you say?"

"I say indeed." The reply was all cheek. *Am I flirting? I'm totally flirting.* It had been a while. *I'm going to play this out.*

"And what about Anna? What does Anna do when she isn't learning German?"

Anna held for a beat before answering. "Anna does what Anna desires." *Say anything with confidence,* Anna thought, *and the world will believe it's true.*

Archie's laugh was sportive, vulpine. "Good to know." They'd reached the head of the line. Anna paid for her coffee then turned briefly back to Archie and presented a terminal smile before walking away.

Back in the classroom, Roland reviewed a list of German prepositions: *under, against, on top of, from behind.*

Later, at the end of their second break, Archie cornered Anna by the trash cans. "What are you doing this afternoon?"

A dozen chaste answers came to mind. Anna ignored every one. She put her hand on Archie's arm and brought her mouth very close to his ear. "You," she whispered. And that was all.

Well how about that? Anna thought as she walked away. A woozy, tinny thrill shot through her. *Yes, how about it.* The inquiry was irrelevant. The answer to every question that day was yes.

But they were not arduous assents. She'd said yes before.

After class, Anna telephoned Ursula and told her there were errands she needed to run in the city and she wouldn't be back until three. Then Anna and Archie took the number 10 tram from Sternen Oerlikon, where the streets ray out from an interior middle like a five-point star, to Central, a stop at the north end of Zürich's Niederdorf district. From there it was a five-minute walk to Archie's flat. What followed was an hour and a half of uninhibited sex.

On Tuesday and again on Wednesday Anna followed Archie home after class. On Thursday and Friday, they skipped school altogether.

ANNA TWIRLED HERSELF IN the swing, winching the chains so that they lifted her higher off the ground than she was to begin with. Then she pulled up her feet and let herself spin quickly down. She accomplished this multiple times unto dizziness.

Eventually the church bells rang their midnight toll. A low, wormish feeling of a reckoning approached her. Only in the present tense is the subject married to its verb. The action—*all* action, past and future—comes at the end. At the very end, when there is nothing left to do but act.

Even so, Anna was back inside the house before the chime of the twelfth bell.

3

ANNA COULD NEVER *REALLY* LOVE A STEVE, A BOB, A MIKE.

She abhorred the casual apathy a diminutive implied. How a nickname more often than not announced "I am the sum of every Matt you've ever met, the arithmetic mean of a Chris, a Rick, a Jeff." It wasn't the length—names don't get much shorter than "Anna." She felt a person's name should resonate with dignity and significance. It should be able to heft the weight and bear the pressures of his personality. A Steffi would never be appointed to a presidential cabinet; a Chad would never appoint her.

Anna named her children with a seemly eye. Their names were American, but many Swiss had nonnative names; one-third of Zürich's population is foreign, thanks to the banking industry. The Credit Suisse in which Bruno worked, for example, employed many Swiss, several Germans, some Brits, a few Americans, and an impossibly handsome Nigerian whose skin was as smooth and dark as Sprüngli chocolate. Everything's eventually normalized by diversity. The names of Anna's children were uncommon in Switzerland, if not rare. She chose them with that in mind. She liked their names. They seemed to fit.

A name is a fragile thing. Drop it, and it might break.

Like Steve. The name of a man Anna could never love.

ANNA BROUGHT AN EXTREMELY convoluted dream to her analysis. It was organized chaotically without regard to theme or circumstance, and it was unbound by the geographies of time and space. A dream of pointed symbols, archetypal images, and allegoric nuances, Anna was sure.

There were twenty doors the Doktor could have walked through if there was one. *Let's begin with the significance of the horse,* Doktor Messerli might have said. *What are your associations with balloons and airplanes? What do you think it means that the roller coaster only runs backward? Why, Anna, were you naked in the church?* But the Doktor didn't ask those questions and instead posed the single one that Anna wished she hadn't.

"There is a Stephen in your dream. Who's he?"

Psychoanalysis is expensive and it is least effective when a patient lies, even by omission. But analysis isn't pliers, and truth is not teeth: you can't pull it out by force. A mouth stays closed as long as it wants to. Truth is told when it tells itself.

Anna shook her head as if to say *He is no one of significance.*

AT 5:45 A.M. ON SATURDAY Anna was jolted awake by an unnatural scream. She threw herself out of bed and raced up the stairs two at a time. It was Polly Jean. She was cutting a tooth. Ten months was late for a first tooth; Victor's came in at five months, Charles's at four. Anna slipped her thumb into Polly Jean's mouth and confirmed the presence of a small white nub. Polly countered with a string of wild infant curses. Anna picked her daughter up, shushed her, rocked her, tried to lull her back into sleep. Or a version of sleep.

Make no mistake: everything has a variant. Like versions of truth, like versions of love, there are versions of sleep. The deepest sleep is meant only for children and perfect fools. Everyone else must pay each night her restless due.

The sky was still dark and the neighborhood silent. From the square of window above Polly's crib, the modest spire of the parish church was visible. The Benzes resided, quite literally, in the shadow cast by Dietlikon's Swiss Reformed church. They lived in its figurative shadow as well. For a thirty-year tenure that ended only at his death, Oskar Benz, father to Bruno and Daniela and husband to Ursula, was the congregation's *Pfarrer.* Its pastor.

Churchgoing in Switzerland is a matter of custom, not zeal. Even a practicing Swiss Christian won't engage in religious swagger. That's an American antic. Swiss faith seems more bureaucratic. You are baptized in a church, you wed in a church, you are eulogized in a church, and that's it. Still, when Bruno and Anna went to the *Gemeinde* to file the papers for her residence permit, she was asked her religious preference. The churches are funded by taxes; money is distributed according to citizen affiliation.

As in America, while most Christian Swiss don't regularly attend, even the smallest towns have at least one *Kirche.* In Dietlikon there were three: the congregation Oskar Benz once pastored, a Catholic church half a kilometer away from Anna and Bruno's house, and an Orthodox group so thinly populated that the church didn't have a permanent address and met instead in a rented, unremarkable building just across the street from the cemetery. Ursula went to church on Sundays and sometimes took her grandsons with her. Bruno and Anna stayed home.

Anna had a cursory, teetering knowledge of religion. Her parents, in a moment of conviction during Anna's youth, flirted briefly with the Episcopalians. They attended church sporadically for almost a year before finding other things to occupy a Sunday morning's empty hours (for Anna's mother it was ladies' brunch and for her father it was golf). It was a case of dispassion rather than one of theological opposition. They simply didn't care enough to continue. So Anna's spiritual formation was relegated to cultural expressions of faith: the Christmas Baby Jesus and his gifts, the Easter risen Christ and his chocolate bunnies, and a copy of *The Thorn Birds* pulled from her mother's bookshelf.

Anna didn't oppose religious belief. She endorsed it in principle, if not in practice. While she wasn't sure if she believed in God, she wanted to believe. She hoped she believed. Sometimes, anyway. Other times, belief seized her with terror. *From God there are no secrets. I'm not sure I like that.* Except she *was* sure: she didn't.

But anyone might feel that way on a walk through downtown Zürich; Altstadt is clotted with historically significant churches. Everywhere you turn the Eye of God is on you. The Fraumünster is famous for its Chagall-designed stained glass windows. The clock face on the steeple of St. Peter's is one of the largest in all of Europe. The Wasserkirche was built on the site where Felix and Regula—Zürich's patron saints—were martyred. And the gray, imposing Grossmünster was erected on the very spot where those same martyrs are said to have delivered their severed heads before they finally (and with no further business to attend to) released their souls to death.

Felix and Regula. Happiness and order. *How Zürich of them to carry their own heads up the hill!* Anna thought. *A perfectly Swiss way to die—pragmatic and correct!*

Pragmatic, correct, efficient, predetermined. It was that theology that troubled Anna most of all. Anna had no qualms laying this anxiety directly at the feet of the Swiss; it was their adopted son John Calvin who insisted that it was impossible for sinners to consciously choose to follow God, taught that all are fallen, preached that all are lost. He called us slaves to depravity, helpless to the whims of Divine Will. There's nothing we can do to free ourselves. The fate of every soul is foreordained. Eternity's determined. Prayer is pointless. You've bought a ticket, but the raffle's fixed. *So what's the use of worrying if there's nothing to be done?* That was just it. There was no use. So whenever this crisis presented, Anna would remind herself that one way or the other, it didn't matter. Either her fate was predecided or she had no fate. There was nothing she could do to change it. Therefore when she worried it was never for very long.

Oskar Benz was a beloved pastor. By all accounts. How generous he was. How wise. Discerning. Gracious. Sage. But Anna knew nothing of him as a husband. That wasn't a conversation she'd had with Ursula. She assumed he'd been good to her. They smiled in their photographs. Ursula still wore her wedding band. Beyond that she didn't know. Was he romantic? A good kisser? Kinky in bed? Violent behind closed doors? *This is none of my business,* Anna thought. *If Ursula isn't telling, I won't ask.*

Daniela's eyes glossed with adoration when she spoke of her father. "I loved him *so,*" she pined to Anna. "I miss him every day. A father's the most important man in any girl's life." Anna's only response was sad silence. She was twenty-one when her own parents died in a car accident two weeks after her college graduation. She'd loved her father too—both her parents—but after sixteen years the ardor had dissipated (though Anna would likely have never described her affection for them with that word to begin with). "I dunno," she told Doktor Messerli, when the Doktor asked her to classify her relationship with her parents. "It was normal. Unremarkable."

The Doktor pushed on Anna. "Try harder."

Anna closed her eyes and searched her memory. "Positive. Liberal, maybe. Reserved, occasionally. Polite, always. Sufficient." They were good. They loved her. She loved them back. Anna left this out.

"Mm." Doktor Messerli jotted.

"What?"

Doktor Messerli suppressed a chuckle. She rarely laughed. "Interesting how our souls seek equilibrium. We search out the familiar. The familial. That which we know and have known since perhaps even before we were born. It's inevitable."

"What do you mean?"

"You have described your parents?"

"Yes."

"You've also described the Swiss."

Bruno rarely spoke of Oskar. They'd skied and hiked together, camped and fished. Bruno was a good father; Anna assumed that Oskar was as well. Bruno stopped going to church long before Anna had met him and she'd never asked him what he thought about God. *Not once,* Anna thought. *Is that right? That can't be right?* She had no idea what he believed. Asking would have embarrassed them both.

AT SEVEN A.M. THE bells began to ring. Those bells. Mornings they roused her, evenings they soothed her, and during the dark, marauding hours before dawn they companioned her. They rang on every hour, and twice a day they pealed for a continuous fifteen minutes. They rang on Sundays before church. They rang at weddings, funerals, and national holidays. As many people hated them as were indifferent to them. Few loved them. But Anna did. The ringing of the bells may have been her singular Swiss joy. Anna stopped herself from fully admitting this with her daughter in her arms.

Polly eventually defeated her pain with sleep and Anna tucked her into her crib once more then slipped out of the room. *She'll be okay,* Anna told herself. *It's the newness of the pain that brings the screaming.* A new pain that Polly hadn't learned how to manage. For even infants understand the rotten, instinctive truth: that no pain ever takes full leave of its person. That pain is greedy and doesn't give ground. That a body remembers what hurts it and how. Old pains get swallowed by new pains. But newer pains always follow suit.

"WHAT'S THE PURPOSE OF pain?" Anna asked Doktor Messerli. It was a question that had skimmed the air around her for years like a ghost that trolls the attic of a house it is forever damned to spook.

"It's instructive. It warns of impending events. Pain precedes change. It is a tool." She spoke in textbook phrases. Anna was suspicious of these answers. Doktor Messerli arced a single eyebrow. "Do you not believe me?"

Anna arced an eyebrow back. *No. I don't.*

ANNA PULLED SHUT THE door to her daughter's room and went downstairs to make coffee. The house on Rosenweg was, by American standards, small. The Benzes were five people residing in what amounted to just over 1,300 square feet of livable space. There were two upstairs bedrooms, each not much bigger than an oversized closet—a shared room for the boys and a room for Polly. The attic encompassed the rest of the second floor. Everything else was downstairs: the kitchen, the bathroom, the den with its tiny dining nook, Bruno's study, and the bedroom Anna and Bruno shared. Beneath it all lay a cold concrete basement. It was cramped quarters.

Anna descended the stairs as quietly as she could. Their house was old, and the steps creaked and groaned under anyone's weight. Anna was always conscious of the noise she made, for Bruno, when disturbed from his silences, often became intemperate and took easy offense at everyday, benign occurrences. Anna had learned to tiptoe and step slowly.

Their kitchen was small, narrow, and tucked up. There was hardly room for a countertop, much less a microwave, and their refrigerator was only slightly larger than ones found in college dormitories. Anna made the rounds of marketing twice a week at least. That was Anna's Saturday afternoon plan. All week she had been occupied and let the shopping slip. Their pantries were almost entirely bare.

"A MODERN WOMAN NEEDN'T live a life so circumscribed. A modern woman needn't be so unhappy. You should go more places and do more things." Doktor Messerli's voice didn't hide its impatience.

Anna felt scolded but didn't offer a retort.

SHE CARRIED HER COFFEE into the den. Her German books and all of her notes from the previous night were still scattered on the dining table like clothes cast off and tossed across a bed. The window in the den opened to face the barn of their neighbors, Hans and Margrith Tschäppät. An elderly couple, Hans and Margrith had lived in Dietlikon their entire lives. Hans was a kind and jolly farmer who would wave at Anna from his tractor when they passed each other going up or down the hill behind Anna and Bruno's house. Hans would give Anna jars of *Honig* cultivated by his own bees and twice a year he pruned their apple trees. Margrith, too, was nice. But she was also extremely perceptive, and Anna couldn't help but feel she always knew more about her than Anna would like her to. Anna had never caught her staring through their open windows or peeking into the Benzes' trash bin. It was something instead in the questions she asked, and the keen-eyed way she asked them, neighborly though they might seem: *Wohin gehen Sie, Frau Benz? Woher kommen Sie?* The past Wednesday afternoon, in fact, Margrith caught Anna as she was coming off the train, fresh from Archie's bed. Anna's hair was in snarls and her makeup lost to perspiration. *Grüezi, Frau Benz; woher kommen Sie?* she asked.

Just coming back from my German lesson, Frau Tschäppät, Anna replied, and then each continued on in the direction she was headed before they spoke. This early in the morning Margrith and Hans's windows were still dark. The Saturday sun had not yet risen.

Polly Jean woke for good around seven thirty. Bruno and the boys were up by eight. The weather was gracious; it was a generous, sunny day. Two well-slept boys rattled the walls of the house with the energy they had stored up overnight, like a pair of batteries, recharged. Anna sent them outside to play in the yard. Charles trotted out the door without a word of backtalk. Victor flopped on the couch and pretended he hadn't heard a thing. When Anna told Victor once more to go outside the pouting began. He wanted to ride his bike to a friend's house. He wanted to watch cartoons on the television. He wanted to go upstairs. He wanted Anna to leave him alone. This is when Bruno intervened. *Go.* That's all it took for Victor to relent. A firm, terse word from Bruno's no-nonsense lips.

Charles was Anna's easiest child. He was pleasant, quick to help, and slow to anger. He minded his manners and was rarely perturbed. He was a happy boy. Victor, by contrast, was rarely purely happy. A good son in his own way, Victor was funny, smart, charming, and occasionally perceptive beyond his years (*Mami,* he once said to Anna, *I will always love you, even if Papi doesn't*). But Victor was also self-indulgent. He tended toward pettiness and he didn't like to share. He was rigid and could not easily accommodate the plans or needs of others. And when he felt slighted, Victor became petulant and ill-tempered. At those times Anna found it impossible to like him very much.

Victor was his father's son.

Of Charles, Anna said to Doktor Messerli, "He has absolutely no guile."

"What about Polly Jean?"

"I don't know her yet." Doktor Messerli thought she knew what Anna meant.

"And Victor?"

"Victor, I do know." She was willing to admit nothing aloud but if pressed (and only if pressed very hard) she would have to say that of her two sons, Charles was her dearest. "Of course I love Victor."

Anna was sorry in a hundred ways.

DOKTOR MESSERLI DREW A diagram. It was a picture of a circle inside of a circle inside of another one. It reminded Anna of Russian matryoshka dolls, or her set of nesting Pyrex mixing bowls.

"These circles? They're *you*. The outside circle is the ego. The ego is the suit that your psyche wears. How you are viewed by the world. It is the first part of you that anyone sees." The Doktor leaned forward and tapped the middle circle with her fountain pen. It left a small but spreading blotch of ink. "This is where your problems lie." Doktor Messerli traced the circle again, giving it a messy, jagged seam.

"How so?"

"Chaos bars the ego from the serenity, the solidity, and the *solidarity* of the self." Anna wondered if she'd practiced this speech; it sounded lofty and rehearsed.

"What's the answer?"

Doktor Messerli leaned back into her chair. "There is no fit-all answer."

"What's the difference between the self and the soul?"

"Anna, our time is up."

Whores, Anna once read, *make the very best wives.* They are accustomed to the varying moods of men, they keep their broken hearts to themselves, and easy women always ease through grief.

This thought occurred to Anna unbidden when, in front of the Coop on Industriestrasse, she slipped a two-franc piece into a coin slot, releasing the top shopping cart from its line of brothers. It was a thought called forward by the simple action of shoving a thing into the hole it's meant for.

Ursula had offered Anna a ride to the supermarket. This was a gesture of clemency on Ursula's part, which Anna graciously accepted. She told Bruno she'd be glad to take Polly Jean with her if he'd watch the boys. *Yes, yes,* Bruno said, waving her off and telling her to bring back six large bottles of water, several pots of quark, and three or four dark chocolate bars. In this way Bruno was exceptionally Swiss; Bruno loved candy. Anna took note.

Ursula pushed the stroller. Anna maneuvered the basket. Polly was fussy and still troubled by her tooth. Anna looked at her daughter and wished she'd just stop crying.

Dietlikon doesn't lack for shopping. On the south side of

the railroad tracks, a comprehensive—and for a town whose population barely hit seven thousand residents, obscene—selection of eateries, shops, and services: an electronics store, an IKEA, a very large home improvement store. There is a Toys "R" Us, an Athleticum, a few shoe stores, a fish market, and a nail salon. There is a multiplex cinema with stadium seating, a Qualipet, a bowling alley, a store that specializes in horse tack, a car wash, a pizzeria, a shop for baby furniture, a low-end department store, and a Mexican restaurant. There are several trendy teen fashion boutiques, a gas station, a pharmacy, an adult movie store, a health food store, and in addition to the Coop on Industriestrasse, there's a Coop City one block over where, along with groceries, you can find household accoutrements, clothes, health and beauty products, toys and games. Everything a body could desire positioned to fit inside a few convenient blocks of commerce girdled by a bus route. It is a close, closed circle of small needs and petty wants.

A circle inside of a circle inside of another one. Anna couldn't imagine what looking beyond the tightly circumscribed world in which she lived might entail.

Anna and Ursula shared a complicated relationship. Ursula was a weave of consistent inconsistencies. At times she was devout, open to interaction, easygoing, generous, and helpful. Other instances found her apathetic, impossible to impress, aggressively punctual, blank-faced, and angry. Those were the instances she shared most frequently with Anna.

Mother has moods, too, Bruno said.

"When a person's mood is out of balance, psyche will always attempt to bring it back into equilibrium. An unconscious opposite will emerge. Tensions seek slackening. Sadness clings to any elevated state it can find. Boredom searches for activity. There is a correlation between the severity of a person's moods and a lack of self-knowledge. Notwithstanding," Doktor Messerli added, "a clinical diagnosis of a mood disorder."

Had Anna ever been more talkative or spoken faster than usual? Had she ranged from great doubt to overconfidence? Had there been times when she felt both elated and depressed at once? Doktor Messerli asked the questions too quickly for Anna to absorb them, so she replied simply, "Sometimes I feel sad. Sometimes I feel anxious." Doktor Messerli responded by writing her a prescription for a mild tranquilizer.

THE COOP ON INDUSTRIESTRASSE was, as Anna had known it would be, heaving with people. Ursula and Anna each had a list. Polly Jean was herself preoccupied in eyeing, with an infant's appropriate misgiving, the conflux of shoppers who made the wide rounds of the store.

They were in the produce aisle. Ursula was vetting nectarines. She inspected nearly twenty before settling on the four pieces of fruit she decided to carry home. Anna was considering the mushrooms when she felt a buzzing in the pocket of her jacket. It was her Handy, her cell phone. She reached for it, flipped open its clamshell, and answered without looking to see who had called. "Hello?"

It was Archie. He didn't want to wait the weekend to talk to her. *Come into town, Anna,* he said. *Come over.* Ursula glanced at her daughter-in-law but returned her attention just as quickly to the nectarines. Anna was silent. *Are you there? Hello?*

"Edith, glad you called." Anna spoke flatly. She didn't miss a beat. Ursula returned and set her sack of nectarines in the cart. *Edith Hammer,* Anna mouthed. Ursula shrugged and turned away, pushing Polly's stroller off toward the celery and the leeks.

"You aren't alone?"

Anna continued. "We'll talk Monday, yes?" Anna was flattered. Anna was annoyed. Ursula lifted a bag of green beans in her left hand and motioned Anna to follow her into the spice aisle with her right. Anna clapped closed her phone without saying goodbye.

Twenty minutes later they paid for their groceries and left. It was just after noon.

"BUT *WHO* IS STEPHEN, Anna?"

4

THE FOLLOWING MONDAY, EVERY STUDENT ENROLLED IN THE Deutschkurs Intensiv turned out for class—Anna and Archie included. Archie had arrived on time and was, when Anna showed up fifteen minutes late, quietly filling in a worksheet with everyone else. The door's hinges squealed when Anna entered and the entire class looked up to watch her cower into the room. Anna undertoned an *I'm sorry* and endeavored what she hoped was nonchalance as she took the only open seat available, the empty chair between Roland and Mary, the Canadian woman. But Anna was often as clumsy as she was passive, and as she rummaged through her book bag with one hand, she seemed to have forgotten that her other hand was wrapped around a flimsy paper cup of hot coffee. She spilled the entire cup—on herself, on the table, and on Mary.

Anna and Mary made simultaneous exclamations. Mary yelped *Oh gosh!* And Anna barked out a splenetic *Mother of Christ!* which, even to her own accustomed ears, sounded coarse. Roland pulled an agitated face. The coffee went down the front of Anna's sweater; it caught Mary on the cuff and on the thigh. Her worksheet was ruined. Anna whispered a feeble apology and rose and left the room. Mary followed after her. Archie's eyes remained locked on his paper.

In the bathroom, Anna blotted and dabbed and swiped at the stain on her sweater. Nothing helped. The cashmere was ruined. It was one of the nicest things she owned and Anna, fond of baubles and adornments, owned many nice things. A Christmas present from Bruno, she knew better than to have worn it to class. But she talked herself into it that morning by imagining the limp, silky pleasure she'd experience later in the afternoon when she would be talked so easily out of it, how Archie would tuck his hands beneath the sweater's bottom banding, slide them up the sides of her waist, skate them across the inner side of her upraised arms, how he would lift it over her head and off her body, how he would then impel her to his bed and vandalize her for at least the next two hours.

Anna loved and didn't love sex. Anna needed and didn't need it. Her relationship with sex was a convoluted partnership that rose from both her passivity and an unassailable desire to be distracted. And wanted. She wanted to be wanted.

The longing for diversion was a recent development; her pining to be hungered for was decades old. But both rose from a lassitude born of small-scale grudges and trifling, trivial injuries, the last ten years of which she blamed on Bruno. From that rose boredom and from boredom particular habits were born. This she could not blame on Bruno. Like the ability to flash that sincere-seeming smile, Anna had taught it to herself by settling down, by settling *on*.

The affair with Archie was and wasn't about sex. Anna was weak and she knew it. But she was still young enough to be pretty in certain lights and to the tastes of specific men.

"What do you think makes a person's life successful?" Doktor Messerli asked.

"Do you mean accomplished?" They'd been talking of something unrelated to success.

Doktor Messerli closed her eyes as she searched for the right words. "The kind of success I mean comes from living a life that satisfies a woman in such a way that when, in her old age, she looks back upon her years in contemplation, she is able to announce with certainty, 'I have led a conscious, useful life, whole and complete, and I filled it with as many worthy things as it could possibly hold.' That's what I mean. Do you understand? Is that something you want?"

"I don't know." Anna didn't.

"I don't know whether you want it either," Doktor Messerli agreed.

MARY'S SHIRT WAS WEARABLE, but her jeans were soaked through to her thighs. She blotted herself with a pad of paper towels as she spoke.

"Missed you in class last week." Anna listened for an accusation but there was none. Mary's tone was sunny, though it perplexed Anna how someone she hardly knew would take even a passing notice of her absence. They'd only been in school a few days.

"I'm sorry I spilled coffee on you."

Mary gestured *never mind* as she stepped toward the bathroom door to leave. "Say, Anna . . ." Anna looked up from her sweater to Mary reflected in the mirror. Mary's face was round and she wore her curly sand-colored hair in a prudent bob. She was short and fleshy. Not fat, but large-breasted, generous of hip, maternal, and, despite her thickset frame, undeniably pretty. Anna looked from Mary's reflection to her own and weighed the disparities. "My husband and I wondered if you and your husband and children wouldn't like to come to the house for dinner sometime this week? You have boys? Are they hockey fans? Is your husband?" Anna paused long enough to defeat her. "Or," Mary stammered, "next week. Or not, you know. Whatever you like." There was apology in her voice. Anna had disappointed.

"Oh, no," Anna hedged. "I'm distracted, is all." She pointed to her sweater. "Of course . . . we'd love to come. I'm sure the boys . . . they'd love it." She stuttered as she poured as much kindness into the words "of course" as they would hold. *This woman wants a friend.* Anna recognized that want. It made her wince. Solitude was her anchor. A familiar misery, and anymore the safest, most sensible approach.

But in the bathroom and at that moment Anna felt trapped. Obligated to oblige. "I'll have to check with Bruno. His schedule, I mean."

Mary brightened. "That's it, *Bruno,*" she said as she remembered a name she'd never been told. "Be sure and give me your email. We can make plans."

"I don't use email all that much."

"Really?" Mary asked as if she'd never heard such a thing in her life. "Why's that?"

Anna capitulated. "I don't have much call for it."

"No Facebook? Myspace?"

"No." This was a bit of a fib. Of course Anna had an

email address. Everyone had an email address. Of course Anna used it. It's where the boys' school sent their announcements. It's how Anna confirmed her dentist appointments. Without it, she'd never be able to shop online. But she didn't use it when she didn't have to. Who would she email that she didn't already regularly see? Who would she connect or reconnect with? All those distant relatives with whom she didn't keep in touch? Her school pals and ex-lovers? There was no one Anna was eager or able to contact. And no one looked to get in touch with her. All told, there was less humiliation in the lie.

"Well anyway, let's not forget to swap numbers, okay? Now," Mary breathed deeply, "time to get back! See you in there? We'll talk more during break?"

"Sure." Anna was as stiff as she could be without appearing rude. She was in a bad mood and being unfair. She self-corrected with an "absolutely" and Mary left.

Once more she looked at her sweater. *I've destroyed a beautiful thing,* Anna thought. *I have nothing to change into.*

In a moment of bald yearning, Anna whined to Doktor Messerli, "I wish I were better looking."

"You think there is something wrong with how you look?"

Anna shrugged. "Wrong" was the wrong word. "I'm neither plain nor pretty. I'm irrevocably average."

"Jung said that beautiful women were sources of terror. That as a general rule, a beautiful woman is a terrible disappointment."

Anna dismissed her with a backhand wave.

Then Doktor Messerli asked, "When will you trust me enough to tell me everything?"

* * *

Anna examined herself in the mirror. She was neither too tall nor too short, neither too fat nor too thin. Her hair fell in easy but shaggy shoulder-length waves. It was the color of top dirt and it was graying around her forehead (she dyed it). *What do they see in me, men?* She wasn't being modest. She truly didn't know.

She stared herself farther down in the bathroom mirror for a full minute more before returning to class.

In the classroom, Roland was explaining the declension of adjectives. Anna took notes and tried to follow along. *Declining adjectives. As if they were cups of tea. No thank you, I've had enough.* She ticked through all relevant descriptives. Lonely. Mediocre. Yielding. Easy. Frightened. *No, no, I have plenty already of each.*

But declension, as Roland explained it, was about clarity. Constructing a sentence in a way that the function of every word is unambiguous, impossible to be misunderstood. To classify units of language by their purpose, to pin all words to their syntax by a constant, final syllable like a butterfly tacked to a board. *Here is a masculine subject, there is its feminine object.* Anna smirked. It was a word's grammatical uniform. *The policeman's badge. The crown of a king.*

A wife's gold ring.

Roland droned. "*Ich fahre ein blaues Auto.*" Anna took absent notes; she doodled arrows and crosses and sadly drawn faces of sad-eyed women in the margins of her workbook. There was no reason for this day to be so intractable.

Roland continued. "*Ich fahre ein blaues Auto. ABER—ich fahre das blaue Auto.* You hear the difference?"

Anna did. It was the difference between "a" and "the."

The disconnect between "general" and "specific."

The vast, vapid chasm that divides "this particular one" from "some of them."

The discrepancy that separates any two "him"s. She did not need this pointed out to her.

No, no. I have plenty. Thank you. That's enough.

Later in the *Kantine* Anna sat with Archie, Mary, Nancy from South Africa, and Ed, who came from London. The English speakers huddled together. *Same seeks same; we search out the familiar, just as the Doktor said.* The Asians sat behind them, setting themselves apart as well. And the Australian couple, the French woman, and the lady from Moscow broke away from the group for their own reason—to go out to the patio and smoke. Underneath their table, Archie slid a hand up and down the side of Anna's leg. She drank her coffee without blinking or shifting in her seat. Ed had Archie's ear discussing politics, while Mary quizzed Anna about her children. Nancy bounced between both conversations, alternating interest.

ANNA BROUGHT A DREAM to Doktor Messerli.

A photographer wants to take my picture. His studio is made of sandstone. There are no windows. The room is a closed box. He asks to see my ID. I only have my Ausweis. I show it to him, but for some reason it's not good enough.

Doctor Messerli began with sweeping generalities. "There are no authoritative rules in dream interpretation. I cannot tell you point by point the significance of each symbol. The message of the dream will depend on the dreamer's associations. But there are guidelines. The dreamer only ever dreams about herself. Every person in a dream is a manifestation of an aspect of her psyche. Every character a reflection of her own subconscious nature."

Anna furrowed her brow but nodded anyway.

ROLAND SIGNALED THE CLASS by tapping on his watch. Everyone rose and cleared away their coffee and tea things, the little plates and spoons that always reminded Anna of the toy dishes she played with as a child and the tea parties and coffee klatches she threw for her ladies' league of plush animals. Anna tried to remember what it felt like to be five years old. In turn, she tried to imagine her five-year-old self imagining the physical feel of thirty-seven. Her five-year-old self could not fathom it. It was a future too far away to mean anything to such a little girl.

In the hallway in front of the elevator, Archie caught Anna's attention and mouthed *Stairs* before heading straight out the fire door. *Why not?* Anna thought, and let the elevator fill without her. Mary motioned that there was enough room, but Anna shook her head and said "It's okay," and as the doors of the elevator shut she entered the stairwell. Archie stood on the landing above her.

"I missed you." Archie took hold of Anna, sandwiched her between the concrete wall and him and kissed her. They held the kiss for a brake-screech thirty seconds before Anna pushed him away and together they climbed the stairs and returned to the classroom.

Don't miss me, Archie, Anna thought. *That's stupid.* It seemed reckless and improbable, inappropriate, personally invasive. Anna understood the incongruity. Of everything affronting or improper about their relationship, his missing her (or even, simply, his saying so) was the least indecorous.

Roland gave a lesson on conjugation.

That afternoon it was a hurried love Anna and Archie made, over almost before it began. Glenn had an appointment in Bern; it was Archie's turn to mind the shop. They both rushed to dress. Anna would finish pulling herself together on the train.

In the hallway Archie pointed at her sweater; she'd put it on wrong-side out. The coffee stain was closest to her body. Anna didn't bother going back into the apartment. She stood in the middle of the common, public hallway, removed the sweater, righted it, and put it back on. A minimal gesture of insouciance. *Don't miss me, Archie.* She thought again. *Don't even think it.*

Anna walked to Stadelhofen and missed the Dietlikon-bound S3 by two minutes. Stadelhofen is Zürich's second busiest train station, and the one nearest Archie's apartment. At that hour the station was crowded. Anna was grateful for so many people. She didn't want attention. She bought a pretzel from a vendor and sat down on the north end of platform 2 with little to do in that moment but reflect.

Adultery is alarmingly easy. A delicate dip of the chin, a smile. It takes so little. He cocks his head. There's a perturbation in the air. Your perception blinks. The exertion is effortless. Surrender is your strong suit. Assent, your forte. You abdicate a little more each day. There's nothing you intend. You do not fight it.

Just the tip, Anna thought. *And just this once. But it's never just the tip.*

Anna ate a third of her pretzel and threw the rest away.

Despite what she had said to the contrary, Doktor Messerli pressed forward and interpreted Anna's dream. "A photograph is an honest reflection of a person's face. As is said, cameras do not lie. But he doesn't take your picture because you don't prove yourself. You hand him an ID—your 'id,' if you will—but it is not acceptable. Your Swiss identification card isn't good enough. For you are *not* Swiss and there is little you *identify with* in this country. His house is made of sand. It is not structurally safe. The building could collapse around you at any moment. Windowless, his studio's dark and stifling. So too, the nature of the unconscious."

OVER THAT EVENING'S SUPPER, Anna mentioned Mary's invitation to Bruno and the boys.

"*Im Ernst?*" Bruno's delight surprised her. "No kidding?" His voice bounced. Bruno loved sports. Soccer, tennis, hockey, all of them. He'd taken the boys to the Hallenstadion many times to see the ZSC Lions play. Of course he'd heard of Tim Gilbert. "That is so cool, Anna!" Anna took pleasure in Bruno's genuine gladness. Bruno rose from the table, leaned over, tilted Anna's chin to his and delivered a brief but generous kiss. "*Merci vielmal,* Anna."

Later that evening, Anna telephoned Mary and plans were made for the coming Friday.

"This is our first dinner with friends since the move," Mary said.

Anna couldn't immediately recall the last time the Benzes had had people over.

During the next day's class, Roland presented a lesson on false cognates, German words that sound like English words but whose meanings differ vastly. "*Bad,* for example, doesn't mean 'not good,' it means 'bath.' And *fast* does not mean 'quickly,' it means 'almost.' *Lack* means 'paint,' not 'absence.' "

And das Gift, Anna remembered, *is the German word for poison.*

Anna asked Doktor Messerli if there was a correlation between the English word "trauma" and *der Traum,* the German word for "dream."

"There's always a correspondence between one's dreams and one's wounds."

AFTER TUESDAY'S CLASS ANNA followed Archie home yet again. He took her into his bedroom and stated plainly, *You are wearing more clothes than I'm comfortable with,* and then he pushed a little button through its little hole and then another and when Anna was shirtless, he licked the small, hollow bowl at the top of her sternum and slid his hands into her panties as Anna gave in to the ruddy, florid bud of his erection.

But the following afternoon Mary cornered Anna into taking her shopping. "I want a new dress. We're having a family photo made next week. For our Christmas cards. I need help. I have no fashion sense." Once again Anna felt trapped enough to relent. "I'll even spring for lunch . . . ?" Mary was eager.

Anna suggested they try the Glatt, an enormous American-style mall in Wallisellen, one town over from Dietlikon. It was home to at least a dozen ladies' boutiques and a few department stores. Glatt is the name of the Rhine tributary that flows through the Zürcher Unterland. It is also the German word for "smooth."

"*Glatt,*" Mary said, drawing out the *at* sound. "It's so *gruff!*"

Mary did the talking on the ride. Anna listened but added nothing to the conversation. Mary was green and needy. But her naïveté was tempered by an abiding kindness that even Anna found difficult to oppose.

"Have you truly no friends in Zürich, Anna? No girlfriends of your own?"

Anna confessed the sullen truth. "No. Not really."

"Are there friends that you and Bruno share?"

Edith Hammer passed for a friend. For a version of a friend. Edith's husband Otto worked with Bruno. Anna and Edith had little in common but this: it was each their lot to love a Swiss. Older than the Benzes by a fourth, richer than them by double, the Hammers had a boat and twin teen daughters. They lived in Erlenbach, on the Zürichsee's east bank, that precious stretch of land known as the Goldküste, the Gold Coast. Edith was fussy, class-conscious, and thoroughly, unapologetically entitled. She had an opinion about everything. When Anna mentioned her German classes, Edith scoffed and made an indifferent face. *Why bother? Everyone here speaks English anyway.*

Anna answered the Doktor's question. "Not really."

The mall overwhelmed Mary. She wrung her hands and babbled while they skimmed the racks at a few of the higher-end stores. But Mary's tastes ran less chic and they ended up at an H&M where Mary found a black wool shift that Anna wouldn't have chosen for herself but actually suited Mary well. Mary rounded out her purchase with a pair of ribbed tights and Anna, on a whim, picked up a plum satin bra and panty set.

"Bruno will love those, Anna!"

Afterward, they took seats at a café in the middle of the mall. Mary ordered soup and Anna asked only for a bottle of Rivella, that Swiss-specific carbonated drink made of whey. Mary asked to try it. Anna warned her she might not like it. She didn't. The milky carbonation is an acquired taste.

The pair sat without talking for an awkward two minutes before Mary broke the conversational lull. "Do you get homesick, Anna?"

This was a difficult question to answer. Anna hadn't been back to the States since she'd left them. There was nothing she missed about America so much to want to return to it. But Switzerland had never felt like home, and never would.

"No."

5

WHEN FRIDAY CAME, THE BENZES DROVE TO USTER FOR DINner with the Gilberts. Uster is a village thirteen kilometers from Dietlikon on the eastern bank of the Greifensee, Kanton Zürich's second largest lake. "You look very nice," Bruno said to Anna as they walked up the drive to Tim and Mary's house. Bruno pronounced his English *v*'s like English *w*'s: *wery nice, waulted ceiling, wampire bat.* Most Swiss do. He even slipped occasionally and said *Wictor.* The effect of Bruno's kindness was charming and unexpected. He wasn't cranky all the time—no one is. But everyone has tendencies and irritability was his.

Mary introduced herself, then Tim, then their daughter Alexis, then finally their son Max. Anna, in turn, introduced Bruno, Victor, and Charles. They had left Polly Jean with Ursula.

The Benzes brought gifts. Anna nudged the boys. Charles handed Mary a box of Lindt pralines and Victor gave her a bottle of cherry brandy. Mary thanked them but assured them it wasn't necessary. Bruno replied, "It wouldn't have been Swiss to come empty-handed."

The party moved into the den, where Mary offered drinks. She spoke in a bona fide lilt as she poured beers for the men and sweet wine for Anna and herself. The children hugged the wall until Mary pointed out to Max that he and Charles were the same age and that perhaps Max would like to take Charles into his room and show him his trains. They raced away at the suggestion. "Alexis," Mary continued, "why don't you and Victor go upstairs as well." Alexis was a year Victor's senior. Neither wanted to play with the other. But Alexis had video games, and in a pinch those will always do, so the two children shrugged and lumbered up the stairs.

The adults sat down: Bruno and Anna on a loveseat, Tim in a straight-backed chair, and Mary on the floor at his feet. Anna offered her own seat but Mary *pshawed,* explaining she was comfortable where she was. For at least the third time since the invitation, Mary mentioned that the Benzes were their first guests since the move. *"Zum Wohl!"* Bruno said, leading the toast. And so the evening began.

Anna sipped her drink and examined the surroundings. The den was a homey room, which looked surprisingly lived-in despite the family's short stay. Bookshelves lined the walls. They were filled with mysteries mostly, genre fiction, children's books and encyclopedias, cookbooks and a few volumes of pop psychology. Framed family snapshots filled the gaps where there were no books, including what Anna deduced was last year's Christmas portrait. The Gilberts were dressed in matching cranberry-colored sweaters. Four smiling faces in front of a fixed winter backdrop. The Benzes had never taken a family Christmas photo.

* * *

"How often appearances deceive, Anna." Anna didn't need the Doktor to tell her this. When she first moved to Dietlikon Anna noticed that affixed to many windows were decals of big, black, featureless birds. *Oh, this must be a custom,* she thought. A trend in design. Just something people did in Switzerland, that's what she assumed. It took months—maybe a year—before she realized that the stickers served the practical purpose of keeping actual flesh-and-feather birds from flying into the glass. She'd never lived anywhere where birds habitually smashed into windows.

She admitted this to Bruno when she realized her mistake. He laughed for ten minutes. It was the funniest thing he'd heard all week, he said. Anna was indignant, then embarrassed, then mortified. How small she felt, and stupid. She started to cry. "Oh, Anna," Bruno said, though he didn't quite stop laughing. "I love you very much, silly woman." Then he leaned over and kissed her on the head, the cheek, the lips, the nose. "Very much, you very silly woman." He'd never said anything exactly as endearing as that before. He was still laughing as he walked away. *Wery much, you wery silly woman.*

They weren't real birds. And he wasn't being mean at all. They were versions of birds. And Bruno was, in the moment, being the only kind of loving he knew how to be.

Bruno and Tim were locked into a conversation about the teams in the Swiss National League. Anna listened until Mary suggested she join her in the kitchen. They received automatic nods of departure from their husbands who otherwise didn't disengage from their chat.

In the kitchen Mary motioned to a high side table flanked

by a couple of bar stools with backrests. Anna recognized the set. It came straight from the IKEA warehouse floor. "Have a seat, Anna." Anna sat. Mary busied herself opening doors: refrigerator, oven, pantry. Mary was at home in her kitchen, a good little hausfrau, happy as a rabbit. Mary hummed while she stirred, sautéed, and sampled. She was a pretty woman, but plain somehow, and doughy, a Canadian mother from the sticks. Her clothes were functional; she wore a sensible hairstyle and very little makeup. *Aren't athletes' wives usually flashier? Don't they typically have more style?* Anna saw nothing immodest about her, her kitchen, her house, her family. Anna chalked this up to the Gilberts' Manitoban pragmatism. Mary was four years younger than Anna. This they had discovered during a class break earlier that week.

The news rattled Anna's vanity. *Do I present as matronly as that?* Later that particular afternoon in Archie's apartment, bare-breasted and straddling him, Anna asked whether he thought she did, warning him first to think hard before he answered. He swore upon the bones of some Scottish hero Anna had never heard of that she did *not*. Anna felt a little bit better.

"Bruno seems *very* nice, Anna. And your children—oh!—so precious!"

Anna swigged from her glass and muttered something along the lines of *Seem and be are cousins, not twins*. Bruno *was* behaving sweetly and with charismatic allure. But that was one night out of thousands.

"I'm glad you're here," Mary said and sadness seeped through her words like water through cheesecloth. "The other men on the team have Swiss wives and I don't know any of the mothers from Max and Alexis's school yet. I know I'll meet people and make friends eventually. Everyone is nice enough. But cold, you know?"

Anna told her she did know.

Mary took the roast from the oven and put it on a platter. Anna rose to help but Mary said, "No, no, I have it." Anna eased back onto the bar stool. "Anna," Mary started, "how long was it before you felt like you belonged here?" Her voice hung on the hope that Anna would answer with the words *Not long at all.*

That was not her answer.

"Oh."

Anna retreated. "Mary, it's really not that bad," she lied. "It's just a chilly climate all around. You'll find your footing and your gait. You'll find your stride. It's good you're in German class. I waited nine years too long."

"But Anna—your German is the best in the class."

Anna corrected her. "I'm the only person who's lived in Zürich more than a few months."

Mary picked up the roast and signaled with her elbow to a bowl of salad. Anna took it and followed her into the dining room. "I'm so glad we met," Mary offered. "Let's do something after class next week. It doesn't matter what. I'm happy to have someone I can talk to. Tim, too, it seems." Mary gestured toward the den, where Tim and Bruno leaned forward in their seats. Bruno used the coffee table as a writing desk and jotted on a confetti-edged piece of paper ripped from a spiral notebook. Anna guessed he was giving financial advice. Mary called out, "Soup's on!" and Max and Charles raced down the stairs. She called again for Victor and Alexis. They had been squabbling over whose turn it was to play the game.

Max was in the kitchen, underfoot. "Darling, please get out of Mommy's way." Max danced around. "Mommy!"

"What's it, dear heart?" Mary dodged her son as she carried a pitcher of water into the dining room.

"Charles told a *secret*!" Anna glanced at Charles, who cowered next to the doorjamb, looking mortified.

Mary also noticed Charles's distress. "Max, if it's a secret then you can't even say *that*. Okay? Go wash your hands." Max grabbed Charles and they both sped off to wash up.

Anna wanted—almost desperately—to know what the secret was.

"You are keeping secrets from me," Doktor Messerli accused.

Anna asked her if she realized that bank secrecy was a twentieth-century Swiss invention.

"There's a difference between secrecy and privacy."

"Yeah? What is it?" It was a defensive response.

Doktor Messerli shook her head and wrote something in her notebook.

About five minutes before the end of Friday's class Anna had looked up from her notebook to see Archie staring at her from across the table. He raised an eyebrow. Anna caught the tacit invitation. She made a face that she hoped he understood meant *We'll talk about it after class*. Five minutes later, after Roland ended his lesson, after Anna assured Mary once again that she knew how to get to their house and yes, they would be there on time, after Mary finally left for her train and the rest of the class dispersed, Anna turned toward the trams at Sternen Oerlikon and without any verbal assent led Archie to the number 10. They boarded together.

Anna sat by the window watching the gray streets of the city grate past them as the tram sluiced south toward downtown. It was a monochromatic day. It matched her mood.

They had just passed the Irchel campus of the University of Zürich when Archie leaned over, put his lips very close to Anna's ear, and in a dirty whisper said, "I want to fuck your mouth." Anna responded with silence. He waited a beat and then said it again. "When we get to my flat I'm going to fuck your mouth. Do you hear me?" At Milchbuck, two nuns dressed in dark slate skirts and matching mid-length veils boarded the tram and took the seats directly in front of Anna and Archie. Anna reddened underneath her clothes. Archie ignored all lines of decorum. "You like it in the ass? You want me to shove my dick into your ass?" One of the sisters shifted in her seat. Archie snorted. "I'm going to pound your ass with my fat, hard cock." Anna wondered if the nuns spoke any English.

The closer the tram came to Central, the more explicit the details of their impending fuck became. *I'm going to fuck you in the ass. I'm going to stick my finger in your ass. I'll shove you to the wall, Anna, I swear it. I'm going to bend you over my table and wipe your pussy with my face.* The second nun turned around but looked past them. Archie grinned. Anna couldn't tell what was getting him off—the dirty talk, the belligerent nature of its script, or the audience of others overhearing them. She didn't know him well enough even to make a guess.

Archie kept on when they got off the tram. *I'm going to lash you to the bed frame. Knot your wrists. Tape your eyes closed. Shove a rag in your mouth.* They walked at a clip, Archie steering Anna through the crowd like a husband, his palm at her back on an angle as he guided her from behind. *I'm going to suck your clit until it's plump like a plum, woman.* By the time they got to Altstadt whatever he wanted to accomplish began to work. Anna was in on the arousal, her pulse was high, and she was starting to go light-headed, nearly ready to let him do everything he swore he would.

But it was all and only talk. That day's sex was straightforward, if renegade. By the time they got to his apartment, they were both so flustered that neither bothered to strip out of their shirts—Archie didn't even remove his jacket. He fell back on the couch and pulled her onto his naked lap. She straddled him and he coaxed her open with his thumbs. Anna was sopping; Archie slid in easily. He grabbed her hips like handles and pistoned her forcibly up and down. She didn't realize how tightly he'd been holding on until the next day when she was in the shower and saw the little purple bruises where his fingers had dug in.

"You're hurting me." It was a statement; she wasn't protesting. Archie grunted in a way that Anna took to mean he was almost done, which he was. He pulled out so quickly that he nearly shoved her off of him. He came hard, on her belly. There was blood on his cock. A lot of blood, and all of it a shiny shade of red, the color of a stop sign, a flashing hazard light. "Christ!" It was everywhere. On his cock, her thighs, his lap, the couch. It glistened in her pubic hair and rolled past her knee in a line halfway down her calf. "Shit." The blood shook Archie from his orgasm. They didn't have a towel so he took off his sock and gave it to her. "I'm sorry," Anna said, near tears.

Archie laughed lightly as Anna mopped herself. All violence in his voice had been replaced with a jovial, practically chummy friendliness and concern for Anna's welfare. "No apologies—I'm the one who should be sorry." He winked. "Didn't mean to split you open." He winked again and broke into a rascal smile. It was the wrong wink at the wrong time. Anna's expression said so. Archie homed in on her distress. "You're all right, yes?" Anna shook her head yes, sniffling. This had happened before, rough sex jarring the blood and spongy tissue loose at just the right time of her cycle. It wasn't exactly his fault. The period would have come anyway, but likely not that afternoon and most definitely not on his couch. "No need to be embarrassed." Archie was trying to be kind. He didn't need to be. Anna found it condescending. She wasn't embarrassed at all. *Why would he even think that?* But she *was* something. What it was, she couldn't yet name. She sniffed again and swabbed her thighs with the sock. Archie ticked his head toward the bathroom. "Go take a shower. I'll make you something to drink. That's a good girl."

Anna gathered herself, her clothes, her purse, and fumbled into the bathroom, the sock between her legs and blood now streaking the inside of both thighs. She found a washcloth on the towel rack and a tampon in her purse. She cleaned up quickly, dressed, and told Archie she didn't have time for a drink. "I have to go," she said, but she was already almost out the door. She'd left the washcloth and the still-bloody sock in the sink.

"*En guete!*" Bruno said before the first bite was taken. Mary asked him what that meant and Bruno explained it was Swiss for "bon appétit." Mary was an excellent chef and her dinner was well received by all. The conversation remained friendly and upbeat. Tim mentioned to Mary that Bruno had given him investment advice.

"Oh, good!" Mary's voice rang sincere.

Bruno smiled deferentially. "This is what I do. It is my job. I am glad to help."

The children behaved well, though Victor momentarily reverted to pouting; he hadn't wanted to play with a girl. He hadn't wanted to come at all. Anna frowned at him and Victor took his usual sulky defense and muttered something about having a mean mother and ordered her to stop looking at him.

"Victor." Bruno's voice carried a warning in it and Victor responded with a near inaudible *Yessir* or *Jo,* Anna couldn't tell. It didn't matter. Bruno was agreeable enough that night to defend her. She was gratified. Max and Charles laughed at a series of in-jokes and distractions, behaving like the best of friends. Alexis sat and ate. She wore a blankly compliant expression. Biddable but frigid. Not exactly passive, but not exactly not. Anna recognized the expression and felt a pulse of compassion. *I know this girl,* Anna thought. *I've been her.*

"THE FACE ONE WEARS as an adult is a mask that's cut to fit in her youth."

There are many kinds of masks, Anna thought. *Theater masks and Halloween masks and surgical masks and fencing masks and diving masks and wrestling masks and ski masks. Welding visors and face cages, blindfolds and dominos. And death masks.*

The Doktor continued. "Every mask becomes a death

mask when you can no longer put it on or take it off at will. When it conforms to the contours of your psychic face. When you mistake the persona you project for your living soul. When you can no more distinguish between the two."

The S3 jerked sharply as Bahnhof Dietlikon came into view. It was the architecture of the track and it happened every time the train from Stettbach pulled in. It didn't matter how often it occurred; it always startled Anna. Anna was in a window seat, resting her head against the glass when the train made its usual sudden move. She bumped her forehead, gave a yelp. A teenage boy sitting across from her sniggered. He had a mean, rude face. They locked eyes for an uncomfortable three or four seconds before his Handy rang and he broke the gaze. He answered it, got up, and moved to a different bank of seats. Of all the events in the last hour, it was this that embarrassed Anna most.

Anna stayed on the train. When she left Archie's apartment she'd been gripped by an indulgent desire to do something she'd always wanted to do but never took the time for: to ride the full length of a line, both ways. In this case, to Wetzikon, the S3's eastern terminus, then back the way she came to Aarau, the city at its western end, before returning to Dietlikon. The trip would devour the afternoon. *I don't know why. I just want to. Does it matter?* Anna sassed herself. She phoned Ursula from Stadelhofen, apologized, and told her she'd forgotten that she'd scheduled an extra analysis that afternoon and promised she'd make it up to her any way she could. It wasn't entirely a lie; Doktor Messerli said it once, twenty, a hundred times: *Analysis happens whether the analyst is present or not.* The dinner with the Gilberts wasn't until that evening. Anna had time.

The sex had left her agitated. *No,* Anna thought, *vulnerable.* No woman watches herself bleed without being reminded that there's little but skin and a collection of thin vascular membranes holding her together. And the bright, basic daylight made the blood all the more startling. It hadn't embarrassed her. It had *exposed* her. Archie's precoital prattle hadn't helped. It unsettled her, how easily she buckled under his insistence, his commandeering whisper. But vulnerability's a magnet that always attracts assault. Some weaknesses beg to be seized.

Anna spent the train ride caught in alternating cycles of self-seeking, self-seething, and silence. The metaphor wasn't lost on her. *Passenger. Passive. I am not the engineer of my life. On track or off. It's what I'm trained in.* Anna could not help but smile at these very apt puns.

In their most recent analysis Doktor Messerli pressed Anna to consider the source of her passivity. What did Anna think lay at the root of the problem? Did Anna know? Had she ever thought about it? Anna had tried to lie. *Of course I've thought about it.* But she hadn't. Not really. It was just something she knew about herself. That was it. What more was there? The Doktor called her out, told her no, she hadn't thought about it, neither deeply nor superficially. For, if she had she'd see what the Doctor saw.

"Passivity isn't the malady. It's the symptom. Complicity is but one of your many well-honed skills. When it pleases you, you are quite practiced at defiance." Anna took the statement as an affront and, as if to diffuse the truth of the Doktor's conclusion, accepted it without rebuttal. Childish, she knew, but gratifying in the moment. By the time Anna's train reached Wetzikon she realized that was exactly the kind of manipulating Doktor Messerli was accusing her of. It wasn't passivity at all. It was an iridescent scheming, a mannequin made up to resemble a timid, yielding woman. "Where did this come from, Anna? What might have caused this?" Anna said that she was afraid she didn't know.

"That's exactly right. You are afraid," the Doktor said, and then she said no more.

IT WAS AN ALTOGETHER enjoyable evening at Tim and Mary Gilbert's house in Uster.

Until.

Mary left the table, then returned carrying dessert. Tim asked Anna how she was finding the German class. Anna said, "It's fine, it's good, it's helpful, I'm learning."

Mary took her seat. "Anna is Roland's A-plus number one student, Bruno. Everyone listens when she talks. Some everyones more than others, wink, wink." Mary looked at Anna and winked on her own cue. It grated Anna how Mary spoke aloud the words "wink, wink."

"What's this?" Bruno asked.

"Have you not told him, Anna?"

Anna shook her head and said to Mary that she didn't know what Mary was talking about. "I don't know what you're talking about, Mary." Anna employed a steady, breezy voice.

"Don't be so modest." Mary spoke to Bruno in the manner of an aside. "Anna has an admirer."

No, Mary, Anna thought.

"Ah, is that right?" Bruno asked. His voice glinted briefly of suspicion. Anna was the only one who noticed it. "So who is it then that admires my Anna?"

His Anna. Anna told him that she still didn't know what Mary meant.

Mary tee-heed in a way that, given other circumstances, might have been considered dainty. In the moment, Anna found it hollow and babyish. "His name is Archie and it's *adorable* how he follows her, sits next to her in class. He even waits for her and walks her to the tram every day after school."

"The tram?" Bruno had a question in his voice. Trams don't run to Dietlikon. There would be no reason for Anna to take a daily tram.

Anna interjected. "Train. She means train."

"Oh anyway. The man is smitten, Bruno. If I were you, I'd watch out!" Mary wasn't being garrulous. She was playing.

No, Mary. No, no, no, no. But it was too late.

Mary continued. "Oh, and ha, ha, he's good-looking as well, isn't he, Anna?"

Anna's heartbeat splintered and in that instant of an instant, Anna panicked and was terrified that the entire evening was a setup intended to out her as a liar, a cheat, a whore.

Anna reddened. Tim interceded on her behalf. "Mary, you're embarrassing our guest."

Mary punctuated her joshing with an earnest smile. Bruno's own smile was blithe. Anna didn't trust it. "So," Mary asked. "Who's ready for a piece of cake?" The children (Alexis included) chimed in unison a ravenous "Me!" and the adults *mm-hmmm*-ed. Mary sliced into an iced lemon pound cake and served a thick piece to each of them.

"Merci vielmal," Bruno thanked her, and everyone began to eat. "Mmm," Bruno savored. *"Sehr gut!"*

And so the evening unfolded, the laughter continued, and the banter went on. Bruno gave more banking advice and in thankful return, Tim invited Bruno and the boys to a ZSC Lions game. Bruno waved his hand—Tim needn't do that—but in the end he accepted the invitation with grace. Mary poured coffee and the children were dismissed and asked once again to play upstairs. By anyone's measure the dinner party ended as successfully as it had begun.

But Anna had seen it when it happened. How the air between her and Bruno had tightened when Mary spoke aloud the words "smitten," "good-looking," "admirer," "tram."

I will pay for this, Anna thought.

When it was time for the Benzes to leave, hands were shaken and unspecified plans made for a "next time."

"See you at the game next week," Tim called to Bruno and the boys.

"See you in class on Monday," Mary sang out to Anna.

Max waved to Charles, who waved back. Victor and Alexis parted without ceremony, and the Benzes traveled home. The boys nodded off during the drive.

The air was strangled. Anna attempted conversation. "That was nice, wasn't it?"

Bruno grunted. "Who's Archie?"

Anna spoke carefully. "Oh. No one. A man in our class. He's fond of me I guess. Mary says, anyway. I hadn't noticed."

"I see."

It was a shorter ride returning than going, and soon the Benzes were home. It was nearly ten when Bruno turned onto

Rosenweg, swerved sharply into the driveway, and snapped off the engine. "*Wacht auf,*" he barked over his shoulder as he got out of the car. The boys were sleepy and they dragged their feet. Bruno shut the car door firmly. Anna noted with small relief it wasn't a slam.

Anna called after him as he unlocked the house: "We forgot Polly." Bruno motioned the boys inside and pointed them up the stairs, to bed. Anna closed the car door and chased him up the front steps.

"Bruno?"

Bruno mumbled something that Anna understood to mean *Walk over and get her yourself.*

The direct walk from their front door to Ursula's was two minutes long, if that. Anna had no incentive to hurry. She took a winding, oblique route that led her in the opposite direction up the hill behind her house. It was a path she often traipsed; she knew it well. During the day it was clogged with Nordic walkers and people exercising their dogs. At night, it was empty and the open fields seemed haunted. The feeling was cryptic. On the hill Anna felt disconsolate, isolated, and renounced. *I am blanched by the moonlight,* she thought. *A revenant in a pauper's graveyard.*

"Do you believe in ghosts?" Anna asked Doktor Messerli.

"It doesn't matter whether you believe in ghosts. The ghosts believe in you."

Anna followed the path until she reached a bench at the crest of the hill. This hill, this bench, the middle of many, many nights—Anna couldn't say how many times she'd wandered up the path just to sit. In the rain, in the snow. On weekends or in the middle of the week. During nights of abject despair. On nights when the air was crass or unemotional. When the horrible ache of loneliness bit her on the neck. When the landscape and its hurt heart had its way with her. This was her bench. The bench she came to sit and cry upon. A yellow *Wanderweg* sign pointed in the direction of the woods. Behind the bench, a fenced-off acre that penned a farmer's cattle. That night, the cows were in the barn and Anna was entirely alone. Every several minutes and from just over a kilometer away, Anna heard a night train juddering down the tracks. *Where is it going? Who's inside? Is she asleep? Is she sad?* It always surprised her how clear and close the trains sounded even from the top of the hill. *I can feel it. A woman on that train is sad.*

Anna waited for the tears to come. They didn't. Five trains passed in the valley beneath her before she rose and made her way to Ursula's.

URSULA WAS PREDICTABLY CURT when Anna finally came home that afternoon. Anna had barely said hello before Ursula pushed past her and left. Anna let it go. Ursula had a right to be annoyed.

Polly was screaming and the boys were bickering. Anna looked at her watch—she'd been on the train for three and a half hours. After the first hour she'd lost patience with introspection. She let her mind turn gray. Her pulse slowed. She relaxed her eyes and tried to focus on the spaces between things as the loll of the train rocked her like a mother would. But the house, the noise, the children, her mother-in-law, the lateness of the afternoon and that evening's dinner plans all converged to a sharp, fine point that forced Anna to the wall of her own woe. There was nothing she could do at that moment but allow it to happen. So she let the boys squabble and left Polly Jean to cry herself out. Some tears can't be soothed, they can only be shed.

By the time Bruno came home from the office, his sons were dressed, his wife was made up, and Polly Jean was ready to go to Ursula's for the evening. Bruno volunteered to walk her over. Anna watched them from the living room window. Bruno was bouncing her on his hip and whistling. Polly had stopped crying before Anna finished her shower.

Roland's last lesson that morning was on subordinating conjunctions. *Falls* means "in case of." And *weil* means "because." "Remember to pronounce it 'vile,' " Roland said, which Anna found apropos. When Roland wrote down *damit,* the class chuckled. "Yes, just like the bad word. It means 'so that' or 'in order to.' " Then he reminded them they were adults and they should stop laughing because it wasn't that funny in the first place.

Anna stood at the window in order to watch them as they walked away, her husband and her daughter. Anna stood at the window so that she could see. She watched until they rounded the corner and disappeared from view.

Dammit, dammit, dammit, goddammit.

Anna rapped gently on Ursula's door even as she opened it. Ursula's distaste for Anna aside, they'd long passed the formalities of first knocking, then waiting on one or the other to answer the door. Anna walked into the house and whispered hello. Ursula had fallen asleep in front of the television, her knitting in her lap. Mike Shiva, a popular psychic and tarot card reader, was taking live phone calls. His programs ran every night; there was no escape from his plate-round face and straight stringy hair held back with a woman's headband. Anna thought he was weird and wonderful alike. A psychic seemed so un-Swiss, so unempirical.

Ursula stirred when Anna switched off the set. She woke with a start and for a moment seemed not to recognize her daughter-in-law.

"I'm here for Polly," Anna announced, as if there would be any other reason for her to appear in Ursula's house so late at night.

"Leave her alone," Ursula said. "If you wake her, she'll never go back to sleep."

"Oh." The tension in the car had distracted her. Anna felt stupid that she hadn't sorted this out. Of course. It was understood. Polly was going to stay the night. "Ursula, you're right. I wasn't thinking." She hadn't been. But fetching Polly Jean was as good an excuse as any to get away from Bruno for a while.

Ursula rose, shook her head thoroughly as if to jostle something loose. "Not thinking is one of your worst habits." Then she walked Anna to the door, directed her unceremoniously through it, and locked it behind her in the space of no more than fifteen seconds. Anna walked home without the baby she came for.

* * *

"GHOSTS," DOKTOR MESSERLI CONTINUED, "aren't always the spirits of the human dead bound to the earth. A ghost can be the residual feeling that follows an act you have accomplished but feel bad about. Or the act itself. Something you've been or done that you cannot escape."

6

Two weeks later, on a Sunday, the last day of the month, Anna, Bruno, Ursula, and the children boarded a 10:00 a.m. train. They were on their way to Mumpf, a town in Kanton Aargau near Switzerland's north border, where Daniela, Bruno's sister, and her partner David lived. It was Daniela's fortieth birthday.

Taking a train often made more sense than driving. Today the choice was made by circumstance: with Ursula along they couldn't all fit inside the car. The only inconvenience of the plan was two transfers. David would gather them at Bahnhof Mumpf when they arrived.

On the InterRegio, Charles took the window seat facing forward and Victor, the seat turned toward the back. These were their permanent assignments when the family traveled by train, much to the vexation of Anna's eldest. Charles had a tender stomach and was prone to motion sickness. A window seat helped his equilibrium. Sure enough, five minutes into the trip, Charles's face took on the color of a small sour pickle.

"Watch the horizon, *Schatz,*" Anna counseled. "Draw deep, slow breaths." This seemed to help.

Anna sat next to Victor on the aisle, facing Bruno who, like Charles, always took a forward-facing seat. Ursula settled into the bank of seats across from them, her eyes closed lightly as if in prayer and Daniela's birthday gift in her lap. In his own lap, Bruno held Polly Jean.

The question had never been asked. Not by Bruno, not by Ursula, not by Daniela nor Hans nor Margrith nor Edith nor Doktor Messerli nor Claudia Zwygart nor the postman nor the cashier at the grocery store nor Mary nor Archie nor anyone who knew Anna either casually or closely, acquaintances old and new. None had asked. And had they asked, Anna would have lied.

But there isn't any reason to ask. Anna always went back to that.

Nevertheless, the facts were chiseled into the exquisite alabaster of Polly Jean's face where anyone who wished to challenge the fiction could have and the facts were these: Polly in no way resembled Bruno.

Polly Jean was not a Benz.

"ANNA, WHO IS STEPHEN?" This was the third time Doktor Messerli had asked her.

A man I could never love, but did, Anna thought but didn't say. Doktor Messerli didn't ask again.

THE WEATHER PLAYED TRICKS. A cold front that had blown through Zürich the night before had left Dietlikon windy and wet. But halfway to Mumpf the skies were clear. The Benzes were outrunning the elements.

It was a story she'd told only to herself, but had repeated so often it was rote. The only thing that ever changed was the tenor by which she told it: sometimes with a sympathetic bias, others with hysteria's rancid theatrics, and yet other times with a harlot's detached sangfroid. Occasionally it brought her comfort. More often than not it made her queasy, it hurt her heart (everything always hurt her heart). But whether through sorrow's shiny tears or memory's glazed and hazy panes of glass, Anna was resigned to a progression of unalterable facts.

"There are no accidents, Anna. Everything correlates. Everything connects. Every detail bears a consequence. One instant begets the next. And the next. And the next."

Anna eyed her husband. Bruno seemed to have let his jealousy go. The past two weeks had been spent without incident. They were getting along. They'd gone to market together, worked in the yard together, gone out to dinner as a family, and even went to a movie they'd both wanted to see. No further mention of Archie was made. But the merry, expansive man who showed himself at the Gilberts' had been replaced by the sullen, disgruntled husband who Anna knew too well.

And why shouldn't he be disgruntled? Anna upbraided herself. *Just because he doesn't know what I'm doing doesn't mean I'm not doing it.* During the last two weeks Anna tried to step back, to stand apart from herself, to evaluate her most recent choices and to weigh their benefits against their costs. It had been a close call. *Who's Archie?* Bruno asked. *A no one,* Anna replied. And he was. She barely knew the man. *Is this the hill I want to die on?* she asked herself. *No? Then don't die on it, woman.*

But was the call really that close? Were the incident drawn on a map, Bruno's moment of suspicion would have been no nearer to the fact of the matter than a suburb is to city center. When Anna thought about it that way, the damage seemed minimal, all the way around.

Like that, Anna bounced between consequence and choice.

And in the end, the ball landed on the side of no harm, no foul. *I am a good wife, mostly,* she self-proclaimed. *Everyone's safe, everyone's fed.*

Anna kept seeing Archie.

"When you were a girl, what did you want to be when you grew up?" Doktor Messerli once asked.

Anna gave a plaintive answer. "Loved. Protected. Secure." She knew that wasn't what the Doktor meant.

The Doktor tried another approach. "What did you study at university?" Anna flushed. She didn't want to say. "Tell me."

"Home economics," Anna whispered.

IT HAD HAPPENED ALMOST two years earlier. It was four days before Christmas. A Wednesday. Anna had taken the train into the city. A reluctant voyage, it was a next-to-next-to-last shopping trip, a chore in which she was only marginally invested.

The weeks that immediately precede Weihnachten in Zürich are entirely tolerable. The streets teem with shoppers whose smart, bright coats appear even smarter and brighter against the drab gray landscape of Zürich's usually snowless Decembers. From sooty roasting drums, dark-skinned men scoop hot chestnuts into thin paper sacks. A seasonal candle-making tent stands near the Bürkliplatz Quaibrücke. And for a time, if you found yourself on the Bahnhofstrasse after sundown there was the delectation of strolling beneath the shine of champagne-colored twinkle lights and a one-kilometer stretch of seven-foot-long tubular bulbs. They pended from cables stretched taut between buildings and above the catenaries supplying power to the city's electric trams and were controlled by software that varied the scintillation according to levels of human activity in the street underneath. The array was modern—too modern, in fact. Enough people hated them that the city eventually returned to a more traditional display. But Anna's boys loved it. Even Victor, who was easily bored and for his age notably jaded, allowed himself the indulgence of childlike captivation, wonder, awe.

Anna had spent the day traversing Zürich's entire downtown from west to east on foot, and the trimmings of the holiday season—lovely as they were in smaller doses—began to feel excessive, unnecessary. Still, she shopped. At Piz Buch und Berg she found Bruno's Christmas gift, several close-scale hiking maps of cantons Graubünden and St. Gallen and a guidebook of suggested treks through the Swiss Jura. At the Manor on Bahnhofstrasse Anna fought aggressive crowds to pick out a modest twin sweater set that she thought might make a nice, thought-that-counts kind of gift for Edith.

Chagrin had begun the day. Bruno had put her in a mood

that morning for a reason she'd managed to forget. But the feeling, whatever it was, gnawed on her like teeth. She hashed and simmered, an all-day stew on the stove. She was lonely and remote. Anna was lonely and remote everywhere she went.

"A LONELY WOMAN IS a dangerous woman." Doktor Messerli spoke with grave sincerity. "A lonely woman is a bored woman. Bored women act on impulse."

ANNA TURNED HER GAZE from Bruno to the window. Kanton Aargau was made fuzzy by the handprints on the glass and the speed of the train. Victor and Charles squabbled over an action figure Anna had carelessly forgotten to make sure they brought two of. Bruno threatened to take it away if they couldn't settle their disagreement. Ursula fell asleep halfway to Mumpf. Her thin, wheezy snore was barely audible over the train's natural noise. The boys laughed; Anna shushed them. Bruno rolled his eyes and said, "She sleeps too much, my mother." Bruno was a devoted son, but he was critical on occasion, not just of Anna, but of all the women in his life, Ursula and Daniela included (though Anna most of all).

Anna scowled at him. "Don't roll your eyes at her, she's your mother." Ursula couldn't help but snore. She was an old woman.

"She's not that old." Anna granted Bruno this. Ursula would be sixty-seven on her next birthday. She'd been a young mother, just twenty-three at Bruno's birth. By the time she was Anna's age, her son was an insolent teen. Anna would be well into her fifties before all of the children were out of the house. The thought exhausted her. *Mother has moods, too,* Bruno had groused, but Anna only knew of one, that vinegar humor, her snappy disposition, the scowl into which she twisted her face when Anna did something she didn't approve of, the silence she spat back when Anna said something she didn't want to hear. Anna had given up trying to please her years ago.

"Is there a difference between destiny and fate?" Anna was jumpy, more unsettled than usual. Doktor Messerli asked if she understood the concept of synchronicity. "Not really."

"Events don't always obey rules of time and space. Sometimes the mere thought of a certain friend will cause her to telephone after months of no communication. Or perhaps a man wonders whether he should leave his wife and in the next instant he turns on the radio and hears a notice for apartments. No coincidence is chance. Synchronicity is the external manifestation of an inner reality."

Anna quizzed her with her eyes.

Had Anna forgone a single stop that day, or had any of her exchanges in shops or on the street endured a short minute longer or a long half-minute less, then what happened wouldn't have. Anna was close to giving up and going home. She was hungry. She was cold. The shopping was almost done. All she'd left to buy was Ursula's gift. Ursula was a knitter; Anna planned to give her skeins of wool. She crossed the Limmat at the Rathausbrücke and made her way to the Hand-Art shop on Neumarkt.

* * *

The Benzes were quiet on the train to Mumpf, each locked in the closet of his or her own thoughts. Anna flipped through a German-language women's magazine she'd bought from a kiosk at the Oerlikon train station. She scanned her monthly horoscope. Born October 22, Anna was a Libra and in less than a month she would be thirty-eight years old. *Forest, danger, fire, trial.* Most of the horoscope's words she knew. She got the gist. It ended with a warning: *Gib acht.*

Be careful.

Before Doktor Messerli suggested the German classes, she recommended that Anna begin a journal. "You needn't bring it to analysis and I don't ask you to share it with me if that isn't your wish. Consider it a private, internal conversation. But be absolutely honest. To yourself, you must admit everything." Anna liked this idea and she took Doktor Messerli's advice and immediately after analysis that day she went to an upscale stationery story near the Doktor's office and bought a flat-spine unruled journal with a green cloth cover. It was almost too pretty to write in.

She wrote the first entry on the train ride home. *Admit it all, Anna. Do not hedge.* Her sentences were scattered, disconnected: *Everything I run from catches up to me. My prayers don't have purchase. I carry them on my back. I cannot set them down. I have lost a year of sleep to insomnia. The utter sameness just drags on. I have a face like a key to a diary. There's something it should open. I lack most kinds of stamina. I am beholden to my own peculiar irony: to survive I self-destruct. But the heart's logic follows its own rules. I miss him simply because I do.*

Anna read what she'd written and grimaced. She'd try this again, she was sure. Probably. *Maybe.* In the meantime, she took her pen and crossed out the entire page with an aggressive X.

"WHAT DO YOU WANT from this, Archie?" It was the Wednesday after the dinner party in Uster. Anna lay on her back in Archie's bed with the blanket pulled all the way to her chin. It was time to go home but the room was cold and she was naked and getting out of bed would mean facing both those facts.

"What do you mean?"

Anna didn't think it was a complicated question. "I mean this isn't a relationship."

"But we just had relations." He winked.

Anna was undeterred. "What kind of man has an affair with a married woman?" It wasn't an indictment. She wanted to know.

"Not relevant." Anna blinked. She rebutted. He shook his head. "More people have affairs than don't."

Anna scowled. "That can't be true."

He spun her question on its axis. "What about a married woman? Why does she do it? What kind of woman's she?"

"A lonely woman. A bored woman." Anna spoke with authority.

Archie shook his head. "No, that's not it."

"How would you know?" Anna wondered whether Archie had done this before.

"Bored women join clubs and volunteer. Sad women have affairs."

That's the statement of a reductionist, Anna thought, but didn't feel like arguing the point. "You think I'm sad?"

"Knew it the moment I saw you." Anna asked how that was possible. "A man can smell a woman's sadness."

"And you smelled mine." Anna was offended by the word "smell." As if sadness could be covered up with roses. As if despair might be washed off with soap.

"Yes."

"And took advantage of it." Anna was perturbed and fascinated and something else, though she couldn't pin it down. *Guilty? Found out? Caught in the red-handed act?* Something like that.

Archie corrected her. "And responded to it."

"There's a difference?"

"You're not sad?"

This time it was Anna's turn. "Irrelevant," she lied. She shifted in bed. Neither spoke for a minute or two. "What do you like about me?"

Archie laughed. "So it's that kind of talk we're having, eh?" Anna shook her head and Archie softened. "You're complicated. You can't be cracked."

Like a safe. Except I'm not. "Thanks. I guess."

"You're welcome." They settled onto their backs, each looking up at the ceiling. "Why'd you say yes?"

Now it was Anna's turn to laugh. "What else would I have said?"

THE INTERREGIO PULLED INTO the station at Frick at 10:56. It was an eight-minute wait before the S-Bahn to Mumpf passed through. The Benzes herded out of the car, descended beneath the station to change platforms, and then huddled around an empty bench while they waited for their connection. The barometric pressure had dropped. The weather was changing. Everyone felt weary and it wasn't even lunchtime.

A month before, a mass grave of dinosaur bones was unearthed in Frick. An amateur paleontologist found them. He discovered over one hundred entirely intact skeletons. Fossils of plateosauri two hundred million years old. Some days, Anna envied the dinosaurs their extinction. A comet did not veer from its trajectory. A beautiful disaster that was fated to happen did.

The eight minutes passed quickly and by five past eleven the Benzes were on the S-Bahn headed directly to Mumpf.

THE HAND-ART SHOP WAS filled with pretty colors and soft yarns and everything smelled like lavender and cinnamon, cardamom and mace. *Lovely,* Anna thought. And it was. Lovely and soothing. Tranquilizing. She spent forty minutes in the shop, picking up skeins of exotic wool and touching each of them longingly to her cheek before returning them to their shelves, all beneath the magnanimous gaze of the shop mistress. The tactile experience consoled her and the dread that had blackened Anna's mood began to lift. In the end, she chose skeins of hand painted silk, of alpaca, and of cashmere—luxury threads she knew Ursula would adore but never purchase for herself. Anna left the knitting shop gratified that, for once, Ursula would be exactly pleased with what Anna offered her.

She could take the number 33 bus directly to the Hauptbahnhof; that was Anna's plan. The bus stop is on the eastern end of Neumarkt. So when she left the knitting shop Anna bore a stiff, immediate right. But she was laden with packages and she wasn't paying attention to where she was going and she'd pulled her winter hat right down to her eyes. Therefore, Anna did not notice the man standing in the middle of the sidewalk, whose own face was buried in the crease of a Zürich city map. And he, so absorbed by the two-dimensional zigzaggery of cross streets on the thin, unwieldy paper, did not see Anna bearing down upon him.

Synchronicity often masquerades as coincidence. As right-place-right-time-ness. As an and-then-suddenly kind of incident. In this case, it was a combination of all three that when balled together knotted themselves into a cliché as saccharine as a kitten in a floppy yellow bow. The trite expectedness of it was one of the proofs Anna clung to for ballast in the aftermath. *See? How could it* not *have been true? Things like that* don't *only happen in movies.*

She hadn't been paying attention.

She hadn't been paying attention and she ran into the man.

"*Eggscusi!*" Anna apologized immediately, using one of the few Swiss words she knew. The man steadied himself and waved her apology gently away. It was a simple, charming gesture. Then he, too, apologized, but in English and then he laughed a nervous laugh, and asked Anna in terrible German whether she knew where the Lindenhof was and if so, would she show him on the map? He was black-haired and pale-skinned and six inches taller than she. The map he tried to fold refused to be refolded. He shivered in the mist wearing only a light car coat the color of ash. A left front tooth was slightly chipped and he had a mole at the outer corner of his eye, also on the left side. Anna noticed these things. She pegged his accent as midwestern by its even phonetic keel. There was an upsurge in Anna's heart.

Is it possible to fall in love over a single look? Anna couldn't say. But at the behest of a glance tossed casually down upon her, she was made witness, victim, and slave to the culmination of all her mythologies. And every heretofore moment in her life, the ones that mattered and the ones that only seemed to matter, had added up to the sum of this intense instant, this instant alone. In the short, sharp span of a single heartbeat, she knew that nothing she'd ever said or done, and nothing she would ever say or do again, would carry even half the tragedy of this.

ANNA STARED OUT THE window on the train from Frick to Mumpf.

I wish I'd never met the man.

7

A SECRET'S SAFEST HIDING PLACE IS IN THE OPEN. ATTEMPT A middling effort at keeping a cucumber-cool demeanor, and no matter the secret, everyone will accept you for who you appear to be. Consider the Nazi who flees to South America and lives out his life in quiet compliance, his remaining days steady and blameless. Mornings he wakes, he rises, he walks out into the open day. He mails letters, rides the bus, buys pears at a market. He eats lunch in an open-air café. He takes his coffee black and always reads the sports scores first. When a pretty girl passes, he tips his hat.

No one knows that seventy years ago his jackboot cracked a Warsaw rabbi's ribs or that he seized the watch fob that he wears from the rattletrap hands of a Romany horse groom just inside Treblinka's gates.

So say nothing. Don't flinch. Act your part. No matter your secret. Atrocious or banal, unfathomable or mundane. It's a method for the *Aufseher* and the adulteress alike. If you don't advertise, you needn't hide.

And just like that, your big, black lies grow small and white.

* * *

"Do you know anything of alchemy, Anna?"

"The belief that base metal can be turned into gold?"

Doktor Messerli nodded. "Yes. In medieval Europe there were men who believed in this possibility. They spent their entire lives in experiment. Of course they did not succeed. But the premise of their work became the foundation for other scientific studies. Chemistry, mostly."

"Oh."

"Jung studied alchemy from a philosopher's point of view. He compared it to analysis. A person achieves individuation through a similar process. She transforms the dark matter of the unconscious into consciousness. The soul's gold. If you will." Anna had stopped listening when she said "chemistry."

David waited for the Benzes on the platform. He cheek-kissed both Ursula and Anna (once, twice, three times as is the custom), gave Bruno a firm, jostling handshake, summarily mussed the boys' hair, and took Polly Jean from Bruno's arms, fussing briefly but immodestly over the baby before handing her off to Anna. Then they all slid into the car for the very short ride to David and Daniela's house. It was a tight fit. Victor sat on Bruno's knee, Charles on Ursula's. They would travel only a kilometer and a half; David promised to steer the car with caution.

Daniela and David had lived together since Daniela was nineteen. David was in his mid-forties then, old enough to have been Daniela's father and still married to the mother of his children at the time their relationship began. But the common-law marriage of David and Daniela had endured now for two decades. They seemed to be doing something right.

David was a crumpled, beige man with thick gray hair who was rarely seen without a calabash pipe between his lips. Anna liked David. Like Ursula he had been an educator; for more than thirty years he taught middle school social studies. David was gentle, agreeable, and possessed a pliable carriage not typically found in the Swiss. This made sense: he wasn't. David was French.

In less than five minutes, the car arrived at David and Daniela's house.

THE MAN WAS LOOKING for the Lindenhof. The Lindenhof is Zürich's oldest quarter, the site of what was once an ancient Roman customs post. Now a park, most days (even bad-weather ones such as the very day in question) find the Lindenhof crowded with old men playing garden chess with toddler-sized *Schachfiguren* upon chessboards painted on the ground, and tourists enjoying the view. Zürich's entire Altstadt is visible from the lookout on the square.

When Anna answered in English an unmitigated relief drained the tension from his face.

"Oh Jesus, you speak English. Thank God. My German's no good."

Anna's smile was sweet and amused. "That's obvious."

He smiled back at her. "I've been working up courage to ask for directions."

Anna returned his returned smile.

So began the affair between Anna Benz and Stephen Nicodemus.

"First off," Anna said, taking the map from his hands and turning it around, "you've got it upside down. The Lindenhof's on the other side of the river." A mild, embarrassed expression spread across Stephen's face. Anna examined him closely. He was and wasn't attractive at the same time. But it wasn't his looks Anna fell immediately in love with (if one could have called it love and two years after the fact, Anna was no longer sure it ever was). It was his voice. It was a steady, low, solid voice with a gentle immediacy to it. He spoke with an intimate and confidential baritone. There was a fleshy texture to his words. Anna gave directions to the Lindenhof as slowly as she could. She wanted to draw the encounter out as long as possible before the thread of it snapped. So she leaned into the space of him, and breathed the air of him, tapped her hand and arched her back under the gaze of him, gestures she would find herself repeating sooner than either of them knew, and while dressed in fewer clothes. Anna fished a pen and a receipt from her purse, and wrote down the tram stops he wanted, the transfers he'd need to make. Anna handed him the paper and for a few awkward seconds the two of them stood cold and shivering and, though fully dressed, strangely naked before each other, not knowing what next—if anything—to say. They spoke in tandem:

"I guess I should get home."

"Would you like to grab a coffee?"

They shared an uncomfortable laugh and the inept silence returned once more. But not all will is free. Anna broke the self-conscious lull.

Oh yes, she said. *Let's.*

* * *

David led them through the house and then to the back patio where the other guests had gathered. Ursula put Daniela's gift on the dining room table, and Anna draped her purse and Polly's diaper bag over the back of a chair and followed David and Bruno outside. Ursula paused in the kitchen, not immediately joining the group.

Daniela and her friends sat upon benches flanking a large mahogany picnic table, itself shaded by an equally enormous umbrella. Everyone drank European beer—Feldschlösschen, Hürlimann, Eichhof—and almost everyone smoked European cigarettes—Parisienne, Davidoff, Gitanes. A radio was tuned to a Basel rock station. Daniela sat near the center of the table. She was telling a story. Anna couldn't make out the details, but Daniela's modulation suggested a ribald tale. Daniela waved her arms as she spoke, a half-empty beer glass in her left hand and in her right, the tail of a red feather boa one of her friends brought for her to wear. She interrupted the story with her own laughter. She was sincere in her present amusement, merry and gay. For a jealous moment Anna begrudged her this happiness. Anna hiked Polly farther up her hip and pulled her own sweater closed as if to protect herself from the sting of a joy she did not know. Bruno broke into his sister's story to give her a birthday kiss. She set aside her beer, rose, and greeted the family. She seemed genuinely glad they had come.

"Anna," she began in English equally as grammatical but more heavily accented than her brother's, "I am very happy to see you. You look so pretty. Polly is so big!" She liberated Polly Jean from Anna's arms. Daniela loved her niece and would hold her the rest of the afternoon if Anna allowed it. Daniela worked in Basel for a fair trade organization. She was kind, thoughtful, funny, earnest, easy to like and all around, a very admirable person. Had Anna known her in any other context, perhaps they'd have been girlfriends. But she didn't, and they weren't. They were sisters-in-law. They were friendly. But they were not precisely friends.

Daniela turned back toward her other guests, who nodded and waved politely at Anna. Anna looked around. Bruno had abandoned her for beer and Victor and Charles had run off to the barn, preferring the company of Rudi, David's decade-old Saint Bernard, over the company of adults.

With Polly in Daniela's arms, Anna didn't know what to do with her hands. She felt ill at ease, like a dateless girl at a school dance. She moved to join Bruno but he was already locked into conversation with another party guest, a man whom Anna had met before, but whose name she couldn't recall. He was blond and muscular and only an inch or two taller than Anna. When he noticed Anna he widened the circle and invited her with an open hand to join. He interrupted Bruno mid-sentence, pointed to his beer, and raised his brow. "*Willst du?*" That's what it sounded like he said. He was speaking Swiss. Did Anna want?

Nice, so very nice to be asked.

Anna stepped a little closer while shaking her head no. She wasn't a beer drinker. The blond man nodded and smiled, then motioned Bruno to continue.

Anna led Stephen to a nearby bistro, the Kantorei. They sat in creaky wooden chairs, the legs of which were uneven and annoying. Anna ordered a brandy and Stephen asked for a beer. And then they began to talk. Stephen was a scientist on a short-term sabbatical from MIT with an appointment at the

ETH, the Swiss Federal Institute of Technology. It is one of the world's top schools. Einstein was a graduate. Apart from the banks and businesses of Zürich's financial industry, the ETH is the city's most prestigious institution. Stephen had sublet an apartment in Wipkingen, a quarter on the city's north side, and the namesake of the district's train station. Stephen was, Anna learned, a thermochemist. A pyrologist. He studied combustion. Stephen was an expert on fire.

In the difficult months following the affair, Anna had ample time to consider the symbolic implications of Stephen's work and the effect the man had had on her. Anna's conclusions were these: That fire is beautifully cruel. That fusion occurs only at a specific heat. That blood, in fact, can boil. That the dissolution of an affair is an entropic reaction, and the disorder it tends toward is flammable. That a heart will burn. And burn and burn and burn. That an ordinary flame's hottest point cannot always be seen.

DOKTOR MESSERLI OPENED A book and pointed to a series of related drawings depicting a couple making love in a fountain. In the first they're rained upon. In the next their bodies have fused together and the pair—now singular—rise. "The result of a union of opposites. King and queen lie down in a mercurial bath. They face each other's naked truths. The psychosexual union is a symbol of coming to consciousness."

Anna offered her a quizzical look. "What's this got to do with me?"

"*Schau.* The being dies and takes the body with it. But it returns. Transcendence has been achieved, but at a cost. The cost is death."

"Symbolic death?"

"Of course."

ANNA STOOD TO THE side and watched her husband interact with his friends. It was strange seeing him like this, chummy and familiar, relaxed among old pals. Twenty years sloughed off him almost instantly. She imagined him a young rake, a scamp with a quirky smile knocking back a beer, his hands darting through the air as he told a story, recounted a soccer match, talked about a girl. That was Bruno at twenty-four. Anna would have been eighteen. Had they met twenty years ago, each would have scared the other off. Anna with her needy solitudes, Bruno with the confidence radiating from the very posture his body seemed to be recalling just then in Daniela's backyard.

Bruno downed the last swallow of his beer and turned to the blond man and asked if he wanted another. He called him Karl. Karl nodded, *Jo gärn.* As Bruno brushed by Anna he bent his head to hers and asked her. His eyes were kinder than they were twenty minutes earlier. *It's the beer,* Anna thought. Bruno's eyes always softened when he started to drink. *Water, please.* Bruno nodded, winked, then marched off to grab drinks for all of them.

He'd called the blond man Karl. Anna remembered now. He was Karl Trötzmüller, a childhood friend of Bruno and Daniela. Anna was embarrassed she hadn't recalled his name right away. He'd been to the house a dozen times. She blamed her absentmindedness on the weather.

"How are you, Anna? It is kind to talk to you. You see very pretty." Karl spoke a very strange and extremely slipshod English. By "kind" he meant "nice," and by "see" he intended "look." Both were odd mistakes to make, but Karl was odd to begin with. Seemingly benign but without a doubt peculiar. Even his name was a little off the mark. *It's got too many umlauts,* Bruno once snarked. *It sounds made up. It's not Swiss.* Umlauts aside, Bruno was right: it wasn't particularly Swiss. But it was Karl's. And it suited him.

Anna considered her clothes. She wore a rust-colored autumn dress styled in an A-line pattern, ribbed yellow tights, and black Mary Janes. Anna preferred the feel of dresses on her body. Slacks and jeans were too confining. Swiss women, Anna noticed, were not dress wearers, choosing more often the practicality of pants. Tomorrow, this dress would return to the closet until spring. As it was, the weather was cold enough that Anna had to complete the look with the only sweater she could lay her hands to as they rushed out of the house, a rough red cardigan. It ruined an otherwise stylish outfit. "I look like a Thanksgiving centerpiece," Anna said to Karl, who laughed and made a hedging motion with his hands. "Well, I do not understand about that," he offered, confusing "understand" with "know." "We have not Thanksgiving in d'Schweez," Karl said, using the native pronunciation of Switzerland's name. He, too, wore an outlaw grin and stood in a near-reprobate stance, his hands in his pockets, his feet squarely planted, and his hips thrust forward like a come-on. *Is this a come-on?* Anna wondered. *Is he looking me up and down?* Yes, Karl eyed her as they spoke. *But that's what people do, they look at each other when they talk,* Anna reminded herself. *Not everyone's as haphazardly moral as you.*

Bruno returned with their beers and Anna's water, and the men—*those rapscallion boys*—took up the conversation where they'd left it. Anna paid only vague attention until she heard

Tim's name and figured that Bruno was telling Karl about their dinner with the Gilberts. Bruno spoke in a rapid, scuttling Schwiizerdütsch. Anna didn't even attempt a proper listen. Karl intuited her frustration and asked Bruno if it would not be better to talk in English. Bruno swigged his beer, shook his head no, and answered, in Swiss German, *She is taking classes, needs the practice, it's time she learned the goddamn language.* This Anna did understand. He was smiling when he said it, and the smile was real. Bruno meant all his gestures. Bruno meant every word he said.

ANNA AND STEPHEN TALKED over one, two, three rounds of drinks. Anna phoned Ursula, fibbed to her, explained that the shops were crowded, that every task was taking twice as long to accomplish as she'd planed, and would Ursula mind watching Victor after school? Would she collect Charles from *Kinderkrippe*? *Would you? Would you . . . ?* Of course Ursula would. But she wasn't happy about it.

By then Anna had been drained of the vexation she'd been carrying around. Her heart shifted gravity again, only this time, it rose above her head like a helium balloon. Anna acknowledged the absurdity of this feeling. It didn't matter. She was high on the moment. A wind could come and blow her away. She begged the clock to spin more slowly. She begged the clock to stop.

"WE MAKE THE PASSIVE voice in German with the verb *werden*. 'To become.' So the bicycle *becomes* stolen, if you will. Or the woman *became* sad."

Or the body would become ravaged. And the heart will become broken. Somehow it made more sense this way to Anna. "To be" is static. "To become" implies motion. A paradoxical move toward limp surrender. Whatever it is, you do not do it. It is done to you. "Passivity" and "passion" begin alike. It's only how they end that's different.

Clocks don't stop. Eventually, with great disappointment, Anna tore herself away from the drinks, her giddiness, and Stephen's company. It was time for Anna to go home. She wrote her phone number on a napkin and implored him with a wink not to lose it. She blushed as she made a happy journey to the train station. *Yes, yes, of course. A flirtation. Nothing more. I won't rely on desire to tell me the truth. It rarely does. He will not—he really shouldn't—call.* But as her homeward bound train rolled past the shunting yards to the west of the Hauptbahnhof, Anna felt a tremor in her hand. She attributed it to shivering from the cold. It was winter, after all. But the tremor repeated itself and she realized it was her cell phone. A message that had been sent was received: *What are you doing tomorrow?* Anna didn't respond. But on that message's tail came another: *Come see me.* And as the train slowed to a stop at Bahnhof Dietlikon, the last message arrived: *Tomorrow. 10 A.M. Nürenbergstrasse 12.* Anna was pressed to answer; she could do nothing else. She told herself—convinced herself—she could do nothing else. She sent a singular reply.

Yes.

She did not even attempt to pretend she had no intention of sleeping with him.

8

Daniela's party was ordinary, prosaic even. At two they feasted upon cervelat, the thick, stubbed wurst known commonly as Switzerland's national sausage. At three they ate a buttercream cake baked by Eva, a distant cousin of the Benz siblings who lived nearby. At four o'clock Daniela unwrapped her birthday gifts. It was five. Anna had a headache. When she checked her Handy, she found a message from Archie. *Tomorrow after class?* She texted back: *Maybe.*

On the day after meeting Stephen Nicodemus, Anna left Charles at *Kinderkrippe* and told Ursula, whom she passed on the street returning from the post office, that she had just a little more shopping left in the city but would be home in time to get Charles and meet Victor after school. Ursula nodded and kept walking. Anna scolded herself for being so chatty. It would be weeks before she learned that the secret to telling lies was simply not to tell them: *Omit, Anna, omit. The fewer the details, the more credible you'll sound.* When Anna reached the station, she boarded her usual train. But instead of riding it all the way to the Hauptbahnhof, she got off at Wipkingen, the station just before it. From Oerlikon, the station that immediately precedes it, the ride to Wipkingen was a short two kilometers, three-quarters of which took place in a dark, straight tunnel. Tunnels made Anna apprehensive. Indeed, she found a comfort riding trains, but this occurred in open air alone. In tunnels she could think of nothing but the earth above. *What if the ground collapsed? What if I was buried underneath? What is it like to be buried underground? Will I know it when I'm dead?* In tunnels she worked her best to distract herself. She would imagine, then, the topographies above her, perhaps with a city map in her hand, and trace the train's path. On the S3 she'd picture the hills of Zürichberg, the Dolderbahn, the FIFA headquarters, the empty fields between Gockhausen and Tobelhof. On this train, the S8, she imagined the houses she was passing underneath, the people inside of them. Who was cooking, who was sleeping, who was fighting, who was making love. Who was sitting on a balcony feeling sorry for herself. Who was breaking someone else's heart. Who was having her own heart broken. As maudlin as it was, it perturbed her less than the alternative. *It's through a tunnel a body comes into the world,* Anna thought. *And as a body leaves it?* Anna didn't know, though some people described a tunnel of light. Anna was willing to accept that as fact.

A short walk found her at Nürenbergstrasse. Stephen sat on a bench in front of his building. He was waiting for her. He took her to his room on the first floor.

Anna had never been mad about foreplay. She was not one of those women who needed to endure complicated half hours of rubbing and prodding and explosive plyometrics before her body tensed and the dam holding back her pleasure burst. Her desires were basic. *Put it in, take it out. Repeat for as long as possible.*

This was Anna's first infidelity.

They fucked so hard that afterward neither could walk.

Doktor Messerli pointed to a picture of a three-footed fountain framed by stars, the sun and moon, and a two-headed dragon. Pillars of smoke plumed up either side. "Fire," she said, "is the first act of transformation. And," she added, "in alchemy, fire is always associated with libido."

Anna ate too much. Her stomach ached and she herself was restless. She was ready to go home but they wouldn't leave for another two hours at least.

She rose from the table, stretched her arms above her head, and looked around. "Anyone want to go for a walk?" Bruno grunted. The beer was catching up to him and he was getting tired and cranky. Anna took the grunt for a no. Ursula had no interest. The boys were elsewhere. Daniela had guests to entertain. Even Polly Jean; she was asleep on David and Daniela's bed. Anna shrugged and started off alone.

She'd only made it down the drive before Daniela called after her and asked if she wanted an umbrella. Anna shook her head no. All day long rain had seemed unavoidable. And yet, they had avoided it. She'd take the chance. A few steps farther on she heard the call of her name once more. She turned. Karl Trötzmüller was jogging across the yard to meet her. "I want to come with you," he said. Bruno glanced briefly in their direction, then turned back to his conversation. Anna didn't need his permission. But apparently she had it.

Karl caught up with Anna and the two of them started on the path that led into the Mumpf woods.

"THINK OF A BUCKET, Anna. Your heart is a bucket with a hole in the bottom of it. It leaks. You cannot keep it full."

Anna nodded opaquely. A sparrow landed on the outside sill and just as quickly flew away. "I've got a hole."

"Over time it widens. From the size of a one-franc piece to the size of a small plum, then an apple, then a man's fist. Eventually the hole becomes so large that the bucket has no bottom at all. Then it is useless."

"I have a useless heart." It was a vacant statement.

Doktor Messerli shook her head. "No, Anna. All I am saying is you cannot treat a mortal wound with iodine and plasters. Repair the hole. That's the only thing to do."

IN JANUARY AND FEBRUARY and the first half of March 2006, Anna spent every available moment in Stephen Nicodemus's arms. They were wiry and able—not strong, but *his*. Anna had fallen in love. Or a version of love.

They spoke most often of things both scientific and theoretical. It was how they flirted. It was almost the whole of their windup. It became Anna's challenge to ask him questions no one had asked him before. *Why is fire hot?* she asked. *Is fire ever cold? Why won't wool burn? Does a flame have weight? Have mass? Is there anything that is entirely resistant to fire? Can fire itself catch fire? Can fire freeze?*

Anna made a fetish of all things fire. She passed her palms through the flames of candles she lit in the den. She lifted the covers of the stove and stared at the pilot light. She dreamed of explosions, of houses burning down. She'd wake in the night with ecstatic sweats. *What would it be like to strike a final match and set it to the center of this bed?* Even Anna knew that she might be approaching the rim of her reason.

Stephen tried to explain his work to her. *Pyrology is an applied science, with practical uses in many fields,* he said. Anna replied, *Apply it to me, this science of yours, Professor,* then threw herself open on his bed.

"DIFFERENT SYSTEMS GIVE DIFFERENT names to alchemy's stages," the Doktor said. "But the step that follows the burning is the washing. *Solutio.* The bathing of the calcified elements in water. For example, the water of tears."

DAVID AND DANIELA'S HOUSE abutted the woods. Anna and Karl entered the forest under a vault of foliage, a canopy of trees. They passed a mannish woman walking a Rottweiler. "*Grüezi mitenand,*" she greeted them in the local dialect. Anna and Karl greeted her back. She was the only person they passed. Anna wondered if they should have brought the umbrella. It began to drizzle just a few steps in.

Karl and Anna walked in relative tandem silence for three or four minutes. Karl was a bruising, muscular man, slightly heavyset and almost imperceptibly bowlegged. His blond hair had been bleached by the sun, his hands were calloused, and his was a ruddy, affable face. Karl worked for Kanton Aargau as a *Holzfäller,* a lumberjack. Karl and Anna shared the most minuscule of small talk. He mentioned Willi, his thirteen-year-old son who lived in Bern with his mother, the woman from whom Karl was divorced. He spoke of a vacation they'd taken the year before to California. He told Anna a joke he'd heard on a television program and asked her if she missed the USA. For Anna he named aloud the plants and trees: *Bergulme. Elsbeere. Hagebuche. Efeu. Scots elm. Service tree. Hornbeam. Ivy.* Anna wasn't feeling any better. Her stomach pulsed with queasiness as if her body sensed an encroaching inevitability.

In mid-March 2006, Anna lay on the floor before Stephen in his apartment on Nürenbergstrasse. She wailed: *Take me, take me, take me with you.* It was the worst day of her life. She'd never felt so awful.

No, Anna. That's not going to happen. He spoke patiently, but there was irritation in his voice. He didn't want to be cruel. Anna clawed at ways to keep him. *I'm coming anyway. You cannot stop me.*

That was true. He could not have stopped her. If Anna had found the nerve she would have needed in order to chase Stephen back to America, she would have brandished it, proved herself, made good on her promise to follow. But she couldn't find it. She didn't even have a bank account.

Hi, um, Bruno? Yeah, I need a one-way ticket to Boston. The only thing that made her laugh that day was imagining that phone call. No. Stephen had to be the one to carry her off. *He* had to do it for it to count, for it to be real. *He* had to grab her and drag her out. She needed to be able to say *I had no choice.*

But Stephen didn't do that. And Anna didn't follow him to Boston.

For three entire months they'd spent at least an hour of most days together. They met at his apartment. They met in the woods and went for walks. They met near the ETH for lunch, coffee, drinks, a fast bout of lovemaking behind the closed door of his office. But the inevitable soon inevited: Stephen left. He went home. He did not come back.

I feel so fucking used.

She had no recourse but the comfort of her tears. She hid them in the best way she knew how to hide them: she cried them only at night, only when she walked, only when no one could question them. But there were so many tears.

And so many daily chastenings. *Goddammit, Anna. You're wasting this much grief on a three-month affair?* She tried to be rational. She tried to focus on her family. She tried to feel guilt. All she felt was inescapable woe.

But no real grief is ever a waste. And every grief is real. And this was bigger than Anna was ready to admit. It extended beyond the immediacy of her shattered heart. But she wouldn't know that for a very long time.

By mid-April Anna had a plan. It was selfish and irrevocable. *But it seems so strangely sane and sensible,* she thought. Bruno had a pistol. A World War II–era Luger. Semiautomatic. Light enough for a lady's hands. Toggle-lock action. An iron-sighted Nazi sidearm. *I will walk into the woods one night and not walk out again.* Twice Anna worked up courage. Twice she went into the woods. Twice that courage failed her and she returned from the forest unharmed. Both times her hands shook so hard she couldn't even grip the gun. The irony was evident: *I'm too terrified of the trigger pull to die.*

But she missed a period before she had the backbone to try again (and after the second attempt she knew she wouldn't). Bruno had wanted another child. Anna hadn't. But the guilt of the affair and the stress of the breakup were gaining on her. The baby could absolve her. The baby could be her consolation prize. Her only consolation.

FIFTEEN MINUTES INTO THEIR walk, Karl and Anna reached a *Waldhütte,* one of the hundreds of free-use cabins dotted throughout the Swiss woods. This *Waldhütte* was more rudimentary than most. It was a small three-walled hut in which there were two benches and a fire pit that looked as if it had been used as recently as that morning. The *Waldhütte*'s interior walls were littered top to bottom with graffiti. As fussy as they were about cleanliness and order, the Swiss seemed to Anna to be rather lax about graffiti. It was everywhere. Anna pointed to an enigmatic scribbling on the stacked-log wall of varnished wood. "What does this say?" she asked. She wasn't invested in the answer, but there was safety in small talk, and Anna sought it. Karl moved closer, put his hand in the small of her back and whispered, *It says I want to kiss you, Anna.*

Before Anna could say one way or the other, Karl had turned her to face him so that she was pressed between his body and the wall. He kissed her. His tongue tasted of *Weizenbier,* the heady wheat brew he'd been drinking all day long.

Anna protested. "No, Karl. No." Karl breathed *Yes* in Anna's ear. The *yes* was enough. Anna's passive self gave in. *I'm going to let him fuck me.* It was like handing an open wallet to a thief.

Anna thought a half dozen thoughts at once: *I should stop*

this. I should feel ashamed. I should feel infringed upon. I should feel bad about Bruno. I should feel bad that I don't feel bad. What time is it? Where are my sons? It's raining and I'm in the woods. It's Daniela's birthday and I am letting this man fuck me. Karl kissed Anna again. When Anna kissed Karl back, these thoughts flew away like little birds.

It was a quick, hard fuck. Karl peeled off her tights and panties. Anna kicked away her right shoe and wiggled her leg and foot free from the nylon. She hooked her calf around Karl's ass and hitched him toward her. He'd already loosened his belt and was shoving down his jeans and briefs. His cock was stiff and wet. That was enough to make Anna wet, too. *Yes, that's it, put it in.* She spoke so quietly her voice was audible only to the air around her lips.

They rummaged through each other's clothes until they hit skin. Anna panicked only once; she thought she heard the crackle of footfalls on the trail. "Just the trees," Karl said, and he was right. So Anna closed her eyes and opened the valve of her thighs even wider. Karl took the invitation and pushed himself deeper in.

Then something happened. Anna felt a shift. A limbic slip. A displacement. Tremendous feeling began to move beneath her skin. It wanted out. *Harder, Karl. More. Now.* He did as he was told. Every thrust knocked something else loose. A worry, a fear, a conundrum, a despair, a sadness—whatever it was, each fell away, one after the other. *Mary who begs for the friend I don't want to be. Archie who can smell my sadness. Victor who I sometimes just don't love that much. Stephen who I will love until I die. Ursula who should just shut the fuck up. Doktor Messerli to whom I've already told too much. Polly who but for that Wednesday would not even exist. Hans.*

Margrith. Edith. Otto. Roland. Alexis. My dead parents. My age. My face. My breasts. Bruno. I've done everything but eat a plate of glass for you. Just look at me! Love me anyway! Anna started to cry. Karl stopped and looked at her but Anna hit him with her fist, *Keep going!* He did. Anna tumbled through the litany once more. The harder he fucked her, the truer her thoughts became. Each statement cracked open a new catharsis. It was as honest as she'd been in years. She let them cover her. She lay down in them. *I'm a queen in a goddamn mercurial bath.* She remembered what the Doktor said: *The being dies and takes the body with it. The cost of transcendence is death.*

Anna gave over to a soundless, unexpected orgasm. Karl shuddered and grunted when he came. Anna squeezed him, then pulsed around him then let him slip from her like a soaped finger sliding through a tight ring.

Anna caught her breath getting dressed. Karl zipped himself back into his blue jeans and handed Anna her shoe. "I've wanted to do that for a craving time." He meant "long." Anna didn't believe him but it didn't matter. "Let's do it again," he said. The assent Anna gave was automatic. *Okay.*

Anna never told Stephen about Polly Jean. In fact, she'd never contacted him at all.

By a quarter after seven the Benzes were homeward bound. The boys, Polly, and Ursula fell asleep after the transfer in Frick. It would be past nine by the time the Benzes got home. On the train Anna watched a Swiss Army cadet talk on his cell phone. She passed her time imagining the party on the other end. *Is it his mother? His father? His girlfriend? Is today his sister's birthday, too?* Anna held her sleeping daughter. Victor rested his head on Anna's shoulder. An affection surged in Anna for her eldest child when, lowering her nose to his head, she noted that he smelled like David's dog. Charles was asleep as well. He'd had a difficult afternoon. While Anna was on her walk he'd fallen off the branch of the tree he'd been climbing. He'd cut his palm. He was howling in the bathroom fighting Bruno as he tried to wash the wound when Anna returned. Anna took over. "You have to let me clean this, *Schatz,*" she cooed. He shook his head. "I know it hurts. So close your eyes. We'll do this quickly, okay?" Charles sniffed and held out his hand and closed his eyes. Anna rinsed and dried the cut, then put a little ointment on it and dressed it with gauze and tape, all in less than a minute. When Anna asked Charles how it happened that he fell he said he couldn't remember. Anna mustered her sternest face and reprimanded him for not paying better attention. Then, she gave him a giant hug.

Anna looked across the row to Bruno, who wore a blank, drunken expression. Despite the day's cloud cover, he was sunburned.

"How," Bruno asked sleepily when they were almost halfway home and for the first time since Anna had begun them, "are your appointments with the psychiatrist? What do you talk about?"

He wants to know whether we talk about him, Anna thought. "We talk about ways I can steer myself into a trajectory that forces me to participate more fully with the world," Anna said, quoting Doktor Messerli.

This seemed to satisfy him. He yawned and pointed to her leg. "Your tights are ripped." Anna looked down. There was a hole the size of a ten-rappen coin on her right shin and a run laddering after it. She must have snagged it on her toenail, dressing.

"I didn't notice," Anna said. This was not a lie.

ANNA SPENT THE PREGNANCY reconciling herself to herself. *This would be his parting song,* she thought. The adieu he didn't bid. It would be, she argued, the only part of him worth keeping. Despondency nauseated her. Morning sickness made her cry. She'd been weepy with the other pregnancies and her daily tears were no surprise to anyone.

ANNA TOLD DOKTOR MESSERLI a dream of a fire-ravaged cabin in an unknown wood and asked her what she thought it meant.

Vhat dooo yooooo sink, Anna?

ANNA WAS IN BED less than half an hour after walking through the door. She hurried the boys through their baths and put Polly in her crib. Bruno was asleep when Anna came into the bedroom. She undressed as quietly as she could, changed into a thin cotton nightgown, and slid into bed. Bruno rolled over and draped his arm around her. It was an action born of habit. Anna curled into herself and faced the wall.

How did I become so unprincipled?

Tomorrow Anna would begin her second month of German classes: Advanced Beginner, II.

Oh Bruno, Bruno, she mouthed silently as she waited for sleep to steal her. *This is your mess too.*

A MONTH BEFORE POLLY Jean's birth Anna left the house in the middle of the night and walked up the hill to the bench where she always went to cry.

To the night, to the cold autumn air, to the stars, to the trains in the distance, to the forest behind her, and to the sleeping inhabitants of the town below, Anna confessed:

I love him. I love him. I love him.

Like people in pain love opiates.

october

9

"A MISTAKE MADE ONCE IS AN OVERSIGHT. THE SAME MISTAKE made twice? An aberration. A blunder. But a third time?" Doktor Messerli shook her head. "Whatever's been done has been done to an end. Your will is at work. You beg a result. A repercussion." Anna held her left hand with her right and rested both on her lap. "A precedent has been established. You will get what you want. And there's no need to seek out these mistakes. For now it is they who seek you."

THE BEGINNING OF OCTOBER was as easy as the end of September had been uncertain. It is often like that. Every month begins at its own beginning. Chalkboards are washed clean. Work kept Bruno occupied and distracted. Victor and Charles were busy with school. Every morning Ursula came to the house on Rosenweg to mind Polly Jean. And Anna had begun the second term of her German class.

Most of the graduates of the September session enrolled in

October's. The remainder of the class was made up of graduates from other sections. Everyone's German had improved. Anna's as well. Anna's especially. It became less difficult to sit through Roland's lectures. They began to make more sense. The mood in the Oerlikon classroom was sociable and friendly, even as the autumn days grew bleak.

The consequence of Anna's lessons was, as Doktor Messerli rightly predicted, that Anna was becoming accustomed to speaking German aloud. And the consequence of that consequence was that Anna began to feel a little less out of place, perhaps even somewhat comfortable in her daily life in a way she hadn't before. On one day she spoke to the mothers in the square. On another she made chitchat with the cashier at the Coop. That was an absolute first. The checker offered a forced, availing smile in return.

But Anna wasn't entirely at ease. In the same market on another day, she'd mistakenly weighed her pears under the code for bananas and a different checker—a fat, belligerent woman with close-cropped hair—huffed and rose from her stool to make a big, bullying point of walking to the scales and weighing them herself. Anna felt scolded and two feet tall. She carried the agitation all the way home and didn't speak another word of German for the rest of the day.

Bruno noticed the upward, progressive arc of her speech, her level of comfort, her general mien. "I am impressed," he said. "But it's not Schwiizerdütsch." It was a cynical, ungracious comment, but it was true. She didn't know any more Swiss German than she did when she began the class. "Still, it is a start." Then he added he'd be glad to pay for more lessons. As many as would keep Anna happy. And Anna was, perhaps, happier than she'd been in a long while (if indeed "happy" was the word for what she was, and Anna was almost sure it wasn't). The classes were the axis around which her present life—public, private, and secret—spun.

"You see?" Doktor Messerli cheerfully pointed out. "What you've needed all along was simply a way of facilitating an ease of speech, of feeling more comfortable with your own vice."

It was a slip of Freudian magnitude.

And it was sometime around the start of October that Anna's relationship with Mary began to deepen into a genuine, unmistakable friendship. It had happened with no fanfare, over cups of coffee in the Migros Klubschule *Kantine*. Anna had never had many close friends, even before the expatriation. But now in Mary, Anna had someone with whom she could enjoy a late lunch or see a film or sit in a park and talk about things that casual girlfriends might share with each other (they'd done none of these things, but that wasn't the comfort; the peace came from knowing that they *could*). Anna was charmed by Mary's sympathetic bent. She'd forgotten that people could be so genuinely kind.

But there are things that Mary will never know of me, Anna thought. *We'll never truly be close.* Anna's psychology demanded reserve. She held Mary at a short but distinct distance. But Mary didn't seem to notice and remained her supportive, cheerful self even as Anna kept her own self separate. But Mary wasn't mannerly all the time. One day after class, she dropped her purse outside Bahnhof Oerlikon and her wallet, her makeup, and every little thing she had stashed inside the bag spilled out onto the street. The powder in her compact broke and a snap-shut photo album she was never caught without landed in an oily puddle. *Shit!* Temperate Mary with her milquetoast demeanor cursed so loudly that a doorman at the Swissôtel across the street looked over to see what had happened. No one is even-keeled at all times, Anna knew. Nevertheless, Anna couldn't dare open up. *There are burdens that even the best of friends shouldn't share.* In that way, Anna was lonelier than ever.

ANNA BROUGHT A DREAM to Doktor Messerli:

I descend a staircase into a maze of dark passages. It's dank and foreboding. Each step forward sinks me deeper below the earth. I'm apprehensive. The farther I go, the more terrible I feel. I never reach the end of the labyrinth and I never find my way back out.

"Which is it," Doktor Messerli asked.

"Which is what?"

"Is it a maze or a labyrinth? They aren't the same thing. A maze has an entrance and an exit. It's a puzzle to solve. In a labyrinth the way in is also the way out. A labyrinth leads you through itself."

IT WAS A WEEK into October before Anna followed Archie home again. She hadn't intended this. A tumbling series of obligations and impediments had wedged themselves between the pair. First it was Mary, who begged Anna to ride the train with her to Üetliberg. Anna explained that in the foggy weather they wouldn't be able to see much of anything and that standing in miserable drizzle 1,500 feet above the Limmat Valley is a good way to catch a bad cold. But Mary had her heart set so Anna gave in and went with her. The day after that Anna stayed with Charles, who was home with a fever. "I want *you*. Not Grosi," he said. Anna would never have refused him. On Wednesday Charles felt well enough for school but in the middle of German class Anna started to feel woozy herself so she left after the first break ("Do you think it was because I made you go with me to Üetliberg?" Mary fretted). Yet another day found Anna rushing home so Ursula could get to Schaffhausen in time to meet a friend who was visiting from America. And one day, it was Archie who couldn't make their rendezvous; Glenn had a doctor's appointment and needed Archie to mind the shop. They hadn't cooled. They'd simply back-burnered each other.

But after German class on the second Tuesday of October Anna followed Archie to his flat and on the spring heels of a kiss in the doorframe that might have shattered glass, Archie carried Anna to his bed and the two of them made love like ravenous teenagers, the air on fire with a thick, erotic charge. She sucked him off. He licked her until she came. He pressed her to the bed and laid his body atop her like a blanket. Anna could barely breathe. That was okay. It was the price she paid for feeling safe, subsumed. A muscle in her soul was massaged, a particular crack in her wailing wall patched.

But the thing about cracks in walls is that they happen when foundations shift. The concrete slabs become abstract. From the first crack, others spider out. *This? This is my fault,* Anna thought when she felt the ground wobble beneath her. And she meant "fault" in every sense.

So two hours later, and against her best judgment, Anna stepped off a train onto platform 3 in Kloten, a town just on the other side of the woods north of Dietlikon, and crossed underneath the station to the Hotel Allegra, where Karl Trötzmüller waited for her. She'd received the SMS while Archie was in the bathroom. *Come, Anna,* it read and gave the address.

I'm cheating on the man I'm cheating on my husband with, Anna thought. *I grow less decent every passing day.*

Anna was frequently saddened by flux. How autumn's spinning leaves ripened first to red then dried to a crackling brown. How spring flowers hidden all winter would bust through the ground unannounced. Bruno told her she was insane. *Everyone loves spring, Anna. Stop being foolish.* But it wasn't spring (or fall or winter) that perturbed her. It was their mutability. How one became the next, became the next, the next. It was a shifty enterprise; she didn't trust it. And change is always an occasion for panic, she tried to explain. Even the changes that one should surely be accustomed to, like the daily rising and setting of the sun. Especially the setting. *Tell me, Bruno, in what culture isn't the sunset a harbinger of doom?* Bruno would roll his eyes and drop the argument. So even as October so easily began, the shortening of days steadily jostled the cogs of an apprehension in Anna that couldn't be denied.

Anna didn't get home from Kloten until after four thirty. She'd stayed to take a shower. Ursula was irritated. "I wish you'd be more considerate. Stop dawdling in the city. I'm not their mother, you know." Ursula left so quickly she forgot her jacket. The boys were in the yard and Polly Jean in the den inside her playpen content and chewing on the foot of a stuffed tiger. The house was so quiet that Anna could hear the clocks tick.

That morning's German lesson left Anna pensive. The German language, like a woman, has moods. On occasion they are conditional, imperative, indicative, subjunctive. Hypothetical, demanding, factual, wishful. Wistful, bossy, of blunted affect, solicitous. Longing, officious, anhedonic, pleading. Anna tried to make a list of every mood she'd ever been in but ran out of words before even half of her feelings were named.

Anna made a mental note to return home directly after class the next few days as she reached into the playpen and lifted her daughter out. Polly Jean began to cry. "Hush," Anna said. "I need someone to hold." She sat in a rocking chair, pinned Polly to her chest with a small blanket, and out of exhaustion, compassion, and perhaps even boredom, all three, cried too.

"WHAT DO YOU THINK you will find at the center of the labyrinth, Anna?"

Catastrophe pushed her down the wending path. She knew that whatever she found, it wouldn't be pleasant. Anna said as much.

"Psychoanalysis isn't therapy," Doktor Messerli replied. "The intent of most therapy is to make you feel better. Psychoanalysis intends to make you into a better person. It's not the same thing. Analysis rarely feels good. Consider a broken bone improperly healed. You must break the bone again and set it correctly. The second pain is usually greater than the initial trauma. It's true the journey isn't pleasant. Anna: it is not meant to be."

* * *

Using convoluted logic, Anna could justify a single affair: *It feels good in the moment. It distracts me from the things that weigh me down. Bruno has ignored me for years. Can I not have something that belongs entirely to me? It doesn't count if Bruno doesn't know. It won't go on forever, just a while. A while. Just a little while.* Anna was clever and could dance around a dozen arguments.

But even clever Anna knew there wasn't any way to justify two affairs at once. Allow them? Succumb to them? Capitulate? Concede? Yes, yes, yes, and yes. But she couldn't absolve or exonerate herself. So she didn't. Instead, she pushed every scruple aside and did her best not to worry about it. A task made easier somehow by the affair itself.

When Anna surrendered in the Mumpf woods, a strange, implausible mercy grabbed her by the throat. *How futile to flee from my impulses.* The epiphany was sharp. A knife. It cut through the ropes at her wrists. *My guilts are undeniable. They are unassuageable. They are mine to feel. Mine to own.* And that's what she decided to do. Possess them. Experience them. The sex begat the clarity. *I may not be as passive as I think I am. The bus is mine. Goddammit, I'll drive it.* And so the worse she became, the better she became. She was still sad. She was still skittish. She was still herself, and in full danger of being trapped beneath the rubble of her poor choices when her makeshift shelter caved in. But from this terrible awareness Anna drew strength. It was this that set October's mood. This that jury-rigged her machine. And for as long as it worked—perilous as it was—she'd employ it.

* * *

The next day Anna came home directly after class. She was tired and sore and wilted and she had promised Ursula that she would. Archie didn't hide his disappointment. "Oh come on, we'll get together later in the week," Anna hissed at him by the coffee machine in the *Kantine.* He frowned and whimpered the way her sons did when they weren't getting something they wanted. The waggishness grated Anna's patience. "Jesus, Archie, get past it." She rubbed her temples as she spoke. Archie turned away without responding, paid for his coffee, grabbed a newspaper someone had left on a counter, and took it to a table in the corner and sat down, his back to the room. Anna felt bad. She hadn't meant to hurt his feelings. Mary sidled up to her. "What's wrong, hon? Got a headache? I think I have some aspirin." She began to rifle through her purse.

Anna stopped her. "I just need some coffee."

"Well, then let's get you some!"

On the way home Anna stopped at the Coop on Dietlikon's Bahnhofstrasse. She'd written a list on the train. *Eier. Milch. Brot. Pfirsiche. Müsli. Die Fernsehzeitschrift. Eggs. Milk. Bread. Peaches. Cereal. A TV guide.* Anna swallowed a self-deprecating snort. This is an old lady's shopping list. There was truth in that. Anna felt her age that day, plus fifteen, twenty years more. She shopped as quickly as she could.

Five minutes later and from behind her in the checkout line, Anna heard her name.

"*Grüezi* Frau Benz." It was Anna's neighbor Margrith.

"*Grüezi* Frau Tschäppät."

Margrith volunteered an odd but not unfriendly smile. She

inquired after Bruno, the children, Ursula. Anna told her everyone was fine and then asked Margrith what sort of things she and Hans had planned for the rest of the season. It was a go-to topic of conversation. Anna never knew what to talk to strangers about. And the Swiss were always strangers. The conversation was polite and cursory, the way conversations in shopping lanes are intended to be.

Margrith continued talking even as Anna turned to pay. "Oh," Margrith by-the-wayed as Anna inserted her bank card into the reader, "I saw you, I think, was it yesterday?" Margrith paused. "Yes. In Kloten. You were walking toward the trains." Anna entered her PIN and didn't look up. "I have a sister in Kloten, you know."

Ahh, yes, Anna responded, though she didn't know Margrith had a sister. *How is she?*

"Oh, she is getting along, thank you for asking. Do you have a friend in Kloten?" "No," said Anna. And then, "I'm afraid, Margrith, that you are mistaken. That wasn't me." Anna said it firmly, calmly. *Das war nicht ich.* She left her face blank and tried to remember if Karl had walked her out of the hotel. He hadn't.

"Oh, well," Margrith said, laughing away the mistake she surely must have made. "It must have been your doppelgänger!" Anna bagged her groceries and smiled briefly at Margrith before the two of them bade adieu and Anna left the Coop and made the five-minute walk to Rosenweg in three.

10

The history of doppelgängers is phenomenological. Doppelgängers rarely appear in the same place as their genuine halves. Most commonly, the doppelgänger will appear when someone is gravely ill, or when she is in tremendous danger. It is said that a person's spirit can will its own bilocation in times of great distress. The sighting of a doppelgänger by one's family or friends bears ill fortune.

It is an omen of death to see one's own self.

Anna would turn thirty-eight in less than two weeks.

Anna hated birthdays. They dejected her. Not once had she celebrated a birthday, the joy of which was not also accompanied by a tremendous crash of disappointment, like a sledgehammer heaved onto a glass sculpture.

It wasn't the thought of getting older that consumed her with dread. Age is the natural consequence of being alive, Anna knew, and the alternative was grim.

But consider: *Every year you have a death day as well, only you don't know which one it is.*

Anna made Bruno promise that he wouldn't make a fuss. This was not a difficult pledge for him to swear: he hadn't intended to. As for Anna herself, she decided she'd deal with the day when it came and not a minute before.

"GRIEF THAT FINDS NO relief in tears makes other organs weep," Doktor Messerli said.

Anna wrote it in her journal. *How very many ways this is true.*

IT WAS SATURDAY AND Anna and Bruno had been invited to Edith and Otto Hammer's home in Erlenbach for a cocktail party. Bruno walked the children to Ursula's house while Anna dressed. Her heart wasn't in it. She didn't want to go, but the Hammers expected them and Bruno promised they wouldn't be late coming home.

Anna made a habit of dressing well. She owned nice clothes and her fashion sense was irreproachable. She felt safest in her prettiest outfits, and if she couldn't be glad all the time, at least she could feel—relatively, occasionally—impervious. She'd take it. She chose a slim-fitting black dress with cap sleeves and gold accents on the hemline. She wrapped a black wool shawl around her shoulders, piled her hair loosely atop her head, and fastened it with a rhinestone-studded claw clip. She considered herself first in the bathroom mirror, and then in the bedroom's. Every looking glass treated her differently. In the bedroom she was thin but wan. In the bathroom she was healthy-hued but her arms seemed thicker and her face swollen. Neither face was hers and yet they both were. *You are not my doppelgänger,* she said to each reflection. She took the sum of both and divided by two. She was presentable.

Bruno and Anna took the car. The radio was tuned to a hip-hop station. It amused Anna how much the Swiss loved black music. After school and on weekends when the weather was nice, a group of Dietlikon's teenagers met in the church playground across the street from their house. They dressed in urban youth wear, their pants baggy, their sneakers white and wide-laced, and their baseball caps cocked hard to an idle side. They turned their radios as loud as the knobs would allow and thumped their heads against walls of air as they drank Red Bull and vodka, smoked cigarettes, and sang along to rap songs whose words they might not really understand the meaning of. Anna never talked to them. They scared her. Bruno left the radio tuned to its station and Anna tried to lose herself in the music's pulse and throb.

WHEN ANNA THOUGHT OF Stephen anymore it was most always in passing, a transitory notion that traveled her mind from one side to its other, like a pedestrian crossing the street. Sometimes she thought of him while making love (it did not matter with whom). Sometimes it happened during her walks in the woods. Other times, it was when the train stopped at Wipkingen station or when the news reported on a forest fire or when she took the number 33 to Neumarkt or when she was combing Polly Jean's hair. It happened on downtown trams when she smelled his soap or his cologne or heard a man speaking in the same register as he. Anna would whip around and scan every face but Stephen's was never among them. This didn't happen often. But it happened enough.

"WHAT IS THE DIFFERENCE between love and lust?"

"You tell me," Doktor Messerli said to Anna.

"Lust's incurable. Love isn't."

"Desire isn't a disease, Anna."

"Isn't it?"

EDITH HAMMER RARELY THREW understated parties. This party, while not inconspicuous, was at the very least relatively small. Fewer than twenty guests moved through the rooms of the Hammers' Gold Coast home. It was a party of no occasion. It was no one's birthday, no couple's anniversary, no celebration of any sort. The party came to pass simply because Edith wanted one. Otto always indulged her: *Wife, your heart's desire is my wish.* But despite the sheen of contentment, the Hammers weren't entirely happy. Otto's temper flared hotter and more often than Bruno's. Edith was frivolous with money and often cruel in her speech. Their daughters were delinquents and lived most of the year at a boarding school in Lausanne. And the Hammers drank too much.

But together they made a handsome, finespun couple, and Edith was one of Anna's only two friends. Snippy and pitiless though Edith usually was, Anna had little recourse but to keep her.

When Anna and Bruno walked through the door, each was swept from the other's company into the large living room, Anna by Edith and Bruno by Otto. It was a segregated room.

The men crowded near the bar and the women by the kitchen. Switzerland is undeniably a modern country, but gender roles make occasional appearances. In some cantons women didn't get the right to vote until the 1970s. Anna knew she'd been in Switzerland too long when this stopped appalling her.

Doktor Messerli had harped on it to the point that the conversation was formulaic: Did not Anna worry that she perpetuated the stereotype of the fragile, subjugated woman? That excepting her manner of dress and the language she used and the Handy in her purse there was little to distinguish her from a woman who lived fifty, seventy, one hundred years earlier? They didn't drive cars or have bank accounts either. Didn't she understand she could be anything she wanted to be? Didn't she think she had a responsibility to be *something*?

Anna's response never varied. *I can see your point. You may be right.*

Edith was in friendliest form that night. She moved about the room with a cheer Anna had never seen her flaunt as she handed out glasses of wine and passed around bowls of olives and peanuts and wasabi-coated peas, snacks that Anna would have sworn were too common for Edith's tastes. Anna stood among a crowd of women she knew only by sight. These were the bankers' wives. They nodded and smiled and widened their circle to include her, but they carried on their conversation in Schwiizerdütsch.

Anna understood maybe five percent of what she heard. It was well and good her German had vastly improved, but that was little use inside a coterie of *Schweizerin.* Anna reverted to smiles and nods as well. It was easiest that way.

Across the room she caught sight of Bruno. He was making exaggerated gestures with his arms and the men around him were laughing as he told a story, just like the men at Daniela's party had done. A cigarette teetered on the edge of his lips. It annoyed Anna when he smoked. But Bruno only smoked at parties and so when he did it tended to be a sign that he was having a good time. *I'll take it, cigarette and all,* Anna conceded.

ANNA LONGED TO CONTACT Stephen, but she never did. *What would I say beyond hello? Would I tell him about Polly Jean? Would I admit that I miss him? Would I beg him to return?* She imagined differing scripts. *What would happen? What harm would it do?* Anna knew the answers.

The desire to reach out to him pulled at her. Anna was an expert at pushing the yearning away. Still, she stored the number to his MIT office in her Handy. She filed it under Cindy, the name of a cousin Anna had long ago lost touch with. She'd pried the number from him just before he left. With a few pathetic punches of the keypad she could reconnect herself with his intrusive, ubiquitous voice.

She never called.

TWICE THAT WEEK THEY'D made love, Anna and Archie. They had fallen into the pattern noncommittal lovers can't avoid. Their attraction for each other was undeniable. But affection wasn't something to discuss. They were not in love. That was off the table. Their meetings were no less intense, but they were a little less frequent.

How many times have we done it? Anna hadn't counted.

How many indiscretions make an affair? It was an irrelevant question. *Fondness but not love. Not for Archie, not for Karl.* Some women collected spoons. Anna collected lovers.

ROLAND EXPLAINED THAT IN German, the conditional is used to show the dependency of one action or set of events upon another. It's an if-then scenario. "*Zum Beispiel,*" Roland lectured. "If I am sick tomorrow, then I will not go to school. Or, if the weather is nice, then we will go to the park."

Anna found little relief in this. *If I am caught . . . then I am fucked.*

ANNA RETURNED HER GAZE to the bankers' wives, who huddled into the company of one another. The women were young. Their husbands wore the jewelry of their beauty like elegant wristwatches.

Edith had set down the tray of food and returned to the group. "Anna," she said as she motioned to a more private corner of the room. Anna dipped her chin and stepped away, literally bowing out of a conversation she wasn't even part of.

Edith hurried her over with her hands. She was agitated. "Come here!" Anna moved more closely into her space. Anna was already as close to her as she felt like she wanted to be.

Edith, always unmistakable, was that night flushed with an immoderate sense of urgency and giddiness. "Don't be obvious, but turn around and look—no, not yet!—to the left." Anna shook her head at Edith's schoolgirl antics but played along. She paused a beat then turned to look over her shoulder.

"What am I looking for?"

"Really, Anna. Look again!"

Anna looked again. She saw Bruno and Otto on the couch. Standing next to the couch was Andreas, a bank employee under both of them. And next to Andreas stood a man she did not know. He was blonder and shorter and younger than the other men. He wore a trim sports coat and dark jeans and trendy designer eyeglasses. He threw his head back to laugh and Anna noticed a gap in his teeth and a chin cleft. He was handsome, yes. And twenty-five years old, if that.

"Who is he? Does he work at the branch? What does he do?"

"Oh, I don't know what he does." Edith waved the question away as if it were a housefly. "Some bank thing." Anna scowled. "His name is Niklas Flimm."

"Flynn?"

Edith shook her head. "No, dammit. Pay attention. *Flimmmm.*" Edith drew out the *m*. "He's *Austrian,*" she said with italic emphasis as if somehow whatever she said next would carry more weight, more meaning. "We've been sleeping together for a month!"

ANNA COULDN'T DESIGNATE A single romantic relationship she'd ever entered into that did not begin in sexual earnestness on the very day she'd met the man, whichever man he was. Bruno. Archie. Stephen. Her college boyfriend, Vince. They'd hooked up at orientation. Later that night he'd kicked his dorm mate out and Anna's hand was in his pants. It's true, she'd met Karl before that day in Mumpf. But they'd never actually had a proper conversation until Daniela's party. A mistake made once is an oversight. But three times, four, a dozen? *Dog, you are begging for the bone.*

"A WHOLE MONTH!" EDITH repeated.

"Huh." Anna said it with a matter-of-fact thud. Affairs no longer surprised her. Edith smiled harshly. *She's expecting more of a response,* Anna thought, then fished for something relevant to say. "How did this, um, happen?" Anna stumbled on the word "happen." She didn't know what else to offer. "Are you and Otto having problems?"

Edith laughed and smiled glibly. "Oh, no. We're fine. What Otto doesn't know can't hurt him. And look at my skin! It's the best it's been in years!" Anna didn't deny this, though she hardly knew what that had to do with anything.

"Er, how is he?"

Edith gave her a you-must-be-kidding look. "Anna, look at him! He's gorgeous. And young! Isn't he amazing?" Niklas turned momentarily from his conversation and saw Edith and Anna looking at him. He raised both an eyebrow and his wineglass to the women. "It's thrilling, isn't it?"

Yes, Anna thought. *Adultery's a blast.*

"Let's get you one, Anna."

"A lover?"

Edith rolled her eyes. "No. A fucking houseplant. Yes, a lover." Edith smirked. "It'll cheer you up!"

That's exactly what it won't do, Anna thought. Even weak, Anna was occasionally wise. "Are you in love?" Anna asked, in all provincial sincerity.

Edith laughed a tipsy laugh. “Heavens, no!” It sounded quaint and arcane, like something Mary would say. “It is most certainly not about love!”

Anna’s German homework regularly consisted of vocabulary drills, verb conjugation exercises, declension practice, and the writing of many, many, many sentences.

Love’s a sentence, Anna thought. *A death sentence.*

11

EDITH FUSSED WITH THE COLLAR OF HER BLOUSE THEN LOOKED around and dismissed herself from Anna with a pat on Anna's shoulder. "Other guests!" she said as she flitted away and left Anna alone to hug an empty corner of the room. The Hammers had arranged two heaters on their patio but no one was outside. Anna crossed the room as inconspicuously as she could and slipped out the back door.

Christ, I'm good at being alone. This was the truth. As a child, Anna preferred to spend most of her time by herself. Eventually her parents took her to a psychologist. It didn't seem healthy, such remoteness in what seemed like an otherwise normal girl. *Is she depressed, Doctor? Will she be all right?* Their concern was legitimate. At home Anna set herself apart. Daily she retreated to her bedroom and locked herself behind the door, where she'd read or listen to the radio or write in her journal or sit in the windowsill and do nothing but stare into the street. *What are you doing in there, all shut away and alone?* they'd ask. "I'm studying," Anna always replied. *And dreaming,* she'd think but not say. *And wondering who I'll be in twenty years.* The psychologist asked three dozen questions and in the end told Anna's parents she was fine. "It's puberty," he said. "It'll pass." Then he handed them a bill for two hundred dollars. But Anna's aloneness didn't blow over. After her parents died and until she met Bruno four years later, Anna lived alone.

Anna wandered into the Hammers' yard, nursing the same glass of wine she'd been drinking inside. A mid-October chill defined the night air. Clouds hid the stars. The darkness was tense and fragmented. Anna was staring into the indeterminate sky when she heard a man's cough. It startled her. "Oh!" She whipped around.

"Hallo, Anna." It was Niklas Flimm.

"Hello." It bothered Anna to hear someone she hadn't been introduced to use her given name. It was an unfair advantage. In some indigenous tribes, a person's name contains more than their identity, it's the vessel of her spirit. Niklas hadn't been given the right. Anna's ire was already up.

"My name is Niklas."

"I know." His English was high-pitched and nasal and he was better looking up close than he was from a distance, and even then it was possible to mistake him for a male model. *Well done, Edith,* Anna thought.

"Edith say you are Bruno's wife?"

Anna smirked. "Sure." Niklas's English was clunky. His "Edith" sounded like "eat it," and he dropped articles in his speech as frequently as Karl confused vocabulary. Anna stared, not knowing what else to offer. The Austrian accent was difficult for her to get past. Anna listened but avoided his direct gaze by focusing her eyes on his forehead.

The talk they made was tedious. Niklas spoke of Vienna,

skiing, and how sometimes he did not understand the Swiss. Anna kept her face blank as she remembered the punch line of a joke that she'd heard Bruno tell about the Austrians. She'd forgotten the joke's lead-in. Anna traced the rim of her wineglass with her thumb and wondered what time it was and how much longer Bruno planned on staying.

THE WEEKEND BEFORE EDITH'S party, Anna and Mary took their children to the Greifensee, Kanton Zürich's second largest lake, the bank of which lay no more than half a kilometer away from the Gilberts' front door. The three boys brought along their bikes. Mary and Anna walked the path behind them. Anna pushed Polly in a stroller. Alexis stayed home.

"How did you meet Tim?"

Mary blushed. "We met in high school."

This didn't surprise Anna. "You've never been with anyone else?"

Mary shook her head. "Nope. No one else. Just Tim." This admission seemed to shame her. *Just Tim.* Anna focused her gaze on the path ahead of her. Of course she'd had lovers before Bruno. College boyfriends, men she saw for a few months then dumped or, alternately, was dumped by. Male friends who, under differing circumstances, she might have seen less circumstantially. But then there was Bruno. Mary redirected the conversation. "How did you meet Bruno? How did you fall in *looove*?" Mary drew out the word "love" like a sixth-grade girl.

Anna answered the first question. "At a party." This was the bland truth. They met at a party of a mutual acquaintance. Drunken groping followed on that very same night. And even now, despite differences both petty and consequential, the lusts upon which they founded their love still thrummed near the surface of their skins. The second question required some circumnavigation. Mary waited on Anna to continue. "Well, he's handsome, and responsible . . ." Anna dodged the question by trailing off. Mary nodded deeply. "And," Anna sighed the sigh of resignation, "here we are."

"As simple as that?" Mary asked. Anna blinked. "How did he propose?"

"In an orchard. In Washington." They walked a few steps forward. "We were on a trip."

"How romantic!"

It should have been, Anna thought. For any other pair of lovers it would have been. A few months after they met, Anna and Bruno moved in together. A few months after that and while on vacation and walking through an apple orchard near Wenatchee, Bruno turned to Anna and said, "I think you would make a good wife for me. I think I want to marry you." It was spur-of-the-moment and matter-of-fact. The idea crossed his mind and he spoke it aloud in the same way he might announce that he'd be up for seeing a movie. There was no ring. A thousand round, ripe apples looked on from above. *I agree,* Anna thought. *I would make a good wife. I would mostly make a good wife.* And Anna loved Bruno. Was in love with Bruno. Was in a version of love with Bruno. Inasmuch as she understood it, Anna felt confident enough to name what she felt for Bruno to be love. The sex was good and in those days that mattered as much as anything else. Anna said yes. They married two months later.

Anna felt the crush of dry grass beneath her shoes. Polly Jean fussed intermittently. "Charles!" Anna cried out. "You're too far away—come back!" Charles couldn't hear and didn't turn around. Anna yelled for Victor to catch up to his brother. When he did, Charles looked back and he waved. "He's always doing that."

"Riding off?"

"Not paying attention."

"Ah, a butterfly chaser! His mother's son!" Mary giggled.

Bruno's proposal may have been matter-of-fact, but Anna said yes without hesitation. The orchard air was peaceful. The sky was promising. The apples introduced the possibility of joy. She remembered them all: *Honeycrisp, Honey Sweet, Golden Supreme, Ambrosia, Sunrise, Gala, Fortune, Keepsake.* Their names so improbable, the queer potential of happiness foretold by each. *Yes, Bruno, I'll be your wife.* They held hands on their walk back to the car. At the end of the path, Anna stopped to pick a black pearly pebble from a pile of lackluster others. She buffed it on her shirt and cached it in her pocket. Anna had carried that pebble with her since. It rattled around in her coin purse against the change.

One day while Stephen was in the bathroom Anna pilfered a blue linen handkerchief from his sock drawer. It was embroidered with initials that weren't his. It might have been his grandfather's. She felt bad, but only for a bit. Like the pebble, she'd carried it in her purse since the day she took it.

I think you would make a good wife for me, Bruno had said.

But that's not why Anna said yes.

She said yes because she couldn't imagine a man more suited for her than he.

* * *

"MEN DON'T USUALLY HAVE affairs because they are lonely or want emotional connections. For a man, the reason often reduces to simply this: the challenge of the seduction." Anna had told the Doktor about Edith and Niklas.

"What about women?"

The Doktor looked sympathetically and directly into Anna's eyes. "I'm worried about you, Anna."

THE CONVERSATION WITH NIKLAS continued, pained though it was. Niklas had lived in Switzerland for less than six months. He peppered Anna with questions. He asked about day excursions from Zürich, specialty shops for foodstuffs, where he might buy a mountain bike. He was chatty and curious. Anna tensed. He was much too young for Edith. Much, much. Niklas worked for Otto. How flagrant of her. It was an unexpected instance of correctness. It swelled in Anna's throat. *Christ, what a hypocrite I am,* Anna thought.

But even hypocrites have moments of clarity. Anna could live with the hypocrisy. It was the clarity she couldn't dodge.

NEAR THE END OF their walk that day, Anna and Mary herded the children into a café near the *Schiffstation* and across from Greifensee Castle, a twelfth-century tower house. They ordered orange sodas for the boys, coffees for themselves, and Anna pulled out a small container of animal crackers and placed two on the snack tray that snapped onto Polly's stroller. Polly picked them up and began banging them against the plastic. They crumbled into immediate bits. "No, Polly." Anna grabbed two more cookies and put one near Polly Jean's mouth. Polly took the animal cracker in her chubby fist and tapped it against her lips as if to eat it, then smashed it, like the others, on the tray. "I give up." Anna handed over the remaining cookie. Sometimes that's what Anna did: she just gave up.

Mary offered sympathy. "Oh, they're like that sometimes, you know. Willful. Girls, I think, especially." Anna would have to think on that before she agreed.

When the drinks came Anna reached for her wallet. "No, no—I've got this," Mary said and Anna backed down. Mary carried a large, unwieldy purse. When she reached inside the bag for her wallet, she tipped it and some of the contents fell out, including a travel-sized container of hand sanitizer that landed in Mary's lap and a paperback novel that fell to the ground. "Oh shoot!" Mary reached for the sanitizer as Anna nabbed the book.

"*His Illicit Kiss*?" Anna was amused.

Mary blushed. "Just something to read on the train."

Anna thumbed to a dog-eared page and read a paragraph aloud. "Her stubborn fingers sought the flesh under his shirt. His pleasure was evident. 'I want you,' she purred as she stepped even farther into his space. She gyrated her hips against his groin and the protuberance between his legs caused her to sigh, knowing that soon he would be atop her thrusting and moaning in the agony of desire . . ."

Mary yanked the book away. "Anna, the children."

The children were absorbed in their own childishness. They weren't listening. "*Protuberance?* Why are you reading this?"

Mary put the novel back into her bag and sighed. "Oh. Because. You know." Anna shook her head in a way that meant both yes and no. Mary tried to explain away her embarrassment. "Sometimes I wish I hadn't settled down. So soon I mean." The admission shamed her. "I missed all my chances to be . . . more sensual." Anna's heart dropped for her friend. Mary hooked her bag on the back of her chair. "But. It doesn't matter because I *did* settle down and I *am* incredibly happy and I *would not* trade this life for any other. So, I read these. It's a small indulgence against . . . I don't know what."

Anna knew what. "I'm sorry, Mary."

Mary pretended not to hear her. "And anyway. These books? They're full of nonsense."

"How so?"

"They all end happily. The heroine gets everything she wants. An amazing job. Loads of success. Fame, money. She's always beautiful and her fella is the man she's dreamed of all along. An absolutely perfect life." Mary's wistfulness was palpable.

"Wow. If only." Polly Jean gurgled and kicked against the stroller, scattering cookie crumbs everywhere.

"I know, right?" Mary blew on her coffee, then took a tentative taste. Anna drank hers hot. It hurt her mouth, though she pretended it didn't.

BECAUSE SHE HAD NOTHING else to do with either her hands or her mouth, when Niklas Flimm asked Anna if she wanted another drink, she said, *Yes, please.* A half minute later, Anna held a fresh glass of wine. That second glass of wine turned into a third. And three glasses of wine turned into a whiskey and by then Anna was drunk.

Anna and Niklas were still on the patio. Bruno was inside, drinking and telling stories to his friends. Edith looked through the glass back door occasionally, Anna assumed, to make sure that Niklas wasn't trying to pick her up as well. She tried to assure Edith with her body language that was in no way possible. Niklas and Anna were running out of things to say. "So Edith is good friend?" he asked.

When drunk, Anna's tact and civil elegance were the first of her social skills to flee. They were usually replaced with the same kind of gadabout forthrightness Edith was known for. Anna wore a sloppy, rickety grin. "What I heard is that Edith is *your* good friend!" Her drunkenness made her irrepressible.

Niklas smiled with slightly narrowing eyes. "She tells you." His voice was even. He wasn't demoralized. She hadn't disconcerted him.

"Don't worry," Anna was quick to add. "I'll keep your secret. I'll keep it."

"I'm not worry."

Past that, Anna had nothing to add. They stood there a minute longer in silence. Anna spoke. "I'm going inside. It was nice talking to you." Anna slurred her words. The tipsy was catching up to her. She left Niklas alone on the patio.

Anna wasn't so drunk that she couldn't walk straight. She walked just fine. Finer than usual, in fact. The alcohol had given her swagger; with every forward step she ticked her hips side to side like a clock's pendulum and wondered who, if anyone, watched her as she passed. In the Hammers' bathroom, she glossed her lips and finger curled the strands of hair that had worked their way loose from the clip. She gazed into her own eyes like a lover would. *I look glassy and mischievous.* Somewhere between the whiskey and the wine, a switch had flipped.

When she left the bathroom, she sidled up to Bruno and put a hand on his shoulder. Bruno looked up, saw that it was

Anna, then returned his attention to the conversation. Anna sat on the arm of the chair in which he was sitting and leaned into him and whispered in his ear. "Let's go home and fuck."

Bruno looked to her once more. He chortled. "I think you're drunk."

Anna's smile was cagey. "I am. Let's go home and fuck anyway."

A handful of seconds ticked past during which Bruno considered her proposition. He locked his eyes on hers. How long had it been? A month? Two? Anna made so much love of late that she couldn't keep track. Bruno's assent was silent.

"Let's go," Anna said.

"Do you know the German word *Sehnsucht*?" Anna shook her head no. "It means disconsolate longing. It's that hole in your heart out of which all hope leaks." Anna became queasy with dread. Doktor Messerli sensed this. "Anna," she consoled, "it only feels hopeless. It doesn't have to be."

Doesn't it? Anna answered silently.

Bruno and Anna bade slapdash goodbyes to Edith and Otto and all the other guests and drove home quickly. Anna let her hand glide up her husband's thigh. Bruno made a hard, hot groan. Anna bit his ear, sucked the lobe. *I want you to fuck my mouth,* she said. *Fuck my mouth then shove your cock in my ass.* Bruno kept his eyes to the road but sped up all the same. *I want you to scrub my pussy with your face, Bruno. I want you to suck on my clit until it's as fat as a cherry.* When they got to the house he pulled in fast and parked the car at a crooked angle. This was something he never did, too regimented and square cornered he was. They began undressing before they even fully stepped inside. Jackets were abandoned in the boot room. Anna cast her shoes and dress aside in the entryway. Bruno's shirt fell away in the hall. There, Bruno grabbed Anna's arm above the elbow and pulled her roughly into the bedroom behind him.

There were freshly washed and folded clothes on the bed. Bruno swept them to the floor and shoved Anna to the mattress without ceremony. Anna let down her hair and tossed the clip toward the nightstand, where it bounced and then slid right off. She reached for the waistband of her pantyhose, the back fastening of her bra—she was too aroused to decide which she'd take off first. *Stop,* Bruno commanded. *I will undress you.* Anna complied limply as Bruno unzipped his pants and pushed them along with his briefs down his legs.

God, he's so fucking handsome. Anna allowed herself this swoon. *I forgot how handsome he was.* Even for a Swiss man Bruno was tall; at a slouch he stood six foot four. His eyes were hazel—yellow and brown like a tiger's-eye jewel. His chest was broad and beautiful, silken and downy. The hair on his head, the hair on his body the rustic brown of fresh-turned soil. His forearms were veiny, strong like a carpenter's. His nose, more Aryan than Alemannic, ran straight as a taut line of string from its bridge to its tip. His were the features of an aristocrat; he was the physical heir of another era. And his cock. Anna loved Bruno's cock. Of all the cocks belonging to all her lovers past or present, Bruno's was the largest. Erect, it was nearly as long as a dinner knife and as big around as the face of a man's pocket watch. Uncut. Precision straight. It was obscene, aggressive, and in just a minute it would split her apart. Anna had never been able to slide more than half of it into her mouth. Her orgasms were painful, exquisite affairs.

Bruno spread her legs. Anna, still drunk, wanted nothing more than to lie there and let his will overpower her. Her knees fell open as Bruno climbed between them, entered her, then slammed his cock in and out of her as hard as he could. After two, three, four minutes of this he pulled out entirely and flipped Anna onto her stomach. He hitched her pelvis to the edge of the bed, knelt on the floor and pushed her legs each to their own side before burying his tongue inside her. Anna moaned, sighed, bucked her hips against his face. But she didn't come. Bruno shoved her forward on the bed and forced her knees underneath her. Anna started to lift herself up onto her hands but Bruno barked *No* and with his left hand he pushed her shoulders down, even as with his right, he positioned his cock to enter her again. Anna allowed herself the ecstasy of powerlessness. Of all her men, it was only with Bruno that this could be fully accomplished. Of all her men, Bruno was the most threatening. Bruno pushed so deeply into her that Anna felt like she might split into halves. Anna growled. Bruno moved his left hand to the small of her back and reached his right around her and found her clit with his fingers. He twiddled it, flicked it, pinched it. "I'm gonna come," Anna rasped and reached back with her own hand and pushed his away. Bruno took hold of her hips, fucked her harder than he had in years. Anna's orgasm called forth Bruno's. They stiffened, flushed, first called out each other's names and then the name of God, before collapsing in a singular, satisfied cry.

When it was done, Bruno let the weight of his body press Anna between him and the bed. They remained that way until Bruno's cock stopped pulsing and it softened enough to fall out on its own. When it did, Bruno rolled off her and onto his back. Anna turned her head to look at him. Bruno, empty of energy beside her, stretched his body out its full length and capped the motion with a shiver. By the light of the dim but undeniable moon, Anna saw what passed for a smile on Bruno's face.

"Bruno," she whispered. "What's the purpose of pain?"

"This is pillow talk?" Bruno yawned. "Go to sleep, Anna." Anna asked him again. She wanted to know. Bruno took several breaths before answering. Anna thought he'd fallen asleep. "Pain is the proof of life." His voice was unguarded. "That's its purpose." It was a more satisfying answer than Doktor Messerli had given her.

"Bruno," Anna pressed. "Do you love me?" He answered Anna's question with a snore.

12

The postanalysis letdown is often palpable. As in the aftermath of sex, you are tired, spent, and for the moment relieved it's over. You leave the analyst's office aware of your singularity and your solitude alike. It's you who lives in the prison of your skin. No one gets the afterglow they want. Everyone dies alone. Analysis is a process. The process is a slow procession. It is a cortege.

Vhat are yooo sinking? Doktor Messerli had asked.

Anna shook her head. There was nothing she wanted to admit thinking of. The session was almost over. Anna stood, rubbed her neck, and stretched herself in several directions. "My back hurts. I'm tense. That's all." Anna bent to gather her things and leave.

Doktor Messerli rose and followed her to the office door. "Even the loveliest shoulders can bear but so much."

Anna was still drunk. She couldn't sleep. Bruno never had this problem. He was an easy sleeper. In sleep, he died to the world. That's what lovemaking did to him. But sex often made Anna restless and insecure. *The consequence of sex is always doubt,* she thought. With greater intimacy came greater doubt. When Bruno fell asleep Anna was alone. The white noise of worry kept her awake.

Anna rose and pulled on a pair of jeans and a sweater and her boots. She didn't bother with underwear or socks. She found her coat in the hallway where she'd stripped it off an hour earlier and pulled it on as she left the house. *Where can I go?* Anna felt trapped no matter where she was. Even at the end of such an evening as this.

In the darkness she traipsed the familiar path behind the house. She passed a rotting barn and the back units of an apartment complex. A motion-detecting light flashed on. The sudden spark of brightness startled her, as it always did. She looked across the sunflower field to the newer houses south of Loorenstrasse. Most were fully dark, but a window here and there was softly lit. *Where am I going?* Anna had nowhere to go and no reason for the going. *Everywhere I go is nowhere.* This was true. But her own ennui annoyed her and so she dismissed it.

The sky was so clear it shone. Anna crested the hill and sat on the bench at a curve in the path. Her bench. One of the most familiar things to her in all of Switzerland. She gazed at the autumn constellations and wished she knew their names. Above her hung the moon. *I have nothing to say about the moon,* she said to herself and in saying that she had nothing to say, somehow said something. She watched the red blinking lights of three airplanes at varying altitudes blip across the dark star-spotted field. Anna was accustomed to airplanes. They lived only a few kilometers from the Zürich airport. She always watched for movement in the skies. In the seventies and ten kilometers away in Bülach, a man named Billy Meier told everyone that spacemen in honest-to-god flying saucers came to visit him. He had hundreds of pictures of so-called proof. Anna had seen the photographs on the Internet. The image was familiar—an empty, pastoral scene, a metal dish poised in a way that toyed with perception and pending from wires that while invisible surely must exist. Anna, having spent nine years considering the words "alien" and "alienated," took to Billy Meier's story. And almost six years earlier in Bassersdorf, the town immediately north of Dietlikon, a Crossair flight crashed four kilometers short of its runway. Pilot error. Anna remembered that night. She'd heard a terrible noise and ran outside. She could see nothing in the dark. Bruno read about it in the next day's paper. There were pop stars aboard the plane, though neither Bruno nor Anna recognized their names. And so Anna scanned the vault of sky above her, searching for signs. She found none.

The air made everything seem lonelier than it already was. Anna reached for her Handy, which she'd put in her pocket before leaving the house. She opened the phone on its hinge and pressed a single button twice.

ONCE, FOLLOWING AN ALMOST painfully tender morning of lovemaking and as the sun passed through the shutter slats and fell upon their bodies, Anna turned to Stephen. "Tell me about spontaneous human combustion."

Stephen laughed, kissed her on the forehead, and rose. "It doesn't happen. People don't just catch fire."

"I've seen pictures."

Stephen shook his head. "Nothing spontaneous about it. There's always a catalyst. Smoking in bed, faulty wiring, stray sparks, lightning. Something. It's not magic, Anna. It's chemistry. Nothing ever just explodes."

Anna knew this wasn't entirely true. Her heart had exploded in her chest when they met. Or it felt like it. She would do anything for him. She'd set herself on fire if he asked her to. Or told herself she would at least.

Anna got dressed and went home.

EARLIER IN THE MONTH, Anna received a card in the mail. It was from Mary. On the outside of the card, a close shot of a ladybug. Inside, Mary had written a short note: *I'm sending this card for no reason except to tell you that you are loveable and dear and I delight in our friendship. Have a great day, Anna!!!*

THE PHONE RANG ONCE, twice, a third time. On the fourth ring Archie picked up. "Yeah?"

The "yeah" blew her back. "It's me." Anna paused, then added with sheepish specificity, "It's Anna."

The connection crackled on Archie's end. He said something Anna couldn't fully understand and she asked him to repeat it. It was still unintelligible. He was in a room with other people. A bar, maybe. Anna couldn't distinguish the competing voices. She barreled forward. *Talk to me, Archie. I am drunk and cold and alone and horny and in the dark and drunk and lonely and Bruno's asleep and talk to me, talk to me please, please.* She knew he didn't owe her this. But she could ask, couldn't she? *Talk to me. Please. Please?*

There was a pause during which Anna heard Archie turn away and ask the people around him to be a little quieter. Anna couldn't differentiate between individual responses but she did make out a woman's laugh, rowdy and high-pitched. "Sorry," Archie said. "It's loud here." Anna nodded as if he could see her nodding through the phone. "Hey," he cleared his throat. "Can I call you later?"

"Are you on a date?" The note in Anna's voice accused. She had intended it to.

Archie pretended not to hear her. "Can I call you tomorrow? I can't talk right now."

"No," Anna said, and reminded him she'd be at home with Bruno and her kids and if he didn't talk to her just then, he wouldn't be able to until Monday.

"Then I'll talk to you on Monday, all right?"

"Okay," Anna responded. But she didn't mean it. It wasn't okay. She ended the phone call quickly, before Archie could end it himself. An immediate, unfair jealousy possessed her. Hot tears welled in her eyes, then boiled over, then slid down her face. *Dammit, Anna.* In her heart she heard the unbidden, disembodied voice of Doktor Messerli: *Your histrionics cripple you.*

Yes, yes, Anna said aloud to the inner voice. *He's trifling. A nothing. A no one.* But her heart hurt anyway.

She opened her telephone again and in a darkness illuminated only by the bright gray screen she scrolled through her address book until she found Karl's entry. The SMS was easy. *Wo bist?* She received an almost immediate answer. *Basel. Tomorrow in Kloten. Hotel?* Karl's father lived in a convalescent home there. That's what brought him to Kloten so often. And he always stayed at the same hotel. *Isn't it expensive?* Anna had asked. It was, Karl said, but the sister of one of the men he cut trees with was a manager and always found him a room in the off-season and gave him a deal. Most often the deal was *Don't worry about it.* Anna assumed he paid her in other ways. Maybe he fucked her too.

Yes, yes, Anna replied. *Text me. I'll meet you anytime.*

"ARSON AND PYROMANIA AREN'T the same," Stephen said. "Arson's a crime. Committed, usually, for insurance fraud." Stephen often testified in criminal court as an expert witness. He would take the stand and attorneys would question him about the behavior of fire. What it did under stress. How it reacted. What things set it off. "Pyromania, on the other hand, is a disease. I'm not a shrink so I can't say much more than a pyromaniac sets fires on impulse. It goes beyond his common sense. Also, it's rare. It's not something he can easily help."

"Pyromaniacs are always men?"

"Overwhelmingly, yes. Most all fire setters—arsonists included—are male."

"And what about pyrologists?"

Stephen grinned. "Ah. The overwhelming majority of pyrologists are men who know how to channel their impulsivity into avenues of potential orgasm." And with that he put his head beneath the blanket under which they lay and began sucking Anna's nipple even as he ran his hand between her thighs. Anna purred. It was a good afternoon.

ANNA WOKE WITH A hangover. Her head throbbed, her eyes pulsed, her stomach was sour and brackish. It was seven A.M.

The children were at Ursula's and Bruno was still asleep. Anna took some aspirin, drank a liter of water, and had two cups of coffee. By the end of the first cup of coffee her equilibrium returned. The morning came into slow focus.

She'd left her cell phone in the pocket of her coat when she returned from her walk. When she retrieved it that morning the message light was blinking. It was a text from Karl. She squinted. The memory of the night before rolled slowly into focus. The sex. The bench. Archie. Karl. She blushed against the recollection of her frantic scrambling to keep from being alone.

Bruno's mood was coltish when he awoke—without a hangover—forty-five minutes later. He brushed by Anna on the way to the bathroom and gave her bottom a smack. Minutes later he was in the kitchen cooking breakfast, whistling as he fried eggs and bacon for the pair of them. Anna marveled at this man. *Where'd he come from? How long is he staying?* She pushed those questions from her mind. It was better not to know. As in the case of a magic trick, once the ruse is learned, the spell dissolves.

They flirted over the meal like newlyweds. Bruno ran his hands up and down the outside of her thighs. She sucked butter from his thumbs. Anna blushed when, leaning in to kiss him, she smelled herself on Bruno's face. That was enough. She was done with the food. She was ready to fuck again. She was ready for Bruno to fuck her again. She mentally drafted an SMS to Karl: *Change of plans.* That would be all she needed to say. Bruno bit her lower lip then drew little circles on the tip of her tongue with the tip of his own tongue.

Anna was manic with desire. Bruno's smile was natural but

perplexed. "What are you thinking?" he asked in his usual, accented English.

Sinking? Anna thought. *I'm not sinking—I'm swimming!* Bruno wore flannel pajama bottoms and a ratty white undershirt. Anna had on nothing but a robe. She'd stripped to nakedness and resignation after her walk the night before. She stood, took hold of Bruno's shoulders, then swung her right leg over his lap and eased herself onto him, pressing her chest into his body. She kissed him once, then again. She undulated. Her robe fell open. It was the act of her body beckoning its finger. She felt his cock begin to stir.

Bruno kissed her back, but it was a pat and friendly kiss. He shook his head. "Not now. We do that later, *jo*?" Anna frowned. "Don't pout," Bruno said as he winked and tap-tap-tapped her outer thigh in a way that meant *You get up now, okay?* and with that, Anna rose. Bruno stood and stretched and yawned and then he reached out and ruffled her hair as if she were one of their sons. He slugged back the last swallow of his coffee. "Maybe you can clean up since I did the cooking?" Then he went into his office and shut the door behind him. Anna sank back into the chair. At the sound of Bruno's office door clicking into place, something in Anna slammed shut too. A closed door reminded her of everything about her life she hated. And she hated it twice as much as she had the day before. The brief vacation from heartbreak made the desolation that remained all the more acute.

Anna washed the dishes then dressed and walked over to get the children. "Did you have a nice time?" Ursula asked. Anna told her nicely that the party was nice and it was also nice to get out of the house for a nice evening out. If she said "nice" enough times she was sure she'd decide that it had been wholly wonderful.

"You're out of the house every day."

Anna caught the indictment. She stood in the doorframe, Polly Jean on her hip. The boys barreled past her. They ran down the street to the house. "Ursula, is there something you want to say to me?"

Ursula backed down. "No. Most days you do leave the house. This is true. That's all."

Later that afternoon, she informed Bruno that she was going for a long bike ride. "Two hours. Maybe more." Bruno was clicking through computer files and sorting papers in his office. She asked him to listen for the children. Bruno grunted. "Polly's upstairs napping," Anna said as she tied her shoes. Bruno grunted again.

Anna returned home more than three hours later. "I had a good ride," she announced in the direction of Bruno's office. He grunted once more.

THERE WAS LITTLE WAY around Anna feeling awkward and adolescent in Monday's German class. She hadn't messaged Archie since she'd hung up on him, and he hadn't tried to reach her either. It was petty, this fuming, Anna knew. But a minor bruise still hurts when you poke it with your finger. For the first full hour Anna didn't even look in his direction and instead watched Roland lecture on German particles, those sly idiomatic words that serve as a sentence's emotional barometer. *Yeah? So? Of course! Really? Duh! Just. Whatever.* Archie watched Anna not watching him. Mary sat between them, unaware of the tension. At break, Archie pulled Anna to the side in the *Kantine* before either of them went through the line.

"You didn't need to get mad at me."

"I wasn't mad. I was drunk." That wasn't a lie.

"I was with Glenn and his wife and their friends."

"I didn't know your brother was married." There was so much of Archie she didn't know.

Archie cleared his throat. "Glenn doesn't know. About you." Anna stared him down in a way she had no right to. Archie gave in. "It was a fix up. It ended with a hug. She might have wanted more." He hadn't needed to tell her that.

"Really. And what did you want?" Anna wearied of herself. She had no claim on jealousy.

Archie gave a moderate sigh. "I'd have liked to not have been there at all. If I can't be out with you, I'd rather be home alone. Really."

It shouldn't have, but this satisfied her. In any case, Anna couldn't admit to what she couldn't explain. "Let's just get coffee."

ANNA HAD LOVED STEPHEN, or thought she had. Anna thought she still loved Stephen, though she wasn't sure. But Anna did love Polly Jean, and in a way that was like loving Stephen.

AFTER THE BREAK, THE group returned to class and Roland moved from particles to a review of the four German cases, beginning with the accusative case. *What a word,* Anna thought. *Accusative.* It pointed a bony finger in her direction (as everything and everyone seemed to be doing of late). She copied out the chart that Roland drew on the board and tried to summon even a little self-empathy.

I'm nothing but a series of poor choices executed poorly. It was an indictment to which she could not object.

But after class and as was now the general custom, she traveled with Archie back to his Niederdorf apartment. They small-talked their way through every tram stop. Inside, they didn't even bother kissing. They made banal, quotidian love. It was the sexual equivalent of a shrugged shoulder.

I owe this man nothing of myself, Anna thought.

13

It is possible to lead several lives at once.

In fact, it is impossible not to.

Sometimes these lives overlap and interact. It is busy work living them and it requires stamina a singular life doesn't need.

Sometimes these lives live peaceably in the house of the body.

Sometimes they don't. Sometimes they grouse and bicker and storm upstairs and shout from windows and don't take out the trash.

Some other times, these lives, these several lives, each indulge several lives of their own. And those lives, like rabbits or rodents, multiply, make children of themselves. And those child lives birth others.

This is when a woman ceases leading her own life. This is when the lives start leading her.

The day before her birthday, Anna woke to the Sunday morning surprise of two little boys standing over her. Charles held out a vase of semi-wilted flowers that must have been purchased the day before. Victor offered her a tray of toast and jam and coffee. Bruno stood behind them holding Polly Jean. "What's this?" Anna sat up in bed. Charles spoke first. "It's for your birthday, Mami."

"Oh!"

Victor piped in, sure of himself. "Your birthday isn't until tomorrow."

Anna suppressed a scowl. Victor was always the room's first pessimist. He held out the tray and Anna took it from him. "Thank you!" She waved her sons over for a kiss. "This is so thoughtful!" Charles grinned and kissed his mother before setting the flowers on the nightstand. Victor received his kiss passively and shuffled from foot to foot. Anna looked up to Bruno. He told her it was all their own idea and then he reached into the pocket of his pants and pulled out a little box.

"Here, Anna." Anna took the box. It was a small square jeweler's box, unwrapped. The tiny hinge creaked when Anna opened it. Inside, pressed into a padded slot, was a gold ring set with three stones—a garnet, a diamond, and a yellow topaz. They were her children's birthstones. It was a mother's ring. Anna slipped it onto the ring finger of her right hand. It was a snug, even fit. She looked up at Bruno and Polly and down to the faces of her sons and told them the truth in a metered, earnest voice.

"It is the nicest gift I've ever received."

"You like it?" Bruno's voice was flat, but not unkind.

"I love it."

"Very good. Happy birthday. Enjoy your breakfast." Bruno leaned down and gave his wife a modest kiss on the lips. Anna didn't fight the tears that came.

* * *

Anna had written letters to Stephen she'd never sent, all but one of which she composed during the immediate weeks after his departure. She hid them in her high school scrapbook (melancholy's most appropriate storehouse), itself at the bottom of a box, which in turn rested underneath a stack of a half dozen other boxes in a deep corner of the attic where Bruno would never find them. Anna sometimes pulled the letters out and sat on the attic floor and spent moody hours rereading them. They were maudlin and overcomposed, and she remembered where she wrote every one. In Platzspitz: *They used to call this Needle Park. Where the addicts got their drugs. I am addicted to you and I shake on the floor in your absence.* And another, written from a bench facing the river Sihl, the muddy river that feeds into the Limmat: *Brown like your eyes, brown like the hurt in my heart. Murky and silty and sad oh sad.* The day was drizzly. A man in a green hat staggered past Anna to a tree fifty yards away and took a piss. Another letter opened like this: *I write to you from the Lindenhof, the very place you searched out the day we met.* And yet another letter began at Wipkingen station: *Your station, Stephen. Do you remember?* That letter took her weeks to write. She finished it on the bank of the Zürichsee at Seefeld, in the Riesbach harbor, by the large, abstract sculptures. Anna remembered each incident, each place, most every pen stroke, the clothes she wore, the weathers, how they turned, how they stalled, how they felt against her skin.

It had been at least five months since she'd read the letters. Maybe six. The last time she read them was the first time they embarrassed her.

* * *

One morning the previous week, Anna arrived at German class with a stomachache. She felt as if she'd eaten pebbles or swallowed hourglass sand. She took her notes silently and without flourish. Roland spoke of indefinite pronouns. *Something. Someone. No one. Everybody. Whoever. All. Enough.* And: *Nothing.*

Nothing, nothing, nothing.

Mary knew that Anna's birthday was approaching. During a class break, she volunteered to have a party at her house and to bake Anna a cake and what was her favorite kind, anyway?

"No, Mary. You'll do nothing. Please. I beg you." Mary seemed baffled, but she capitulated. She let the matter drop.

They spent the rest of the German class in pairs, pretending to telephone each other.

"Do you know what it's like?" Anna spoke quickly, breathlessly. "It's like having so much feeling in your body that you *become* the feeling. And when you become the feeling, it's not *in* you anymore. It *is* you. And the feeling is despair. I almost can't remember a time I didn't live here. But even my walk gives me away as an American. I've forgotten how to think in dollars and yet I barely understand how to count in francs—my husband's a goddamn banker!" Every thought Anna had, she had at once. "Am I in Hell? I must be in Hell. I don't know what else you want me to say. I can cook and shop and read and do simple math and I can cry and I can fuck. And I can fuck up. Can I love? What does that mean? What does that matter? What do I matter? All I ever do is make mistakes."

Doktor Messerli inched herself to the edge of her chair and urgently motioned her to keep talking. They were close to a breakthrough, she was sure.

YES, ANNA HAD ASKED that nothing be done for her birthday, but Mary, sweet Mary, wouldn't hear of it so she suggested an outing in lieu of a party. Both families. A day of minimal but undeniable celebration.

"Besides," Mary offered, "it's something we might have done anyway." So Anna conceded as Anna often did.

The Benzes had arranged to meet the Gilberts at a quarter past eleven at Stadelhofen. From there, it would be a half-hour train ride to Rapperswil, where the families would walk around for a while, then board a boat that would carry them back to Zürich. The trip would last the afternoon, the boat stopping many times to let people on, to let others off. Mary had packed a basket of sandwiches, beer, sodas, and snacks to enjoy on the ride. A day would be made of this travel and when they returned to Zürich, the Gilberts would come back to the Benzes' for drinks, a simple dinner, and cake. Ursula stayed home with Polly Jean.

Rapperswil is a picturesque city on the eastern end of the lake about thirty kilometers from Zürich. Built on a Bronze Age settlement, its sinewy alleyways date to medieval times. There's a castle there and Rapperswil is the home of Circus Knie, the largest circus in Switzerland. Anna had never visited.

The families made easy conversation on the train. Mary talked of volunteering at Max and Alexis's school, Bruno and Tim spoke of skiing. Anna split her attention between the competing conversations. Max and Charles amused their parents by telling silly jokes: *Why did the train choke on its food? Because it didn't choo-choo it!* Anna smiled at her middle child. "What a clever boy you are," she said, and Charles broke into a proud, pleased grin. Victor sat alone and played with a handheld video game. Alexis had brought a book. Anna tried to engage her in conversation with little success. She asked her about school, about Canada, whether she liked Switzerland or not, if she was enjoying her book. Alexis's responses were polite but terse. Anna let her be. The child didn't want to talk. A familiarity flashed before her once again and Anna's heart reached out invisibly to Alexis's. Anna said nothing more.

ANNA SOMETIMES WONDERED IF Stephen ever thought of her. *Has he forgotten me entirely? Do I ever invade his thoughts? Like a song he can't shake from his head?* This line of questioning never did her any good. She avoided it most of the time.

But when she couldn't, she settled on believing that months ago he realized he'd made a terrible mistake but was too timid, too embarrassed, or too frightened to come back to her. *It's possible,* Anna reasoned. She understood that insurmountable feeling of being penned in, captured and unable to act. Anna had lived in the house of her own inevitability for years. Maybe Stephen had as well. Anna made a choice to believe that this was the reason he'd never called or written.

She knew better, of course. But there were times when she forgot that she knew better and she forgot that she was pretending.

* * *

"WHAT'S THE DIFFERENCE BETWEEN a delusion and a hallucination?"

Doktor Messerli made a noise that relayed her frustration. And that's what it sounded like, the click of a relay switch closing a circuit. "Hallucinations are sensory. A person sees or hears or smells things that do not exist apart from his own experience. A delusion, per contra, is a false belief. A conviction that someone adamantly holds despite strong evidence to the contrary." Anna gave herself the rundown. She'd never heard the voice of God or smelled a vase of ghost roses. "A hypochondriac will convince himself he's dying though every test proves he's perfectly healthy. Someone else will swear that the government pursues him. Another person might be steadfast in his belief that the object of his most zealous love returns his deep affection even though she does not."

"I see." This hit a little nearer to the nail.

"Are you having hallucinations, Anna?"

"No."

This time, it was the Doktor who answered with *I see.*

THE SUN SHONE LIKE a song. The boat skated over silver, glinting water. Anna wore layers but there was a wind and despite the sunshine, she was cold enough to shiver. Bruno saw this and drew her close into him. This was the Bruno she had fallen into a version of love with. Being with the Gilberts brought this out in him. A wonderful, comfortable ease that they could never seem to find when they were alone. Anna was glad in a way she had forgotten how to be. Happiness moved through her body from her head to her mouth to her throat to her chest, down through her belly to the deadbolt room of her pelvis, where she tended to file her grievances with the world.

Anna took the day for what it was: a gift. A present. In the present. She couldn't remember the last time she'd felt so glad. On the boat, no one sulked. Alexis set her book to the side when Victor gave her a turn on his game. Both were being kind to their younger brothers. Charles and Max darted around the boat pretending they were pirates. The children drank sodas and the grown-ups had beer and everyone snacked on bags of paprika-flavored potato chips. Bruno stole one kiss, then another. Anna let him. She let him again. Everyone laughed and smiled. Everyone enjoyed the lake. *It is unfair of me to feel so happy. I do not deserve this. This is a mercy I don't merit.* Anna had a flash of understanding. *This is what they mean when they talk about grace.* She thanked aloud the god she wasn't sure she believed in. Anna caught Mary checking her watch four times in the span of thirty minutes. *The boat ride lasts two hours,* Anna said and Mary replied, *Oh.*

At every *Schiffstation,* a few people boarded and a few others disembarked. The Benzes and the Gilberts made a game of guessing who they were. They decided the young, tall man with the shaved head and his female companion with the black-blue hair were on their fifth date and that an older couple on the ship's port side were British tourists celebrating a fortieth anniversary, and that the thirtysomething woman smoking a cigarette near the prow nursed a broken heart with solitude and sea spray. Or at least that was the conclusion Anna came to.

At the end of the boat trip, their faces sunburned and stung by lake wind, the families took the tram from Bürkliplatz to the Hauptbahnhof and rode the train back to the Dietlikon station, all eight of them. It was near six and growing dark. There was cake and champagne waiting at the house.

Anna couldn't believe how enjoyable, how perfectly pleasant the day had been. She hadn't expected it to be. She had forgotten that was possible, if ever she had really known.

She was still engaged in the experience of the day's supple joy when they came up the hill on Hintergasse past the town square and rounded the corner to Rosenweg. On their right, the church parking lot was filled with cars. If Anna noticed this—which she didn't—she would have assumed that the church was holding evening services. They passed the little playground, walked toward the house, mounted the steps, and opened the door.

The house was dark. Bruno threw the light switch and, after a half-second pause, almost two dozen people yelled the word "Surprise!"

Christ, Anna thought. *They threw me a fucking party.*

The architect of this surprise was obvious. Before she could take stock of the guests, before Anna could rightly register the faces of the people who had come into the house without her personal invitation, Mary leapt into Anna's line of vision. She jumped around and clapped in the manner of a jack springing from his box when the handle's been cranked.

"Are you surprised? Are you? Did you guess? Look how surprised you are!"

Yes, yes, Anna mollified her friend. *Big surprise.* She gave Mary a mechanical hug of thanks and then talked herself silently through the situation. *Okay, Anna, you can manage this. It's been a good, good day. I can manage this. I can be thankful for this.*

Anna scanned the room. Ursula was there as well as Daniela and David, Margrith and Hans and their daughter Suzanne and her husband Guido, neither of whom Anna knew well but who until last year had lived in the cottage behind Hans's barn with their three little girls, who had also come to the party. Bruno and Anna's neighbors Monika and Beat were there and Edith and Otto as well. Most of the people from Anna's German class including Nancy and Ed and the Australian couple she rarely spoke to and the French lady who always smoked during break and the Asians who kept to themselves and who had, in fact, never once uttered a conversant word to Anna had come to the house. And Roland. And Archie. And Karl.

A FACE SEEN OUT of context creates confusion. And most paranoiacs have reason to be.

14

IT'S TRUE: A FACE SEEN OUT OF CONTEXT CREATES CONFUSION. A momentary blip of disorientation. Transitory befuddlement. Personal perception is called into question. Like being in a bar when a priest and a rabbi actually walk in. *Is this a joke?* you ask yourself. The answer is yes. The answer is no. The answer is both.

Is this a joke? Anna asked herself. Nearly every person in her house that night was divorced from his or her circumstance. Anna's bearings faltered as the floor beneath her tried to shift and she fought the onslaught of a literal swoon. Mary beamed. She was pleased with herself and still under the impression that when Anna had said *Do nothing for my birthday* what she really meant was *I want you to throw me a party.* A blush rose from Anna's chest to her face. "I know you said you didn't want a fuss, but really it was no trouble at all!" Mary waited for a response. Anna offered a weak, tactful smile. "And I wanted to do this! You're my best friend!"

Mary drew Anna into the living room and put a paper crown on her head. It was pink and sparkly, made for a child.

Anna immediately removed it. Bruno shook hands with the men he knew and before long, Bruno, Guido, Otto, Beat, David, and Karl had beers in their hands and were moving toward the door. When they passed Anna, each wished her happy birthday and gave her a quick hug and the customary three-cheek kiss. When Karl came in for his Anna hissed into his ear, *Why are you here?* To which Karl responded, "She invited Daniela and David and they invited me." Bruno led the group outside, the children following along. Edith sidled up to Anna and handed her a glass of sparkling wine.

She smirked. "This is rare, Anna." Anna was inclined to agree. Anna downed the champagne in two quick swallows and handed the glass back to Edith with a face that read *Now go and get me a real drink.* Edith laughed her Edith laugh and slid away into the kitchen.

A moment later she returned with a Scotch. Anna sipped it. The whiskey was peaty and smooth. "Where'd this come from?" She didn't need to ask.

"He brought it." Edith gestured toward the other side of the room where Archie stood with Roland and Ed. Anna started to say something but thought better of it. Edith, too, opened her mouth to speak but was interrupted by the arrival of Mary. Anna introduced them. Mary and Edith were, respectively, effusive and detached. This was not unexpected, but at the moment, Anna didn't have the heart to referee disputing personalities. She excused herself under the pretense of wanting to change out of the clothes she'd worn on the boat ride and slipped into the bedroom, closing the door behind her and leaving Mary and Edith to discover how little they had in common all on their own.

Anna found a nicer sweater and changed into it. She checked

her face—it was still flushed. *I'll blame it on the Scotch,* Anna thought, and then, reexamining herself, *This will have to do.* A knock on the door startled her, "Who is it?"

"It's Arch."

"For fuck's sake." Anna huffed to the door, jerked it open, and yanked him inside.

"Anna—," Archie started, but Anna held up her hand.

"Why are you here?"

"Mary invited me." Mary was every present problem's lynchpin. "It would have seemed odd if I hadn't shown up."

"Really, Archie?" Anna said. "Go tell that to my tall Swiss husband with his beefy Swiss friends getting drunk in my Swiss front yard." Anna couldn't stop saying the word "Swiss" but she didn't know why. Anna was angry. She had worked very hard to keep her secret life—lives—separate. "I need to get back." Anna opened the door and shoved past him into the hall. *Am I the only one my secrets make sense to?* Anna asked herself before remembering that she was the only one who knew the secrets in the first place.

The party's chatter had picked up. People drank and ate and while the party retained a strained, dull ambiance, conversation loosened and people began to relax. Anna lagged back for a second, exhaled deeply, and then steeled in herself a will to interact. She bumped into Edith as she rounded the corner into the den.

"Everything all right, Anna?" She spoke disingenuously.

"Everything's swell," Anna said simply.

"You know"—Edith leaned in—"I've been surveying the livestock." Anna made a face. "I'll bet there's at least one man we could hook you up with."

"Edith. Really." Anna reminded her she had a husband.

"Yes. I suppose you do." Edith kept on. "What about that fellow Roland?" Anna threw her a you've-got-to-be-kidding look. "All right, then. What about the Scotsman? Didn't I just see him coming out of your bedroom?" There was a dance of light in Edith's eyes.

"Enough, Edith." Anna had flint in her voice.

"God, Anna. Lighten up. That Mary's done her prudish number on you."

"It's not prudery," Anna said. "It's decorum."

"Ha, ha!" Edith's laugh was scattershot. "Trust me, Anna. I know the score." Anna looked at her and decided that she probably did.

Edith returned Anna's stare. "Mary, on the other hand . . ." She trailed off affectedly. Whatever she was going to say, she didn't need to finish it.

"Be nice to her, Edith."

"God, Anna. You bore me."

"Edith, I have guests."

Edith smirked. "Fine, whatever." Edith brushed past Anna into the hall, pulled her cell phone out of her pocket, and began to text Niklas, Anna assumed.

"WHAT'S THE DIFFERENCE BETWEEN an obsession and a compulsion?"

As a child Anna had been prone to counting things. Rocks in her path. Telephone trills. Words in sentences. Sentences in paragraphs. Every action had to be ordered. Every thought both metered and meted out. It was painstaking. She was always on call. It was a fair enough compromise. The counting, sorting, and classifying helped Anna manage her panics. The psychiatrist decided that it, like Anna's depression, was a phase. It was. It didn't persist. She moved past the habit by picking up other habits.

"An obsession is a defense against feeling out of control. A compulsion is the failure of that defense."

AT THE END OF a recent class, Anna asked Roland to translate some graffiti she'd seen scratched onto the back of a train seat. Graffiti in Swiss trains is rare. Anna had copied it onto the back of her German notebook. "'*Was fuer ae huere Schweinerei . . .*' What does that mean?"

Roland frowned, shuffled his papers, and started for the door. "It means something not very nice." Anna stood there waiting for a response. Roland sighed and relented. "It means 'what a fucking mess.'"

EVERYONE HAS A TELL. In poker, the underpinning rule for assessing them is this: a weak hand means strong action and a strong hand means weak. Does he shake? Does he glance too furtively at his stack of chips? Does he stare too intently at his cards? Does he throw down his bet like a chef drops a hot potato? Does he or does he not look other players in the eye?

Of course, there are other tells. Your son says *Tell me a story, Mami,* and you settle down next to him and begin: *Es war einmal eine Prinzessin . . .* There is show-and-tell, where for perhaps the first time in your life you publicize an inner aspect of yourself, not yet aware of exposure's possible consequence. Once, in second grade, Anna brought her favorite doll to class. A bisque-head doll, her hands and feet were also made of porcelain and her hair was human, black and perfect. Anna named her Frieda and while she did not love her in the way that other girls loved their own baby dolls, rocking them and pretending to feed them and scolding them when they were naughty, Anna felt something lovelike. She was fascinated with the curves of Frieda's face, the softness of her hair, and the lacy pink dress she wore. It was a detached, scientific interest, but a deeply enthralling one nonetheless. And when on the playground that day she dropped her by accident and a boy named Walter—also by accident—stepped on Frieda's right hand and crushed it to irreparable bits, Anna felt the sort of loss that little girls do when their dolls break and she spent the rest of the day in tears. At home, Anna returned Frieda to her shelf and never played with or examined her again. She'd loved her more than she'd realized.

And then there is Wilhelm Tell, the Swiss national hero who, having refused to bow to the overlord, was forced to shoot an apple off his young son's head. With a single bolt of his crossbow, he split the apple into perfect halves. If there was a moral to that story, Anna couldn't say what it was.

HE NEVER TOLD HER he did not love her.

But he never told her he did.

ARCHIE, MARY, NANCY, ROLAND, and Ed congregated near the snacks. Archie had turned his back to Anna, granting her the wish of extreme discretion. Outside, Bruno and his friends stood in the street looking at Guido's new car. Bruno balanced Polly on his hip. Daniela leaned in and tickled her. Polly Jean was a dozen smiles and giggles.

The party continued dully. As was the case with Edith's party, Anna's had split into halves—though here it was geography and not gender that divided the room: the native friends of Bruno's stayed outside, and Anna and her foreign acquaintances remained indoors. *How emblematic,* Anna thought. *They're free to move in open air through their own world. We are locked in a box of otherness. There's a line of demarcation. They tolerate our presence but will never welcome it.*

Mary announced she'd brought board games. Edith groaned from the station she'd assumed on the couch, and Anna shot her a stare she didn't look up from her cell phone to see. Nancy's position was sympathetic and she said she'd be up for playing, if other people were. Mary arranged the choices on the coffee table. *Life. Risk. Trivial Pursuit. Sorry.* Even the board games pointed a finger at Anna. She caught Archie's eye and mouthed *Please leave.* Archie blinked against her request and in turn mouthed *In a bit.* Anna responded by retreating into the kitchen.

A minute later, Mary joined her. "There you are! You're missing all the fun! If I didn't know better I'd say you were trying to avoid your own party."

"Mary," Anna spoke with exasperation. "I told you I didn't want a party."

Anna opened the refrigerator. Inside, a layer cake so large that the refrigerator's upper shelves and everything that rested upon them had been removed so the cake could fit. *Where's my salad dressing? Where's my mustard? I want to know where my mustard is.* Anna shoved the door closed. The fridge made a dramatic rattle.

"Are you mad, Anna?" There was a tremor in Mary's voice. Anna didn't want to hurt Mary's feelings. She had little choice but to inhale the whole affront. "No, Mary. Not at all. It's a good surprise. Thank you."

"WHAT ARE YOU GOOD at?" the Doktor asked one afternoon.

Anna scanned her memory, attempting to recall the last time she'd been asked, if ever. She gave a catechumenal answer, born of repetition and praxis.

"I don't know," Anna replied, and both women understood this to mean *I'd prefer to not talk about it.*

The Doktor pressed. "I'm not letting you off this hook," she said, then crossed her legs and arms and leaned back in her chair as she settled in for the protracted wait that prefigured any conversation with Anna that required initial coaxing. The windows were closed and the room was damp and clammy. The Doktor redirected. "Okay. Let's try this one. What is it you *like* to do? Whether you're good at it I don't care."

I like to fuck, was Anna's on-the-spot response, though she kept it to herself. Instead she squinted and bit her lip and tried to think past the fucking as the Doktor waited for her to answer.

"When I was *younger*"—Anna drew a pause, emphasizing "younger" as if it were key that a *then* and *now* distinction be understood—"I liked to sew."

The Doktor clapped her hands together once. "Finally! An

admission!" The levity came off as inconsiderate. "Now. Were you good at it?"

Anna hadn't sewn in years. The last time she pulled out her machine—*Where was it now, anyway? The attic? The basement?*—Victor was an infant and she still had the determination necessary to cultivate a certain kind of home life. Anna told this to the Doktor.

"And why did you stop?"

Anna mumbled a response along the lines of a lack of time and energy.

"And what's keeping you from sewing now?"

The answer remained intact. "Time. Energy." She was empty of both. She offered freely to her men all her free hours. She stored up no stamina for herself.

(Anna had never considered the correlation, but as they sifted through this part of Anna's past the parallels were evident and the correspondence clear: *I've traded sewing hems for sowing hims.* Anna grinned on the inside. There was comedy here. Clarity, too. *Bias. Pattern. Seam.* She could have simply told the Doktor that she was good at word games, and that would have been true, too. But that confession would have wrung out another one: that her wittiest moments were her slyest and most often they served her in the way the ink serves the octopus. Smoke screens, she hid behind them. *Dart. Edge. Bolt.* These days, *needle* had become *need.* A *pleat* was now a *plea.* But Anna startled herself as she thought through this. In this case, these weren't clever comebacks or coincidences. There were the bad, bald facts, and they aligned exactly.)

"Did your mother teach you to sew?" The Doktor's question snapped Anna back into the room. When Anna didn't immediately respond, the Doktor asked again. This time, the inquiry forced a dimming memory forward. Anna was young. Six or seven. She could no longer say. The afternoon in question had been as hazy as was her current recollection of it. That afternoon. It had been late enough in the day that when the light cut through the window it hit the room at an angle and the air's dust and floating motes appeared as playful and lovely as tiny flakes of snow. Anna's mother was stationed at her sewing machine, a now-obsolete Singer she'd inherited when her own mother died. She was crafting pillows for the sofa from the most beautiful velveteen fabric Anna had ever seen before or since—soft as down, it was the color of burgundy wine still in its cask. Anna, in tandem, sat in all seriousness on the floor at her mother's feet and busied herself over the body of her teddy bear, fitting soft, purple remnants to its form with safety pins. Later, Anna's mother took her on her lap and together they stitched those scraps into a tiny skirt, Anna's hands atop the fabric and her mother's hands on top of hers guiding both through the motion of the needle's piston punch. When Anna's father came home from work he kissed his girls and asked about their day. There was a roast in the oven and the air whirred with the steady, supple buzz of the ancient Singer and an indeterminate tune Anna's mother was fond of humming. It was a benevolent afternoon. But the fact of that day had long dissipated. In its stead, a metastasized wistfulness that, if she dwelt too long on it, devoured Anna with despair. Of course her mother taught her how to sew. And it made her just as sad as almost anything else. A pleasant husband. A darling daughter. A faithful wife. What a happy home.

"Can you tell me a little more?"

Anna could, but didn't.

"Anna, have I never asked? Where did you grow up?"

She had asked. Anna had dodged the question. Anna ran her fingers through her hair and tousled it, as if the act would shoo the memories away. "Does it matter?"

"Of course it matters."

It was one of the few times Anna disagreed with the Doktor openly, to her face and aloud. Most other contentions took the form of lies. "No. It doesn't." Where you were is never as relevant as where you are. Anna fully believed this.

To Anna's relief no one wanted to play games, so the suggestion was forgotten and the party lumbered on. Archie still hadn't left. Anna wondered if Bruno knew he was there. She had no doubt he remembered his name. Fifteen minutes later everyone crowded into the den and sang "Happy Birthday." Ursula brought in the cake. Anna was half blush, half fume. *Please go home, Archie. Please go home, Karl. Please go home everyone.* Anna couldn't breathe. There were too many people in the room. Archie kept far away from Bruno. This was a mercy. Anna ate half a piece of cake and went outside. She'd been to more parties in the last three weeks than she had the entire year. She was tired of watching people stand around rooms and talk.

David was standing in the driveway smoking his pipe. Anna was disappointed. She'd hoped to be alone for just one minute. The air had turned very chilly very quickly after the sunset and Bruno and his friends hadn't come back outside once the cake was served. Instead, he'd taken them into the basement for a reason that didn't hold water (to show them this or that, Anna wasn't listening closely when he said it). She could hear them, though, and see their silhouettes through the tempered glass of the basement window. Anna knew her husband. His motive was transparent and entirely Swiss: he didn't want to interact with anyone he didn't already know. "I'm sorry. I didn't mean to interrupt."

Anna averted her eyes and looked back to the basement window, flush with the ground, and thought of Doktor Messerli and labyrinths and mazes, the symbolism of the mumblings of subterranean shadows. David shrugged gently as if to say *This is your house, I am your guest, there is no interruption here.* Anna shrugged back at him and sat on the porch steps. She didn't want to talk. She didn't have anything to say.

David smoked and paced and whistled an ominous tune in a minor key that Anna had heard before but couldn't place. When he began to speak, it was apropos of nothing and directed at no one. "The French, we are expert at many things. Food and philosophy. Wine. Desire." David winked and Anna smiled thinly. "But the best lovers are so often the worst liars, Anna. It's a universal law." David offered a single sagacious nod and said nothing further.

It was a dream Anna wrote down but didn't share with Doktor Messerli: *I am in a room of absolute darkness. I fumble as I walk, unsure of the ground beneath me. I hold my arms in front of me, searching for something to grab on to. I touch a wall and it gives under the pressure of my hands. It's like the wall of an inflatable castle, the kind you rent for a child's birthday party. Except the more I press on it, the more it gives until eventually I break through. On the other side of this dark room is a new, bright, other, outside world. I am at the*

Zürichsee. The water is intensely blue. It's the bluest water I have ever seen. There are swimmers, boaters, sunbathers on the shore. And the sky, too, a stupefying azure. I have moved from absolute darkness into absolute light. I have stepped into a numinous world. It is amazing. I am amazed. And yet it isn't my world. I do not belong. I was safer in the blackness. But the wall's been broken, and the darkness is gone. I can't return to its safety. I am prisoner to the consciousness of this light.

15

Anna was ready to skip Monday's German class. She didn't want to see anyone. She could say she'd planned a day of leisure for herself, a trip to the spa, whatever. It was her birthday, she could do what she wanted. But she hadn't planned anything and the prospect of staying home alone depressed her more than the idea of facing the class made her anxious. And Mary had made Anna promise she'd let her take her out to lunch. It would be a disappointment if Anna canceled. So to Oerlikon Anna went.

She hadn't slept. She lay in bed the entire night, the day's events tumbling in her head like clothes in a dryer. It had been a day of revelation. *I brushed against happiness and I liked how it felt and I want to feel it again.* When the last guests left Bruno drove the Gilberts home. Anna waved goodbye through the kitchen window. The boys were upstairs, playing quietly. Polly had been asleep for an hour. Bruno wouldn't be home for at least forty-five minutes. She had the house effectively to herself. There was ample space and time for her to think.

She'd heard what David had said. It is dangerous to keep

secrets. And she hadn't been keeping hers very well. She ticked through a mental list. Edith hinted. David intimated. Ursula's voice, on several occasions, had intoned suspicion. Margrith had even seen her in Kloten. She'd thought she'd been strategic and cautious. She'd been nearly proud of her discretion. *That's the problem,* Anna thought. She could hear the phantom voice of Doktor Messerli: *Hubris is every heroine's assassin.*

Anna didn't need a walk up the hill or a cry on her bench to figure this out. *No more affairs,* she thought, *and never again.* When Bruno returned from the Gilberts' they made love. It was fun, pleasant, pleasurable sex. They came together. Quietly. Kindly. It was a respectable and ceremonial way of starting over, Anna decided. *No more. Never again.*

All through the night she worked on a plan. She would be active, not passive. She would invest herself fully in the day-to-day life of the home. She wasn't planning to can figs or cross-stitch wall samplers (though thoughts of redecorating the bedroom occupied a good half hour of her sleeplessness), but the vow she made was this: *To my family I give the entirety of myself. My time, my talents, my attention. I'll distract myself from the sex with which I distracted myself from the sadness of my life by fully living my life. How circular! How . . . Jungian!* Doktor Messerli would be thrilled at the turn of Anna's inner events. *Perhaps it's even time to tell her everything.* Anna came to, then backed away from, then approached with tentative caution that conclusion once again. This cycle occurred the entire night.

Anna arrived at school early and waited for Archie outside Roland's classroom. When he got there she pulled him aside.

"I want to talk." Anna had intended to stand on as little ceremony as possible, but there was no privacy in the hall outside the classroom, and while there wasn't much she planned on saying, Anna preferred not to advertise herself. Archie waited for her to continue but Anna shook her head. "Not here." She rubbed her temples and thought for a moment. "Mary's taking me to lunch at the zoo. Meet me in front of the zoo at one thirty." The drama was ominous. She didn't mean for it to be. Or she didn't think she did, which isn't at all the same thing.

Far less theatrical, however, was the untangling of her entanglement with Karl. Anna had sent him an SMS before Bruno came back from taking the Gilberts home: *I'm sorry. We have to stop. Bruno. Kids. Everything. Okay?* She wasn't exactly sorry and the quizzical "Okay?" at the end of the text served only to soften the blow. Not even a minute passed before the response came through. *Jo. I bring it.* "I bring it" was a stretch, even for Karl. Anna finally worked out that he meant to type *I get it.*

ANNA AND STEPHEN RARELY arranged to meet except to have sex, though once they met each other at Friedhof Fluntern, near the zoo. Anna had suggested it. James Joyce was buried there. It was a Zürich landmark. She'd never been.

It was mid-January and a light snow had fallen the night before. Anna had just dropped Charles off at *Kinderkrippe* when she ran into Ursula on the street (how often this seemed to happen!). She told her mother-in-law that she was on her way to return some books to the downtown library. If Ursula doubted what Anna did during her time in the city, she never challenged her. In any case Anna had several stories on hand: I went to see Edith. Or: Went to buy spices at a specialty shop. Or: There was a film not playing anywhere else. Lies thin as gauze but in a pinch they would have to do.

Stephen was indifferent. "Why not?" he said as if one way or the other, he had no opinion. This was a tendency Anna didn't realize she didn't like until the affair was over. Friedhof Fluntern is situated in a grove of trees on the Zürichberg, the mountain that lies exactly between Dietlikon and the city. Could she have climbed the trees, Anna would have been able to see her house.

They walked to the grave without talking. Anna had read Joyce in college, though beyond "famous Irish writer" she couldn't say much. The grave was easy to find. It was marked by a statue of the author in thought. There was snow in his lap. His wife and his son were buried next to him.

"Hey," Anna said, her voice fully mischievous. "Let's do it here."

Stephen looked up, faced her, and then returned his gaze to Joyce's grave. "That's about the most inappropriate thing I've ever heard." A moment passed, then Stephen pulled his coat tighter around his body. "Let's go. It's cold." Anna followed after him, dragging her feet through the snow.

MARY HAD MADE RESERVATIONS for two at 12:15 at the Altes Klösterli, a traditional Swiss restaurant close enough to the zoo to hear the elephants. The first trip Anna made into Zürich by herself was to the zoo. It was her third or fourth week in the country. The household was falling into order bit by bit. Anna had found an English-speaking obstetrician. Ursula radiated helpfulness and took Anna marketing and showed her the town and painted the nursery with her. Anna breathed into those early days. Her eyes bounced upon all she saw. Every road led to possibility.

She'd been into the city before, with Bruno. He took her on a single slapdash tour that ended with him giving her a map and a ZVV pass and telling her that she was on her own (a truer prophecy would never be spoken!). "Go explore!" he said. Anna wasn't usually an explorer. But things were running so smoothly and happiness seemed potential if not plausible. And if ever there's a time to move beyond one's boundaries it's when one has, literally, moved beyond them. Anna took the challenge. Where would she go? What would Anna do? Window-shopping on the Bahnhofstrasse? A visit to the art museum? The knife museum? The clock museum? For her first outing alone, Anna chose the zoo.

The day was beautiful but blistering. Pregnant Anna moved slowly through the gardens, took pictures of the animals, relaxed at the café, and drank one lemonade and then another. She felt a surge of self-satisfaction. She made plans inside herself to stop on the way home and buy peaches for a pie. She thought ahead to the evening and a box she'd not yet opened in which was packed a black silk nightgown that she thought but wasn't sure she hadn't grown too big for. But self-satisfaction is a dangerous conceit. Anna was too pleased with herself. When she left the zoo she took the right bus but rode it in the wrong direction half a dozen stops before she realized her mistake. Then she got off at an inconvenient intersection and had to walk for blocks before she found a tram stand. And when the tram came, she took that, too, in a direction she didn't intend. Eventually she landed at Bahnhof Wiedikon, where, seeing her in tears, a woman (whose limited English vocabulary unfortunately matched Anna's equally inadequate German) sat with her and together they puzzled out a way for her to get home. The going home was the easy part; the S8 ran through Wiedikon. All Anna needed to do was to ride the (correct) train all the way to Dietlikon. It was almost impressive, how she managed to traipse so far across the city, so accidentally. The cleverness Anna had allowed herself to feel dissipated in an instant.

It was the beginning of the end of Anna's confidence.

ANNA, ON FOUR OCCASIONS since his departure, had taken the S8 to Wipkingen, disembarked, and walked to Stephen's apartment on Nürenbergstrasse as if nothing had changed. The first time she did this was the day after he left. She went to the door and rang the bell and when no one answered she pretended it was because he was at the market or the laboratory. Other times, she'd stand in front of the building and feign a phone call or check her watch as if she'd told someone to meet her there. Anything to lend legitimacy to her lingering. She would walk slowly around the block. She would close her eyes and imagine that it was a month ago, eight months, a year. Yesterday. The last time she'd done this, Polly Jean was seven months old. What had provoked the trip? Anna could barely recall. *The house was noisy. Bruno was cold. Ursula had scolded me for something I'd done. I wanted to return to the scene of the crime. I wanted to return.* She left her sons with their grandmother and took Polly Jean into the city and rolled her stroller past Stephen's apartment. *And here is where we invented you, Polly Jean.* It was an indulgence she allowed herself, this reveling in her stagnant, inalterable past.

* * *

Lunch with Mary was pleasant, affable. Their conversation was casual but that was all right because Anna didn't have the heart for anything profound. Mary spoke of Rapperswil, of Anna's party, of that day's German class, of how pretty Anna's ring was. They ate *Gschnätzlets mit Rösti,* a traditional Zürich dish of minced veal and hash browns. Mary had never had it before. Anna had eaten it a hundred times if once. To her it was ordinary, regular, same.

When dessert came Mary gave Anna a birthday gift. "Oh Mary, you really shouldn't have," Anna said. Mary's generosity sometimes exasperated her. She never knew how to respond.

Mary replied, "We're friends. Practically sisters. Of course I should have." Anna opened the small, shiny box tied with an apple-red grosgrain ribbon. Inside were a dozen antique handkerchiefs embroidered with Anna's initials. Mary had done the needlework. The handkerchief on top was baby blue. Anna traced the A with her thumb and the B with her forefinger. She sighed so deeply it sounded like a sob.

"Are you okay, Anna?"

Anna brought the handkerchief to her nose. It smelled like lavender. She closed her eyes and nodded, then sighed again. "You know, I used to do this stuff."

"Really? You sew?" This admission amused Mary. As if Anna were teasing her, or playing a joke. "It seems like such an un-Anna thing to do."

Anna opened her eyes. She could understand how it would seem that way. "No, it's true. I sew. I mean, I know how to sew. I don't do it anymore."

Mary's grin was self-satisfied without being smug. When

Anna called it to her attention, the grin became an outright smile.

"What?"

"I like it when I get to see a side of you you're trying to hide."

Anna pretended she hadn't heard this and set the baby blue handkerchief atop the stack of the other ones and changed the subject.

"These are almost too pretty to take out of the box."

"Nonsense!" Mary said. "What good is a useful object if it can't be used?"

"NARCISSISM ISN'T VANITY, ANNA. We're all narcissists to a degree. A measure of narcissism is healthy. But out of balance, what was once appropriate self-confidence becomes grandiose, pathological, and destructive. You have little regard for those around you. You do what you will with a libertine's abandon. Boredom sets in. A bored woman is a dangerous woman."

"You've said that before."

Doktor Messerli nodded.

"And?" It was an impatient "and."

"And there are acts that cannot be unenacted. Outcomes impossible to repair. A narcissist won't see that until it's too late."

"LET'S REVIEW THE TENSES," Roland said, and the class groaned collectively. This wasn't the first time he'd given this lecture. "*Zu viel Fehler!*" Too many mistakes, Roland said. Anna took easy offense at this even though she knew that there was a tipping point in mistake making when blunders stopped being instructive and became simply habitual. A cards-land-where-they-may approach to moving through language, through love, through life. Unflappable passivity in action.

But mistakes, Anna thought. *They're yours. All yours. Your own belong to you and no one else.* When she thought about it that way—which she had consciously made the choice to do—she felt noble. As if admitting or laying claim to a failure—even if only to the mirror, in solitude and silently—was itself an act of absolution.

So to Roland she said, *Ohne Fehler, ohne Herz.* No mistakes, no heart. *We are marked by our fuckups. We are made from our fuckups.* Anna wanted it to be true. And if she wanted it to be true badly enough, perhaps it would be.

But days came that the plain pain of memory ate through Anna's understanding of her personal history. It was then that she pined for the hour exactly before she met Stephen Nicodemus. *How different it all would be had I just gone home.* Other days, it was such an ache that tethered her to joy. It was despair alone she owned outright. An indefensible comfort, but comfort nonetheless. The only thing she rarely felt was guilt. Love trumped guilt like rock won out over scissors.

"This is basic, class. Present tense. That which happens now. Future tense. What will occur. Simple past: what was done. Present perfect? What has been done."

But how often is the past simple? Is the present ever perfect? Anna stopped listening. These were rules she didn't trust.

ANNA SAW MARY OFF at the bus, telling her that by tradition, she took a solitary walk on her birthday during which she considered the previous year and reevaluated her priorities. She would walk the Zürichberg that day, she said. Anna pointed in the direction of Dietlikon. "I may even walk home." It was a passable lie. She always wanted to hike home from the Zürichberg but never had. If she hadn't planned to meet Archie that day, she might have made the hike. Mary gave her a final birthday hug and blew her ridiculous kisses from the window as the bus drove away. Anna shook her head and walked back toward the zoo. She met Archie by the ticket booth. He paid both admissions. "Let's walk around a bit," Archie said. "I want to see the animals." Anna replied, "Sure," but she meant *Whatever.*

They made a wistful pair, Anna knowing that it wouldn't be long before she told Archie the fun they'd been sharing was over and Archie suspecting that was what she would be telling him. They walked without affect and moved through the exhibits and the habitats barely speaking beyond *Look over here* and *Uh-huh.* The tigers slept behind rocks and couldn't easily be seen. The pandas were shy and didn't come out at all. The monkeys wanted to be watched. They shrieked through their cages and shook the bars.

"YES, YOU DO HATE Switzerland. And," Doktor Messerli paused for effect, "you love it. You love it and you hate it. What you don't feel is apathy. You're not indifferent. You're ambivalent."

Anna had thought about this before, when nights came during which she could do nothing but wander Dietlikon's sleeping streets or hike the hill behind her house to sit upon the bench where most often she went to weep. She'd considered her ambivalence many, many times, and in the end, she'd diagnosed herself with a disease that she'd also invented. Switzerland syndrome. Like Stockholm syndrome. *But instead of my captors, I'm attached to the room in which I'm held captive. It's the prison I'm bound to, not the warden.*

Anna was absolutely right. It was the landscape. It was the geography. The fields, the streams, the lakes, the forests. And the mountains. On exceptionally clear days when the weather was right, if you walked south on Dietlikon's Bahnhofstrasse you could see the crisp outlines of snowcapped Alps against a blazing blue horizon eighty kilometers away. On these certain days it was something in the magic of the atmosphere that made them tangible and moved them close. The mutability of those particular mountains reminded Anna of herself. And it wasn't simply the natural landscape that she attached herself to emotionally. It was the cobblestone roads of Zürich's old town and the spires of this church and the towers of that one. And the trains, the trains, the goddamn trains. She could take the train anywhere she wanted to go.

But when she asked herself, *Where to?* her only answer was impossibly illogical: *I want to go home.* Ostensibly, she was already there.

"Where does fire go when it goes out?" Anna asked. Stephen shook his head. The answer he gave was remote. "Nowhere, Anna. It just goes away. We've been over this before."

They had. And Anna still didn't like the answer. *Why does the fire ever have to go away?* She refused to concede the point. Not when he said it and not—nearly two years later—when she remembered him having said it.

* * *

A WEEK EARLIER NANCY invited both Mary and Anna to her apartment after class for lunch. Nancy lived in Oerlikon, a short walk from the Migros Klubschule. Outside of the twenty-minute coffee breaks and a word or two during class, Anna and she had never spoken. But Mary and Nancy were friends. "Come with me, Anna," Mary said. "Nancy's *great.*"

Nancy was a tall, thin woman, Nordic blond, stylish, with a warm and generous demeanor whose apartment, in a way, resembled Nancy herself: modern, clean, sparse, pulled together, open. She was forty-one years old, unmarried, childless, and, currently, unemployed. When Anna asked how that was possible (Zürich is painfully expensive) Nancy said it wasn't a problem and then, with awkward circumspection, confessed to the women that her family owned tea farms in Africa and while she had worked many years as a print journalist, she really hadn't needed to. "Don't mistake me for a trust fund brat," she was fast to add, "I've busted my ass. I've always earned my keep." So it seemed to Anna; Nancy had worked all over the continent reporting on international politics, mostly from the strange, exotic cities that Americans never think to list when they're asked to name the capitals of Europe: *Tallinn, Sofia, Kishinev, Skopje, Vaduz.* Nancy wasn't just a good sport; she was an adventurer. She didn't *take* the assignments—she had *volunteered* for each of them. If it was someplace she'd never been? That's where she wanted to go.

"So what are you doing here?" Anna hadn't meant for the question to sound like an accusation.

"I heard it was a top city. A fine place." Nancy shrugged. "I wanted to check into it. I had nowhere else I needed to be."

"How long are you staying?"

"I've only been here four months. I have no plans to leave. I like it."

"Really?" Anna hadn't expected that.

"Sure. Don't you?"

Anna didn't answer.

Mary began to fawn in that Mary way of hers. Emptily, repetitively. "You're so admirable, Nancy. I really admire you, Nancy. How you just pack up and go wherever you want and do what you want to do," Mary said. "I wish I could do that. I really admire you for that."

"What's to admire? I'm just living my life."

"Still." Mary sighed. "You're so fearless. Strange places frighten me. I get anxious just taking the bus from Schwerzenbach to Dübendorf!" Mary sighed again. It was hard for her to stray too far from her own front yard. That's what had made the move from Canada so awful, she confessed to Anna early on.

Nancy offered Mary a consolation that fell somewhere between empathy and a reprimand. "Mary. To each her own fear. But I don't want to watch my life unfold. I want to unfold it myself, if you will. If there's something I want to do? I do it. If there's something I want? I chase it. And I catch it. If I believe in something, I support it. If none of those things? Then . . . nothing. Then I let it go."

"Is that why you never married?" Mary asked.

"Sure," she said in a throwaway tone as she rose and gathered the women's empty plates. Anna and Mary were silent. Nancy shook her head. "Really, I want to be clear. My life is no more commendable than either of your lives." Mary twisted her face into a question mark. Anna looked blankly at Nancy and waited for her to continue. "We're modern women in a modern world. Our needs are met and many of our wants." Mary nodded. Nancy continued. "We have rights and the means to exercise them. Each of our lives is our own and as far as I know we get one apiece and no more. We should do something with them. If we can. If we're able to. It's a travesty when a woman wastes herself. That's all."

A travesty to waste one's self. It was a truth Anna couldn't refute.

Nancy took the plates into the kitchen and returned with coffee and biscuits. Dessert was spent gossiping about people in the German class.

"I still think Archie has a crush on you, Anna," Mary giggled.

"I *know* he does," Nancy added. Anna asked them to drop it. Yes, they were pals. But nothing more.

"Oh, god no, Anna!" Mary almost choked on her water. "That's not what I meant! I'd never suggest such a thing!" *Of course you wouldn't,* Anna thought. It was wistful thinking. Mary's goodness made Anna's badness worse. Anna's shameless self felt shame. It was a strange, recursive feeling.

"What's his story, anyway?" Nancy asked. Both Nancy and Mary turned to Anna for the answer. If anyone knew it would be she.

Anna scanned her thoughts for something to tell them but she couldn't come up with any details that weren't sexual. *He likes it when I'm on top. He's into biting, dirty talk. He likes to smell me—should I tell them that? He puts his face between my legs and inhales me like I'm a goddamn bowl of potpourri.* But when was his birthday? What did he study in school? Did he go to school? Had he ever been married? Any children? Are his parents alive? Any known allergies? She knew he had no visible scars. Was this all she knew of him? *Think, Anna. This can't be all.*

"He's got a brother." That was the best she could do.

ARCHIE TRIED TO HOLD Anna's hand. He'd never done that before and the awkwardness of the attempt startled Anna, and so she let him hold it, albeit limply. Barely a minute passed before she wrangled it free. It had felt wrong and his palms were damp.

They walked around the zoo for a quarter of an hour and said nothing to each other.

In the rainforest reserve they stared at lizards sleeping in trees and dodged the birds that hopped freely down the paths. Anna looked at all the placards but recognized neither the German nor the English names for these exotic animals. At the South African habitat they leaned against a rail and watched a mountain goat preside over a congregation of baboons on jagged, beige rocks. The largest of the baboons, a male, stood on his legs, turned to face Anna and Archie directly, and presented his red, erect penis as he hissed and sneered. "Okay, Archie," Anna said. "It's time to talk."

Anna couldn't remember the last time she'd broken up with anyone. *Is ending an affair the same as breaking up?* Anna decided it was close enough and told him as much: "Archie, I am breaking up with you."

Archie stared past the baboons. "So that's how it is." She hadn't expected him to be devastated and he didn't seem to be. "Yes," Anna said. "This is how it is." He didn't ask why, though Anna would have told him if he had. "I need to go,

Archie." Anna hiked her book bag back up her shoulder. She'd been carrying it around the whole time. She looked once more into his eyes and turned to leave.

Archie grabbed her by the wrist and pulled her back toward him. "Not without a goodbye kiss," he said as he laid his lips to hers and held her tight against her own protestations. Anna struggled briefly against his mouth and his arms but then relented, for there was no real harm in a goodbye kiss and she was too emotionally weak to fight him. So in the middle of the Zürich Zoo and on her thirty-eighth birthday, Anna let the Scotsman search her mouth with his tongue and her breasts with his hands for what would be the last, passive time.

Public displays of affection always draw attention; Archie and Anna made an obvious pair. They were the only adults in the entire zoo unaccompanied by toddlers in strollers or schoolchildren on a class trip, like the group who walked up to the South African habitat in the middle of the pair's final kiss. Children around the world are all alike. At a certain age, the sight of two people kissing will invariably invoke giggles and "ewwwww"s and "oooohhh"s and every available finger will point in the couple's direction. This is what happened to Archie and Anna. And yet, they kissed through it. It was a moment. Anna let the moment have its gravity. A last kiss, she thought, is an occasion.

The kiss was on its downslope. Anna was ending it. She drew a breath, then licked her lips then made one, two motions to pull away before finally wrenching her mouth loose from his. "Well," she said, "I guess that's it."

But it wasn't.

A singular thin, tinny voice rose above the chorus of whooping children. "Mami?"

Anna whipped around to look. It was Charles.

She had forgotten. It had been planned for weeks. Anna had been so wrapped up in her private, secret life that she'd forgotten.

Charles's class had taken a field trip to the zoo.

Anna had been caught.

16

"It's quite common for the subconscious to create intentional scenarios that force you to face something you've been ignoring. Your dreams might get louder and more violent. You may become forgetful or accident-prone. Psyche will do anything to get your attention. She will sabotage your consciousness if she must."

"What do you mean?"

"Think of an abscess. Untreated, the wound swells and causes pain and eventually ruptures."

"That's revolting."

"It is. Infections are. This is an infection. Of the soul."

Anna did not immediately know what to do and so she did nothing. That was a crucial moment of composure. She didn't look back at Archie but she didn't have to. "Get lost," she said through the smile she'd put on in order to face Charles. Anna stepped toward her son.

"Hey, *Schatz,* my love!" Anna's voice oscillated as she

bent down and wrapped her arms around Charles and drew him into her so that her body blocked his line of vision and he couldn't see Archie as he slipped away. Charles's teacher seemed to understand what the class had just interrupted. Frau Kopp was young and savvy and European and she knew the difference between Herr Benz and the man Anna had just been kissing. Her eyes were sympathetic, continental.

"Why are you here, Mami? Who was that man?"

Anna ignored the second question. "I'm here to take you home, *Schatz,*" she said, then turned to Frau Kopp for corroboration. "It's okay, yes?" Frau Kopp gave an almost imperceptible nod. By then the children's attention had shifted from Anna and Archie to the baboon with the erection. They howled with laughter until Frau Kopp settled them down and ushered them toward the penguins. It was almost feeding time and a zookeeper had promised the children they could watch. Charles looked perplexed. "Do you want to get an *Eis*?" Anna's mind tap-danced around ways to distract him from what he'd seen, and Charles loved ice cream and would eat it every day if Anna allowed it. "Green?" he asked. Anna forced a grin. "Of course!" Pistachio was his favorite. Charles hopped up and down and Anna took his left hand and led him away while with his right he waved goodbye in the direction of his classmates, who were by then entirely focused on the penguins they would soon watch being fed.

Anna and Charles took the bus, then the tram to Stadelhofen and at a Mövenpick shop near the station she bought her son a small cup of pistachio ice cream, which he ate in the store. Anna chattered the entire time. She left no space in conversation to let Charles speak. Charles, deferential as he was, gave over to his mother's babbling. For his meekness, Anna was grateful.

Charles finished his ice cream and Anna suggested they go watch the trains. Charles grinned and Anna took his hand and led him from the Mövenpick to the train station, and up the stairs, to the gallery-like walkway that overlooked Stadelhofen's open-air train tracks. From above, they watched several trains pull in and roll out, including an S5 on its way to Uster, the train Mary most often rode in and out of the city. The promenade above the tracks was supported by angular steel ribs spaced at even intervals along the entire walkway. Anna thought the effect Jonah-like. *This is torture in the belly of a fish.* Charles answered with a great deal of animation when Anna asked about the animals he'd seen that day. He rambled on about lions and black bears and flamingos and hippopotami for several minutes, but after a while, the imminent question resurfaced.

"Who was that man?"

"What man, Charles?"

"The man you were kissing. I saw you kissing a man."

Anna feigned surprise, tried to tease him. "Really? How strange! I think you're making that up, Charles. I wasn't kissing anyone." This wasn't entirely a lie. It was Archie who kissed her. Anna felt like an ass, relying on the childish logic of exactitude.

Charles had none of it. "I saw him!" He was deeply upset.

Anna stiffened. "Charles." Her voice was firm and stern. It was a tone she never used with him and one, therefore, he was unaccustomed to hearing. He tensed visibly. "Charles," she repeated. "You didn't see a thing." Charles's eyes dilated. He tried to look away. "Listen to me." Anna snapped her fingers and drew his attention back to her face. "Did you hear me? I said you didn't see anything. And you are not to tell anyone you did. Do you understand?" Charles didn't answer. Anna took his face in both her hands and turned it straight to face her own. It was something she'd seen angry mothers do. Her voice was pinched. "Do you understand?" Charles blinked. Her words were hot and hushed. "Listen to me. I am telling you for the last time that you made a mistake. Don't make me say it again." Charles whimpered. "You don't tell anyone. Not Papi or Victor or Max or Grosi. If you do I will be so angry." Anna nodded gravely for effect. "I'll tell them you're lying and they'll be angry too. I'm the mother. They'll believe me." Charles started to cry. Anna shook her head. "Charles, I mean it. Unless you want something bad to happen, you need to be quiet. Don't even say you saw me at the zoo." And then she added, "Don't tell anyone we came to watch the trains."

Whatever Anna had intended, it seemed to work. Charles looked grave and terrified. He sniffed and he shook and eked out a nearly inaudible *okay.* Anna was satisfied. She didn't need to elaborate. She left Charles to imagine what those really bad things might be. She knew her son. She knew he'd never say a word. She'd never been cruel like this before.

"C'mon. Let's go home." Anna stood up, slung her bag over her shoulder, and brushed her hands on the top of her thighs. Charles turned back toward her and she put her arm around him and squeezed him against her hip in a protective, loving way. This seemed to comfort him and together they crossed the bridge that would lead them down the stairs to the platform.

They'd just passed the midway point when Anna startled

herself with a memory. "Wait, come here." Anna stopped, knelt, grabbed Charles's hands and turned her son to face her. "Do you remember the first time we went to Tante Mary's house? The first time you met Max?" Charles hesitated. Was this a trick? Was this, like the kiss he did not see, a memory he didn't recall? "No, it's okay. Tell me. Do you remember?" Charles gave a cautious nod. "Do you remember when you came downstairs and Max told everyone you'd told him a secret?" Once more, Charles nodded, then let his gaze fall to the floor of the walkway. "Good boy. Now tell me what the secret was." It was a paranoiac's question. She was afraid that his secret was one of her own. "Tell me."

Charles shuffled slowly foot to foot. "I told Max that I thought Marlies Zwygart was pretty." His whole body flushed with embarrassment. Anna's ring tightened on her finger. She'd never felt so awful in her life.

THE FIVE MOST FREQUENTLY used German verbs are all irregular. Their conjugations don't follow a pattern: *To have. To have to. To want. To go. To be. Possession. Obligation. Yearning. Flight. Existence.* Concepts all. And irregular. These verbs are the culmination of insufficiency. Life is loss. Frequent, usual loss. Loss doesn't follow a pattern either. You survive it only by memorizing how.

ANNA WATCHED CHARLES VERY closely that night. And the next night. And the one after that. She kept a vigilant eye on him until she was sure that he hadn't and he wouldn't tell anyone what had happened at the zoo. By the third night she started to relax. He'd never once disobeyed her—why would this time be any different? There was no cause to believe that it would.

What else could I have done? Anna rationalized.

That night after the children were in bed she knocked on Bruno's office door.

"Are you going for a walk?" he asked. He didn't look away from the computer screen.

"No." It was a fair-enough assumption. Most usually that was what Anna came to his office to tell him at this late hour. It sank her heart a little, Bruno thinking that's the only reason Anna would ever knock upon his door. It sank a little more, she conceding that it most often was.

"Did you need something?"

She had interrupted him watching online videos of the Schweizer Luftwaffe, the Swiss Air Force. Earlier in the afternoon, the Benzes had heard from inside the house the matchless sound of supersonic jets slicing through the sky. An air show? Flying practice? General maneuvers? Unclear. The noise was tremendous. The whole family went outside to watch. Polly Jean didn't like it one bit. Anna held her tightly against her body and covered her ears. Victor and Charles were captivated, then alarmed. *How fast they flew! How close they came to each other!* Charles reached for Anna's hand, and when one of the planes executed a barrel roll right above the house, Victor threw his arms around his mother's legs. That was unforeseen. In light of the week's troubles Anna welcomed any request for consolation.

Anna didn't like the planes. The noise hurt her ears and she was terrified by how low they flew to the ground. *They're just one sneeze away from crashing through an attic,* Anna thought. Bruno, however, was transfixed. He couldn't tear his eyes away. As a boy he'd been as fascinated by airplanes as Charles was by trains. After ten minutes Anna, Polly, and the boys went back into the house. Bruno stayed outside the whole half hour, wide-eyed and watching so intensely that one might think he believed that it was his vigilance alone that kept the planes in the air.

The monitor's volume was turned almost as high as it could go. He'd waived his own excessive noise rule. The same cutthroat roar that frightened Anna earlier sliced through the office atmosphere.

"Do you believe in God?" Anna looked at Bruno's bookshelves. The books were arranged alphabetically and by subject.

"Huh?" Bruno paused the video and turned to look at his wife. "Where's this come from?"

Anna pointed at his monitor. "I was thinking about the planes today." She moved her gaze to the wall where, affixed by sticky putty that, if removed, would not leave a mark, hung several drawings the boys had done. Victor liked to draw animals. Charles, of course, trains.

"I don't understand."

Anna wasn't sure she did either. The correspondence had made perfect, poignant sense in her head just a moment earlier. Now, as she spoke it aloud, her words became minor and inept. She sounded deranged. "That noise they made." She searched for the clearest explanation. "It sounded like they were cutting open the sky." Bruno's face was rimpled, harried. Anna let all current semblance of logic and composure go. "What do you think is on the other side of the sky?"

"The sky doesn't have another side, Anna."

"No, I mean . . . Bruno, do you believe in God?"

"Of course I do."

"Really?" She didn't know what she expected him to say. Any answer would have surprised her.

"Don't you?"

Anna's shrug told the truth.

Bruno shrugged back at her. "If there isn't a God then what's the point of anything? Without God, what matters?"

Anna didn't know. She said so.

"Without God, *nothing* matters. But Anna? Things matter." He said it in a way that was meant to school her.

"Do you believe in destiny? Salvation? Do you believe that we can save ourselves?"

Bruno shook his head as if to say *Why the fuck are we talking about this?* "My father believed that we are broken people who live in a broken world. I believe that too. That doesn't mean there isn't a God. It just means we aren't him." Bruno cleared his throat. "Is that all?"

"Yes."

Bruno turned back to the screen. "Enjoy your walk." He'd forgotten that Anna said she wasn't taking one. She didn't correct him.

"HOUSE FIRES ARE ALMOST always preventable," Stephen said, though Anna already knew it. "But under certain circumstances, probable."

"Like?" She played along with this lecture.

"Smoking in bed, of course. Cooking. The unsupervised burning of candles."

"You sound like a fireman, not a scientist."

Stephen shrugged. "Fire is fire."

Yes, Anna thought. *And it is never safe.*

* * *

"A PERSON CAN BE fully conscious and still make terrible choices. Consciousness doesn't come with an automatic ethic."

They had been discussing Anna's most recent dream. It began in the grocery store, where so much of Anna's life took place. Her basket was full, but when she got to the checkout, she realized she didn't have any money. She told the cashier she'd return the items to the shelf but when Anna went into the aisle with the basket she hid as much of the food as she could in her pockets. She knew it wasn't right but didn't care. Outside the store she stopped a man who was on his way in and told him what she'd done; she was proud of it. He was shocked and threatened to call the police. Anna said she'd give him a blowjob if he didn't. They went behind the grocery store. Across the alleyway, the local high school. Anna knelt and gave him head while students watched from a classroom window. In order to keep them from telling anyone what they had witnessed, Anna lifted up her shirt and showed them her breasts, which, in the dream, were leaking milk. The dream ended at the bus stop. She may or may not have boarded the right bus, she couldn't remember.

"You do nothing in this dream that isn't the commission of some sort of crime—theft, adultery, exhibition . . ."

Anna interrupted. "You can't seriously judge someone against what she does in her sleep. I can't help what I dream."

"That's not entirely true, Anna. What we dream, we are."

Anna frowned. There was nothing of this conversation she liked.

Doktor Messerli didn't pull her punch. "You recognize each consequence. You do the damage anyway. The dream is emphatic: you're spinning out of control."

17

Every few weeks and sometimes more often than that, the Benzes would receive in the postbox affixed to the wall outside their front door a notice printed on a half-size sheet of white paper, bordered in a bold black line. They were death announcements. *Ein Bestattungsanzeige.* The postman delivered them along with the mail whenever a Dietlikon resident died. It was a small-town courtesy, not a typical Swiss practice. The notices began with the decedent's name and then below that, his or her birth and death dates. They ended with information about the funeral.

Anna saved every death notice they received. She kept them in a shoebox in her *Kleiderschrank.* She had collected at least three hundred of them over the span of nine years. When Bruno found the shoebox, he threatened to throw it away. "You have an unhealthy fixation on death," he said.

Anna was emphatic in a way she usually wasn't. "Don't you dare. I keep these because someone has to. The worst thing that can happen to a person is to be forgotten."

"That's not the worst thing, Anna."

"Don't touch this box. I'm telling you."

ANNA AVOIDED GERMAN CLASS for two days. She dreaded looking Archie in the eye.

As angry as she was with herself, she was equally furious with him. She knew her indignation was unreasonable (*Was it? It was Archie who swooped in and kissed her when she wasn't asking for it, Archie who showed up at the party, Archie who propositioned her in the first place*) but the haughtiness was serving the purpose of keeping Anna focused on the present task of behaving herself. Resentment was her arsenal's secret weapon. When Mary called Tuesday afternoon, Anna gave an excuse that resembled the truth: that the exhaustion of the party caught up with her a day late and she needed rest. Mary volunteered to drop over with notes but Anna told her not to bother. So Anna stayed home and played house with her daughter. Anna baked for the first time in over a year and cooked Bruno's favorite meal for dinner. It was a stab at atonement. The smallest of stabs.

SOMETIME DURING THE WANING hours of her second day in a row at home, Anna began to feel restless, bored, and lonely. *Jesus, Anna, really?* She scrambled to find avenues of acquittal. She blamed it first on the sunset and then on flaws fundamental to her personhood. The brokenness she was trying to mend. It wasn't, after all, just about the sex.

This, she knew, was mostly true.

She couldn't really call it missing them. She didn't miss them at all (*Who were they anyway to miss?*). Anna had read that it takes far longer to break a habit than to make one. In the case of heroin, addiction can occur in the span of three days. *Am I addicted?* She didn't want to use that word. These men were simply the embodiment of urges she no longer wished to deny herself. *It's just a handshake, really. A casual greeting made with alternate body parts.* She could live without the favors of these specific men. The affair with Archie wasn't even two months old and her relationship with Karl barely constituted a dalliance. But the nature of habits is this: they are habitual. They die very hard, those that die at all.

Anna fought her agitation by doing laundry.

On Thursday Anna returned to German class. She'd paid for it, after all, and up until Monday, she'd mostly enjoyed it. So Ursula came over and Anna went to Oerlikon. She summoned the backbone to face Archie but was relieved when he didn't show up for class.

Roland gave a lesson on comparatives. *This* is more whatever than *that*. *That* is less something than *this*. *This* and *that* are precisely equal to *that* and *this*.

They ran out of time before Roland could introduce superlatives, the proclamation of what is *most of all*.

Like so much else, this was a concept Anna already understood.

On Friday Anna woke well before dawn. The clock blinked 4:13 a.m. She looked to her right. Bruno was asleep. Of course.

She rose and dressed and tiptoed out of the bedroom and left the house as quietly as possible. She was practiced at this. She needed to be.

The pre-sunrise October chill had bite. Anna turned up the collar of her coat, put her hands in her pockets, and leaned into the oncoming wind as all around her Dietlikon slept unperturbedly at ease. She had no intentional destination; Anna followed her feet where they led her: first south toward the church, then down Riedenerstrasse past the traffic circle to the town cemetery.

Anna didn't routinely visit the cemetery, especially in insomnia's dark, horrible hours; that morning's walk was unpremeditated. But there are times to talk to the dead, times when the dead want to talk. In these rare instances, the dead will draw you to them; your volition is irrelevant. Anna couldn't tell if this was one of those times, but she was at the cemetery, so all signs pointed to yes. The gate was locked but Anna cut through a sparse hedge. She didn't plan on staying long. *I am not a ghost, I am a guest.*

She passed slowly through the rows of graves. She attempted a measure of somberness but settled on worry and fatigue, which, when coupled, passed for solemnity. This would have to do. Things for Anna always had to do.

Opposite the cemetery gate lay a separate section for the graves of the town's children. In the daylight, there was simply no way to pass these graves without breaking down. In the darkness, however, to stand in their presence was to enjoy a bearable, almost beautiful experience. *They are babies asleep in their cribs,* Anna imagined. *Just sleeping.* Earlier that year, the granddaughter of a friend of Ursula's had drowned in Dietlikon's community pool. Her name was Gaby and she was buried here. It was too dark for Anna to read the names; she didn't know which grave was hers.

ANNA MADE THE MISTAKE of meeting Edith for a coffee after German class. It was often a mistake to meet Edith for coffee because Edith didn't drink coffee, she drank bourbon, and drinking bourbon always agitated her. Anna met her on the south end of the Bahnhofstrasse at Café Münz, a bar and lounge near the Zürich branch of the Swiss National Bank. It was the SNB that housed the Nazis' gold during and after World War II. For her entire first year in Switzerland, Anna was haunted by the notion that cached beneath the streets down which she strode, bankers—the alleged gnomes of Zürich—trolled the subterranean vaults grubbing the treasures of long-dead Jews. She implicated Bruno retroactively until he finally forbade her from ever bringing the subject up again.

Anna ordered a café crème and Edith, being contrary even to herself, ordered a beer. Anna raised an eyebrow and Edith waved her off. "Niklas is teaching me beer," she said as if beer were a school subject like algebra or civics. "I still don't like it. But for him, I'll try anything." Edith winked. Anna understood that anything meant more than beer. Anna didn't want to talk about lovers. She didn't really want to talk at all. But there were empty hours to fill and if she wasn't spending them with Archie or Karl, then she needed to spend them with someone, and Mary was busy that day. *Take one lover, you may as well take twenty,* Anna thought. *They're like salty snacks. You can't stop at one.*

Edith yammered on with her typical self-centeredness, hopping from subject to subject like a frog leaping from one lily pad to the next. She spoke first of Niklas, then Otto, then the twins, then the trip they were planning to Ticino, then of a ball gown she recently bought. Anna hadn't known she was going to a ball. "I'm not," Edith said. "The dress was too gorgeous to deny myself. I'll wear it one of these days." Anna finished her coffee then asked for another. She had little to add and she wouldn't even offer that until or unless she was asked.

Edith moved from beer to wine. They weren't alone in the café. Behind them, a couple enjoyed a late lunch. There was a tall, gaunt man in a business suit standing at the bar, smoking and drinking a beer. Sitting by the window nearest the street, a young woman with a nose ring and thick blond hair pulled back in a low ponytail was pushing the last few salad leaves around on her plate and flipping absentmindedly through a magazine.

Anna was staring at the girl with the ponytail when Edith did something Anna wasn't sure she'd ever done before. "All right, Anna. You're distracted. You're barely here. What's going on?" Edith had never shown Anna any real concern, and Anna was thrown off guard. "Is there something you want to talk about?"

Anna didn't know what to say. She stared at the empty plastic pot of cream on her saucer and the small spoon next to it as if they might get up and walk around. "Edith, what does Otto do at the bank?"

Edith blinked. "That's what's been bothering you?"

Anna shrugged. "Maybe. Kind of."

Edith swilled her wine and blew out a hard sigh. "I don't know. Count money? Why are you asking?"

"I mean specifically. What does he do specifically?"

"Do you know what Bruno does?"

"No, I don't." Anna shook her head. Her voice got low and sober. "Edith, we should know what they do, I think." In all those years, Anna had never asked Bruno to explain. He fiddled with other people's money, that's what he did. And that's all that Anna knew. "We should care about our husbands enough to know what they do." Anna took a slow, deliberate sip from the coffee cup and with an equal measure of reflection, set it back down.

"Anna, you've lost a screw. I don't see what the problem is." Edith didn't. The conversation flummoxed her. "The only thing we need to know is this: they bring home a paycheck." Edith swigged her drink. "They take care of us. Does anything beyond that matter?"

ROLAND HAD TAKEN A tangent. Someone had suggested that Schwiizerdütsch was a German dialect and not a language all of its own. Roland was vehement. *Nei! Nei! Nei!* he yelled, emphasizing each *no!* by slapping his notepad on the table. "Switzerland is not a German colony! We don't live under the *Bundesflagge!* Schwiizerdütsch is ours! They did not give it to us—we built it ourselves!" Roland continued in a broad, philosophic arc. "The language a man speaks defines him. A man's language tells the world who he is."

Anna considered that. Everyone's born into a native language. Most of the people she knew had full command of a second (and according to the bee in Roland's bonnet, a third): *Bruno, Ursula, Daniela, Doktor Messerli.* Even Anna's own sons. To Anna they spoke English. But to each other and to their father when Anna wasn't around (and sometimes even when she was, though she'd asked them very sternly not to) they reverted to Schwiizerdütsch. It deflated her. Even if she managed a proficient level of German, Anna would never have an indigenous Dietlikonerin's command of Schwiizerdütsch. She would never share that spoken bond with her children. It just wasn't going to happen.

Anna didn't disagree with Roland. It was entirely true—the language you're born into (or in Anna's case, the one you aren't) determines your most basic identity. But Roland had stopped short. There was more. Your native speech situates you in your society. But your second language is the one that reveals your character. *Look to the mistakes,* Anna said to herself. *The mistakes a person makes tell you everything you need to know.* It made sense. Leopards don't change their spots, after all. If a person behaves one way in situation A, then why would anyone expect him to behave differently in situation B? Karl, for example. In speech he confused primary and secondary meanings of words and synonyms. It was a habit born of carelessness. He treated words as if they were interchangeable. This one, that one—a word, a woman. One was good as the other. He meant no malice but . . . what *did* he mean? It was always so hard to unravel him. And what about Mary? Her tendency was to stumble over even the simplest of sentences. She flustered easily. She wanted so much to be correct. When she did speak, it was slowly and without flourish. Niklas's English was always nonspecific. Anna didn't know him well enough to say what that might mean. Edith didn't speak German at all. What that said was she didn't give a damn. Nancy was always trying sentences beyond her reach. If she wanted to say something, she went for it. If it came out wrong, she'd warp the syntax and speak past the impediment, as if she were driving around a concrete pylon. There was always a way to work through the problem. Archie's German was the kind of German that men who had affairs with sad women spoke. He was terrible with possessives. It didn't matter what belonged to whom. All was free use.

But Anna. What were her tendencies? It was no mystery. With Anna it was all verbs. She was sloppy in her conjugations, reckless in her positioning. She confused tense with mood and relied too often on the passive voice. Anna laughed at these conclusions. *How evident I am!* And she was. She truly was. Evident, undeniable, sloppy, and sad.

Anna was five months into the pregnancy when Polly Jean started to kick. She kicked hard, much harder than either of the boys had kicked, and she kicked constantly. There was no rest from her kicking. She drummed on the walls of the womb like a madman pounds a padded door. The entire pregnancy was difficult. Anna's morning sickness lasted for months. Her face was by turns dry and scaly, then oiled and pimply. Misery exhausted her. On walks she faced west and spoke aloud in the direction of Boston. *I love you. I hate you. I miss you. I never want to see you again.* She meant every word she said. The middle way played against each end.

This hyperbolic sadness consumed her. Except when it didn't. Which was rarely.

Anna hadn't intended to concede. It came out of nowhere. It came out of everywhere. It came out of the weather. It came from the wave that Charles turned to give her as he left the house for school, and the half wave that Victor tossed back to her as well, a concession he rarely granted. It came from Bruno's impossibility when Anna offered him yogurt instead of quark. She'd mistaken the pots at the grocery store. It was easy enough to do. It came from Ursula's dourness and the rumpled skin that years of frowning had creased into her face. It came out of the German homework that Anna didn't do the night before. It came from wondering why she still bothered with the German class. It came out of knowing that Mary would be disappointed if she dropped it and what came out of that, in turn, was a big, resigned sigh. It came from that morning's every annoyance, the sum of which was a defeat so looming that anyone with even a teaspoon of common sense would run far and fast away from it. But Anna didn't run away. So when it came—this particular dejection—she embraced it like she would have held a long-lost friend (which, in a way, it was) and pulled those many miseries tightly around her shoulders, wrapping herself into a familiar quilt of ineffable, inconsolable longing. By the time Karl replied to Anna's impulsive SMS, she'd already relinquished her grip on the wheel of her will. It was Wednesday, the last day of October. Anna was on the train to Oerlikon when the message came through. It was Halloween, which most Swiss don't celebrate, and Anna had been thinking once again about ghosts.

She changed trains at Oerlikon and took the S7 to Kloten. She didn't even think twice. If she had, she still would have gone.

Anna knocked on the door and Karl let her in. He opened his mouth to speak but she shushed him.

"Don't. Don't say a word." Anna pushed him back and the door closed behind her.

She shoved her face onto his face and they kissed in a reckless, pointless way. There was no mystery here. Anna shrugged out of her coat, threw her bag into a corner, and pulled her sweater roughly over her head, taking an earring with it. She shoved Karl to the bed with enough force to startle him. Anna was damp with abandon.

"Do you know about the Teufelsbrücke?" Anna didn't. Doktor Messerli explained. "There's a mountain pass in Kanton Uri—the Schöllenen Gorge. It's tremendously steep. The walls are sheer and abrupt." Anna nodded. She understood. These days, everywhere she turned was precipice. "There is a bridge that crosses the canyon and the river below it."

"The Teufelsbrücke?" Devil's Bridge.

"Genau." Doktor Messerli continued. "It was built in the Middle Ages. But the landscape is so unpredictable and the bridge so fabulously made that at the time, it was believed human hands alone could never have erected such a structure. So the legend says that the Devil built it himself."

Doktor Messerli continued in the manner of a storyteller, adjusting her intonation and speed of speech for dramatic effect. "But the Devil does no favors. He will always demand to be paid. In this case, he ordered the soul of the first man to cross it." *That seems kind of fair,* Anna thought. "No one volunteered, of course. Who would enlist to be so sacrificed?" Anna had an answer but kept it to herself. "Instead, the citizens of Uri decided to trick him and sent the Devil a goat. The Devil was furious. No! A goat would not do! He'd had it. So he picked up the largest stone he could find and started toward the gorge. He would show them. He created it, it was his to destroy."

"But he didn't."

Doktor Messerli shook her head no. "On his way to the bridge he met an old woman carrying a cross. The Devil was so terrified by the cross that he dropped the giant rock and ran away. The people of Uri never heard from him again. They kept their bridge. They kept their souls."

"So goodness conquers evil is what you are saying."

Doktor Messerli shook her head. "What I'm saying is that our most sinister parts bridge the gap between consciousness and unconsciousness. That's the dark matter's most useful function. But hear me: you do not owe the darkness your soul."

"I'm not planning on giving it away."

"Planning has nothing to do with it. We plan. The Devil laughs at our plans."

ANNA WOKE FROM A muggy, fitful sleep, the only possible kind of sleep in a hotel room in the afternoon of a late October day next to a lover you care nothing about. She took a moment to stretch and adjust her eyes. She looked to the clock. It was a quarter past four. *Shit, shit, shit.* Karl groaned, then sat up in bed.

"Is something immoral?" Anna guessed the word he meant to use was "wrong," but it didn't matter. In this case he was correct on both fronts. She dressed very quickly, put on her shoes, and grabbed her bag with every intention of leaving as she arrived, without fanfare. As she moved toward the door she pulled her cell phone out of her bag to check for messages.

The small red light blinked hotly. She'd missed thirty-two calls.

An unseen hand pierced her heart with an unseen sword.

No. Anna let her bag fall to the floor. "Is okay?" Karl was fastening his jeans. Anna didn't answer him. She scrolled through the list. Ursula had called. Then Bruno. Then it was Ursula, Ursula, Ursula, Bruno, Mary, Bruno, Daniela. The list of missed calls seemed endless.

"I turned my ringer off." Anna said it to herself. There were messages. Her hand shook. Her fingers couldn't find the buttons. But they did. They had to. Anna listened to the last one first. It was Bruno. His voice was rabid with sobs. *Anna. Come home, please. You have to come home. Now, Anna. Come home now.* "I have to go." Anna said it even as she snatched her bag and bolted through the hall and down the stairs and into the waning day. A taxicab would be quickest. She ran across the street to the Kloten station and hurled herself into the first cab she came to. *Dietlikon.* She was out of breath. She spoke between gasps. *Dee. Et. Li. Kon.* The cab driver didn't seem to understand. *Dietlikon!* She yelled and kicked the back of his seat. This got his attention. He put the car into gear and pulled into the street without looking.

november

18

Tears are wet but they aren't water. Both liquid and potable, it is possible to freeze them and, as is said, to drown in them. But they aren't water. Theirs is a chemistry of fat, sugar, salt, antibodies, minerals, and at least a dozen other substances native to a living body, which, for the remainder of this digression, we will presume to be human.

There are three kinds of tears.

Tears that serve only to moisten the eye are called basal tears and they lubricate the lids like oil on a hinge. The tears known as reflex tears erupt when irritants like dust or onion vapors aggravate the eye. And while they may also flow when a person yawns or coughs, the particular function of reflex tears is to wash and clean. Their purpose is ablution.

The tears that come from pain are psychic tears and these need not be analyzed.

There are three kinds of grief.

The first is anticipatory. This is hospice grief. Prognostic grief. This is the grief that comes when you drive your dog to the vet for the very last time. This is the death row inmate's family's grief. See that pain in the distance? *It's on its way.* This is the grief that it is somewhat possible to prepare for. You finish all business. You come to terms. Goodbyes are said and said again. Anguish stalks the chambers of your heart and you steel yourself for the impending presence of an everlasting absence. This grief is an instrument of torture. It squeezes and pulls and presses down.

Grief that follows an immediate loss comes on like a stab wound. This is the second kind of grief. It is a cutting pain and it is always a surprise. You never see it coming. It is a grief that can't be bandaged. The wound is mortal and yet you do not die. That is its own impossible agony.

But grief is not simple sadness. Sadness is a feeling that wants nothing more than to be sat with, held, and heard. Grief is a journey. It must be moved through. With a rucksack full of rocks, you hike through a black, pathless forest, brambles about your legs and wolf packs at your heels.

The grief that never moves is called complicated grief. It doesn't subside, you do not accept it, and it never—it never—goes to sleep. This is possessive grief. This is delusional grief. This is hysterical grief. Run if you will, this grief is faster. This is the grief that will chase you and beat you.

This is the grief that will eat you.

He hadn't been paying attention.

He hadn't been paying attention and he ran into the street.

What had they been playing, Charles and Victor? Was it cops and robbers? Tag? Red light, green light? Anna didn't think children played those games anymore. Maybe they had just been chasing each other around in happy circles. The brothers played well together almost half of the time. *Maybe this was one of those halves,* Anna thought. As if knowing that made much difference, if any at all.

It didn't.

He hadn't been paying attention.

By everyone's account it was an accident. Terrible and unfathomable? Yes. But also entirely accidental. Ursula and Margrith saw the whole calamity unfold. They'd been standing in front of Hans's tractor shed, just twenty feet away. Margrith was holding Polly Jean. Ursula had just gathered the last late vegetables from her garden and had brought them over to share with Margrith. A basket of turnips and potatoes was hooked in the crook of her arm. It happened in a startling instant. Charles ran into the street and almost immediately the car made contact. His little body hit the ground. *He ran in front of the car! He just ran in front of the car!* The driver was a man in his early thirties. *He ran in front of me! I couldn't stop! Jesses Gott! Jesus Christ!*

Victor, too, saw the accident. For the rest of his life, he would remember, in perfect, immutable detail, the shriek of the tires as they seized to a radical stop, the incomparable panic of disbelief that glazed the driver's eyes, and the absurdity of the single red potato that fell from his grandmother's basket and rolled close enough to Charles's head that it had to be kicked away.

It was an accident. The driver—his name was Peter Oesch—had not been drinking, he had been paying attention, and he was not speeding. Charles ran into the road. *He just ran out in front of me! I wasn't going fast!* This was true. Peter hadn't been. But it wasn't the impact that killed him. As quickly as Charles ran into the road, Peter hammered the brake and swerved sharply enough that he didn't hit him head-on. He clipped him. It broke his leg and his hip. That's it. This alone, Charles would have survived. But when Charles fell, he cracked his skull. While improbable, the fracture was not impossible. His little head hit the ground at the exact right angle and with just enough force and velocity to split it apart. A betting man would have never taken the wager. A thousand to one chance against its occurrence. But it occurred. It was an open fracture, a lacerated artery. Paramedics couldn't stop the blood. Charles died quickly, though not instantly.

Anna was asleep in the Hotel Allegra when he died.

19

STERBEN IS THE GERMAN VERB "TO DIE." IT IS AN IRREGULAR verb. This makes sense; no two deaths are the same. *Sterben*'s participle changes vowels mid-word: a usual, expected *e* becomes an *o*'s wide-mouth surprise. *Sterben* forms its compound past with *sein,* which means "to be." *Er ist gestorben. Du bist gestorben. Ich bin gestorben.* He and you and I. The present being becomes the passed.

For dead is something you are. Forever and forever. You are dead and you'll never be anything else.

THE TAXICAB PULLED UP to the scene and Anna jumped out before the car fully stopped. She didn't pay the fare. The driver yelled for her to come back, but when he saw the police, the women clumped in crying circles, and the tall man who stepped out from the crowd to grab hold of the woman who had leapt from his taxi, he guessed the rest. He turned the cab around and drove away. Anna craned to look past Bruno to the place in the road around which the policemen huddled.

Bruno blocked her, even though at this point there was nothing left for her to see. Anna yelled out a half dozen breathless questions. *Where is Victor? Where is Polly? Where is Charles?*

She didn't need to ask; she knew who'd been hurt without being told. This is a mother's talent. *Hurt,* she told herself. *He's hurt. That's all. He's okay. I* will *him to be okay.* But the same mother's talent knew that he wasn't. When Bruno explained what had happened, Anna's yelling folded seamlessly into howling. She buckled at the knees and went limp.

Margrith stepped forward to steady her but Bruno shook his head. "Put your arms around my neck, Anna. That's it. Try." Bruno lifted her and carried her into the house like a new husband delivering his bride across the threshold of their first home. He brought her into the bedroom, laid her on the bed, sat down next to her, took her shaking hands inside his own, and told her everything. Each detail forced Anna's body into a tighter ball. The driver's name. The time of death. Which leg the impact broke. Bruno stroked her hair with his right hand and with his left, he rubbed his own tears back into their sockets. "We tried to call you."

Anna spoke to the pillow beneath her head. "My ringer was off. I forgot to turn it on."

Bruno didn't respond. There was no reason to.

I DREAM I AM *at the Hauptbahnhof with two pregnant women, one quite young and the other a bit older. They deliver their babies at the same time, but the infant of the older woman either dies or was born dead to begin with. She shrugs and says, "It's okay. I'll figure something out." I tell her I'm sorry but I don't know what else to add. When I turn back, the younger woman is gone. She has left a note that says she needs to be home before her husband starts to worry. She has forgotten to take her baby. I get very upset and start to look for her but the older woman stops me and makes me give the baby to her. "See?" she says. "It all worked out." I say I suppose it did.*

MARY CAME TWENTY MINUTES later and joined Anna and Bruno in the bedroom. The women looked at each other and both began wailing with despair. Bruno rose and stepped aside. Mary took his place on the bed and reached to Anna and pulled her into her soft, maternal body and rocked her back and forth as she cried into Anna's hair, and as Anna, in turn, cried into Mary's chest. A policeman stepped into the doorframe and motioned for Bruno to come outside with him. Mary nodded in a way that meant *It is all right; I will take care of her.* Then she looked back down to Anna and continued the rocking.

"Hush. I have you." Mary rubbed Anna's back and smoothed her hair. She noticed Anna's missing earring. "We'll find it later," she whispered and Anna began to sob with even more hysteria.

"I'M TERRIFIED OF DEATH," Anna said.

"Why?" Doktor Messerli responded. "What use, fearing the inevitable?"

But the fear is in the inevitability, Anna thought. "Do you believe in God?"

"I believe in a benevolence around which the universe revolves."

Anna made a face. "Do you believe in Heaven?"

Doktor Messerli avoided the question. "No one knows what happens after death. The dead. They so rarely come back."

Anna repeated herself. "I'm afraid of death."

"Death is transformation, Anna. That's all." This was not the concrete answer Anna longed for. "Death is the soul's way of becoming something new. All living beings die. It's just what we do. It is just how it is."

"I'm still frightened."

For the next several seconds, doctor and patient watched each other with solemnity, waiting for the other to speak first. Doktor Messerli interrupted the silence. "Death is change. Nothing more. Metamorphosis. A movement from one state of being into another. Like walking into a different room in your house, Anna. Does it help to think of it in those terms?" It didn't. Doktor Messerli sighed. "Anna, I only know this: when it is your turn to die—my turn, anyone's—when it is time for you to let go of one life and reach out for another, you will be left with no other choice but to hurl yourself willingly into the mother arms of transfiguration. It's not an end. It's a beginning."

ANNA HAD NOTHING TO do with planning the funeral. She was too unwell to be of any use. Services were held three days after the accident. It was a Saturday and the church—the church of which Charles's own grandfather had been the pastor—was full. So many people came. All the Benzes' friends, their family, the men and women Bruno worked with, the students in Anna's German class, members of the church, townspeople, friends of Ursula—people Anna didn't even know, had never even met—everyone came to the service. Charles's teacher, Frau Kopp, was also there. Anna couldn't bear to look her in the eye, and Frau Kopp was kind enough to avoid all direct gazes. *Thank you,* Anna said inside herself. Archie came to the funeral but slipped away before it was over. Anna had seen him sitting in the back when she'd turned in her seat to survey the church before the service began. His head was down and he was pretending to read the printed-out order of service. Anna's stomach soured. She vowed to never lay eyes on him again. And she didn't. Karl was there as well, of course. He was a friend of the family. The sight of Karl had no effect on Anna. She looked at him and felt an absence of feeling. A blank nothing. A nothing so blank that it was brutal. The parents of most of the children in Charles's class came to the church, though many had left their children home. Tim and Mary also came alone. Anna understood. She wouldn't have brought Charles to a funeral either, even a funeral for one of his friends. *He is too young, too tender,* Anna thought in present tense. She hadn't yet begun to think of him as past.

The *Pfarrer* conducted the service in Swiss German. The bells rang.

The graveside service had been earlier in the day. Anna relied on Bruno and Ursula to hold her up as she cried into one of the handkerchiefs that Mary had given her for her birthday.

Charles was cremated. They buried his urn in the graveyard's children's section.

That was all Anna remembered of either service. After the funeral Bruno and Ursula and the rest of the mourners went to the *Kirchgemeindehaus* for a light lunch, coffee, and more tears. Anna didn't follow them. Mary took her home, helped her out of her clothes, and put her into bed. *Please don't leave,*

Anna asked when Mary moved toward the bedroom door. Mary shook her head and said of course she wasn't leaving but that she would be right back. A few minutes later, Mary returned with a tray of food that Anna had no interest in eating. Mary asked her to try her best to eat a little, reminding her gently that Victor and Polly would need her and that to be strong she could not starve herself. Anna took two bites of the sandwich and drank only one sip of the tea. Mary took the tray away and then returned. She sat in a rocking chair next to the bed and kept vigil over Anna for the rest of the day.

Victor and Polly will need you, Anna. In the days after Charles's death, Anna had caught herself forgetting she had two other children. Anna's neighbor Monika babysat Polly Jean for several days, to Bruno and Anna and Ursula's immediate relief. But they couldn't shield Victor from the experience. He'd shared a room with Charles. He'd shared toys and parents. Victor's usual sullenness had been replaced with a blank, baffled face that revealed a sadness that existed somewhere beyond the reach of comfort. At the church he sat between Anna and Bruno. They hadn't allowed him at the burial. Victor didn't need to see that. Anna hadn't either.

THE DAY BEFORE THE funeral the Benzes received, in their mailbox, Charles's *Bestattungsanzeige.* Anna found it in Bruno's nightstand drawer. She was hunting down painkillers; the crying had induced a migraine. Bruno had slipped on the ice last winter and sprained his back. Anna banked on at least one leftover pill.

The announcement lay at the top of an assortment of other ephemera: a drawing Charles had done in school, a photograph of Anna holding Polly Jean, the card his mother had sent him on his last birthday. He had folded the announcement into careful quarters. When Anna opened it, she couldn't read past her son's name. It was a feeling more closely related to embarrassment than to grief. *This is something I'm not meant to see.* Anna returned the death announcement to its place in the drawer where Bruno kept his private things.

Bruno never once asked where she had been the day Charles died.

20

Twice in the last year Anna had been in the city when a woman (a different woman on each occasion) approached her with a clipboard and asked in Swiss German whether she had time to spare. The women were market researchers seeking ordinary people to participate in taste tests. In both instances, Anna had agreed (what else would she have done?) and each time, she followed the women into a nearby hotel's conference room. For the first test, Anna was asked to sample and rate several coffees. *Is it bitter? Can you describe its aroma? What would you say about the body of the coffee? Would you describe it as "full"?* Anna hadn't begun her German classes yet, and she and the market researcher struggled through the next twenty minutes, the woman miming questions with her hands, and Anna answering those questions with blinks and nods. For her troubles, Anna earned a jar of instant coffee and a large bag of assorted mini chocolates. Anna shoved the coffee to the back of the pantry but—over the next three days—ate the entire bag of chocolate herself. *Why should I share?* she thought. I'm the one who took the test. She considered it her reward for trying. Sometimes Anna tried. Sometimes she tried very, very hard.

The second time Anna was approached (on the same street corner, no less) occurred after she'd completed the first month of her German class. This test ran far smoother than the previous one. Anna smiled through it, stumbling over only a few sentences and even fewer words. She vetted pickles that day and this time received a jar of cocktail onions, which, like the instant coffee, had also been pushed to the back of the pantry. There were no chocolates but that was okay. Her poise, the smoothness of speech—those were her reward.

Anna related this story to Doktor Messerli a few days after the second, more successful encounter. Doktor Messerli asked what Anna thought it meant.

Anna said she thought it meant that things were looking up.

A WEEK AND A half after the accident Victor went back to school and Bruno returned to the bank. What else could either of them do? Bruno tackled his grief by throwing himself into work. At the bank he was focused, efficient, busy. At home he filled the extra hours with chores and fix-it projects. He painted the basement and replaced the rotting boards in the shed. He bought a dishwasher and installed it. It helped his hands to have something to do.

They had tried making love the night before he went back to the office. It was a failure. Bruno lay behind Anna in their bed and locked his arms around her and pulled her toward his erection. He buried his face in her hair and braced his tottering body against his wife's beautiful, brittle back and pulsed gently but with intention into her. "Please, Anna," he said. "I need you. I need to be with you." But Anna could not stop crying and that in turn made Bruno cry. He rolled away. Anna shrank into herself. For an hour Bruno stared at the ceiling as if it might move. Eventually they both fell into tandem, fretful sleeps.

Anna stayed mostly in bed. Time froze. The house palled. She hadn't bothered to ask for a refund for her German class, but she had no intention of returning. It felt pointless, rude to the memory of her son. As if she would have been able to concentrate. Grief consumed every minute. Anna was sick all the time. She ate only broth and toast. She grew thin. On walks she hallucinated birds. Black and erratic, they followed her up and back down the hill. They kept to the margins of her vision but daily the flock grew larger and less peripheral.

Mary volunteered to withdraw from the class as well so that she could come to the Benzes' every day and take care of Anna and Polly Jean (Monika could not, of course, watch Polly indefinitely). Anna talked Mary out of it, reasoning that whatever Mary learned she could, in turn, teach Anna once she felt better, even though Anna doubted she ever would. And Ursula would be coming over; Anna wouldn't be alone. Mary accepted this and did as Anna suggested.

When Victor came home from school he'd bring his snack into the living room and mother and son would sit together on the couch and watch television. Neither wanted to talk. Victor regressed. At night he sucked his thumb and once or twice he wet the bed and the programs he watched on TV were much too young for him. They were cartoons that Charles had liked. Silly children's shows about red tractors or construction men or trains. On the couch Victor would lean tentatively into

Anna as he watched them. Anna would run her fingers lightly through his hair.

He is too timid to ask for comfort, Anna thought. *He isn't Charles.*

"Do you believe in Hell?" Anna asked.

"What's this?" Stephen pulled Anna closer. It was a remarkably cold morning in early February. They spooned beneath an eiderdown comforter made for one.

"Oh. Just fire stuff." Anna smiled as she said it. Her voice was light, relaxed, and happy. It was all she wanted, to be pressed so tightly against him, seamless as the woodwork joinery of a Mennonite table.

Stephen exhaled. "I don't really think about it."

"Hell, you mean?"

"Yeah."

"You aren't religious."

"Not at all."

"Your parents?"

Stephen stretched and shivered and checked his watch. It was time to get up. "Grandparents. Greek Orthodox." He stood and yawned and threw on a pair of sweatpants as quickly as he could.

"You're Greek?" Anna had never thought to ask about his background.

"Cypriot."

"Oh." Anna didn't have any more immediate questions.

"Say, though . . ." Stephen turned back to the bed and Anna sat up. "Here's something about fire you probably don't know. And since you love these divagations . . ." He offered her a perfect replica of the smile he gave her the first time they met.

"Tell me." Anna loved it when he played along. She batted her eyes and indulged her voice a lilt.

Stephen sat next to her on the edge of the bed. "So, in Jerusalem every Easter, a priest takes a couple of candles into the church they say is built on top of Jesus's tomb."

"This is an Orthodox thing?"

Stephen nodded yes as he continued. "He goes down into the crypt alone, says an ancient prayer, and when he comes back up the candles are lit."

"Okay. What's the miracle?" Anna gave over to the lecture with attentive, schoolgirl glee.

"Ah. The miracle is he's frisked before he goes into the church to prove he isn't hiding matches or a lighter in his robes. The tomb too. They check it. So where does it come from, the fire? That's the mystery."

"Where does it come from?"

"What's said is a blue light appears out of a cloud that itself materializes out of empty air. The light and the cloud kind of dance around each other until they contract into a single, floating column of flame." Stephen mimed how the elements might come together.

"Who says?"

"The priests. And from this flame he lights his candles." Anna enjoyed these moderate theatrics. "And then he shares the flame and the people tremble with awe. It's called Holy Fire. Because it comes from God." Stephen yawned and stood up again. "So they say."

Anna was fascinated. "Have you seen it? Do you believe in the miracle?"

"Anna, don't be daft. There is no miracle. He's hidden the matches somewhere."

Anna slouched forward. She'd hoped he would say *Yes, I absolutely believe it.* "But isn't a blue flame unusual?"

Stephen bent and kissed the back of her neck. "There are a dozen colors of fire. This is trick of light, of atmosphere. Group hysteria."

"So you don't believe in Hell?"

"Anna, I don't even believe in Heaven."

IT WAS THE CLOSEST Anna came to a confession. A week after the funeral, a Saturday morning. Mary had come over as she had done every day since the accident. She brought a casserole, a tin of cinnamon tea cakes, another tin, this one filled with walnut fudge, and a bag of various other treats and snacks she thought either Anna or Bruno or Victor might enjoy. "Mary, this isn't necessary," Anna said. She knew she wouldn't eat a bite of it. Mary waved her off and told her it made her happy to do it. *It's how she sublimates her pain,* Anna finally realized. Mary put her grief to use. In that way she was as practical as Bruno or Ursula. But Mary had a tenderness they lacked. *Is it because she's Canadian?* Anna wondered. *No, it is because she's Mary.*

Mary came into the bedroom with mugs of tea and pulled a chair right next to the bed. She told Anna she was there for her. They could talk, or not talk. Mary would listen or they could just share silence. "Whatever you need, Anna."

Anna lay quietly for several minutes and listened as Mary made neutral, inconsequential conversation about Tim and the kids. She mentioned that she talked to Nancy, who sent love and wanted Mary to let Anna know that if there was anything she needed, she shouldn't hesitate to contact her. Anna said thank you; Mary said she'd pass it along. The conversation idled.

"Mary, what's the worst thing you've ever done?"

Mary set her mug on the nightstand and put her elbows on her knees and her chin in her palms like a young girl might and thought for a moment. "I don't know. I've always tried to be respectable. I'm boring like that, I guess," she dismissed herself.

"No, Mary, you're good like that."

Mary blushed. Anna had embarrassed her. "Let me think. Maybe it was the time I . . ." Mary stopped and rearranged herself in the chair. "Oh, Anna, I don't want to say! Why do you want to know?"

"It will make me feel better."

Mary didn't understand what she meant but did not press her to explain. "Okay, Anna. You want to know? I'll tell you. But it's a secret—really, please—you can't tell anyone." Anna nodded. "In high school I set fire to the shed behind my volleyball coach's house."

"Mary!" Anna didn't know whether to be impressed or appalled.

Mary backtracked. "It wasn't just me. The whole team. We all set it on fire. And it was an old, dilapidated shed to begin with, so . . ."

Anna was dumbstruck. "Why?"

Mary sighed. "The girls on the team, most of us, we'd been very, very mean to this other girl. Absolutely cruel. We spread rumors about her, we let the air out of her bicycle tires, we told her a boy she had a crush on wanted to date her when he didn't, we cut her hair . . ."

"You cut her *hair*?"

Mary nodded shamefully. "Anna, we were awful. But we were trying to be. We wanted to make her miserable. She quit the team. She transferred schools, actually."

"But why did you do this?"

Mary shrugged. "It was just one of those high school girl decisions that got made randomly and early on. I didn't make it. I can't even say I hated her." Mary hung her head. Anna could tell she'd felt bad about this for years. "I honestly can't tell you how it happened that she became our enemy."

"But the shed?"

"Oh. Our coach found out and made us forfeit the season. It ruined our record. We were angry. So one night we snuck onto her property. One girl had the gas can, another had some newspaper. I struck a match and set the whole thing going. Then we ran."

"And you didn't get caught? Surely she suspected you . . ."

Mary shook her head. "We covered our tracks. And we kept our mouths shut. We couldn't be charged on suspicion alone. There wasn't any proof." Anna nodded. "So that's it. The worst thing I ever did."

"And you had to think before answering?"

"Well, no. But I try not to dwell on it."

"What happened after that?"

"Well, after that we got a new volleyball coach. So we got rid of her as well. The next year we won every game we played. Then I graduated." Mary stopped to think for a second. "Well, maybe *that's* the worst thing. Running her off. And that poor girl." Mary shook her head. "You know I can't even remember her name."

"That's pretty bad."

"I've never told a soul about this, Anna. Not even Tim."

"Didn't he go to the same high school?"

Mary nodded her head yes. "Like I said. We didn't say a word." Mary exhaled. "We were just so stupid and thoughtless. This girl didn't deserve the treatment we gave her. And we weren't terrible ourselves, I don't think. Just so destructive. One destruction fueled the next one. We weren't thinking. We should have been. But we weren't. Can you understand that?"

"Mary, this is all my fault."

Mary slid to the edge of her chair and reached for Anna's blanket and smoothed it down and around her body like she did with her children when she tucked them into bed, mothering her. "What is, honey? And of course it isn't. I'm sure of it."

Anna wasn't brave enough to continue.

"Anna," Mary cooed. "You can tell me anything." Anna believed that yes, she probably could.

But knew without a doubt she wouldn't.

KARL CAME TO THE house just once after the funeral. He and Bruno and Guido were going to a ZSC Lions game. Bruno wasn't home from work. Ursula had taken Victor and Polly on a walk. Anna was dressed, but shabbily. Karl knocked a timid knock.

"Hallo, Anna. How are you touching?"

Anna looked both through and past him. He could have guessed how she felt, he didn't need to ask. But asking was customary. Responding was optional.

"Come in," Anna said and showed him into the living room. Karl stepped through the hall and into the house. Anna had been watching a game show on television. *5 Gegen 5*. Five against five others. It was a Swiss version of the American program *Family Feud*.

Karl wasn't sure what to do with his hands, so he pushed them as deeply into his jacket pockets as he could and then looked to Anna for a cue. Anna shrugged and motioned him to a chair as she shuffled back to her seat on the couch. They spent the next five complicated minutes pretending that neither had seen the other naked.

Anna hadn't turned the TV off. One of the teams was made up of members of a Burgdorf yodeling club and the other a women's floorball team from Winterthur. The question—asked in Schwiizerdütsch—was, as near as Anna could tell, "Name a favorite ice cream flavor." The top response, chocolate, had already been given. One of the women on the floorball team answered "Strawberry!" It was second to last on the list. Anna stared at the television with bloodshot eyes and wondered whether pistachio was on the board. It wasn't.

"You must never, never, never tell Bruno."

Karl nodded. It was solemn and small. Then the two of them sat in stillness. Outside, the sun set so quickly it was almost audible.

In the back of her notebook, Anna kept a running list of potentially useful German phrases. *Mum's the word! A thousand thanks! Don't mention it! Ah, but there's a catch. No ifs, ands, or buts! Ready, set, GO! Good things come in threes! When in Rome! Do you have a toothpick? An eye for an eye.*

By the skin of my teeth. Where is the drugstore? Where are the trains? How are you doing? I'm doing well! I'm great! I'm pretty good! I'm okay. I'm miserable. I am sick. I need help.

In a session before Charles's death, Doktor Messerli attempted to instruct Anna in the difference between a reason and an excuse. She split these hairs in an Anna-like way.

"I suppose," Anna conceded dully. She wasn't exactly listening.

The Doktor frowned but pressed ahead to make her point. "You're unhappy? Fine. You have grounds for occasional sorrow. Swiss customs still elude you. Yours is a difficult marriage—all marriages are difficult, Anna, even the good ones—and you have few friends and no pastimes. Your children are young. They're demanding. All of it is difficult. But," Doktor Messerli continued, "for every reason you present to justify your sadness, you offer a tandem excuse that serves no purpose other than to prolong your misery. 'I cannot change the intractable Swiss,' you whine. 'There's nothing I can do to make Bruno more attentive'—Anna, have you tried just simply *asking* him for more attention?—'I am too shy to make friends,' 'Taking care of an infant requires all the energy I have.' There's nothing you can do to change your life? That's the biggest excuse of all." Anna couldn't disagree.

Doktor Messerli softened. "Let's work on this, Anna. Just this. That will be enough. You move like a refugee in a war ghetto when, truly, you have every Allied power at your command. There is no reason to live like this." Anna nodded. There wasn't. "A successful life. Anna. I want you to succeed."

In Anna's half-attentive state she heard "secede."

21

Polly Jean's first birthday fell on November 29, a Thursday. Anna had no interest in celebrating it. All motions toward merriment seemed obscene. They'd had small fêtes on the occasions of the boys' first birthdays. Simple dinners, then cake with family. It was the cake that Anna cared about. It was tradition: the birthday child, king of his high chair, his hands elbow deep in a cake he didn't have to share with anyone, icing in his hair, crumbs up his nose, and Anna taking pictures. That's what she was ultimately after, the pictures. Bruno found the custom ridiculous. *It's messy and a waste of cake,* he said. Nevertheless somewhere in the attic was a photo album no one looked at anymore and inside it, snapshots of each of the boys, their entire faces smeared black with chocolate frosting.

It was Ursula who came to Anna a week before Polly's birthday. She'd be happy to bake the cake, she said, and volunteered to have the party at her house. It was a warmhearted offer. Anna's face collapsed under the sympathy of Ursula's suggestion, but she said nothing. Ursula backed quietly out of the room and left Anna alone for the rest of the afternoon.

Ursula, like Bruno, took a sensible approach to grief. She threw herself into knitting and volunteered on a children's clothing drive with the *Frauenverein* and once a week, she met with the same women in the *Kirchgemeindehaus* to work on other projects, some of them charitable, others creative like the following week's workshop on Advent crafts that Ursula was planning to attend. And every day, Ursula walked over to Rosenweg to tend to Polly Jean. During this time she set her usual impatience with her daughter-in-law aside and looked for practical ways to help Anna get through the day. Ursula cooked most of the family's dinners and did the greater part of the marketing and housework. She could offer no other comfort. She'd never been affectionate with Anna. To be familiar and effusive now would seem peculiar and forced.

The subject of Polly Jean's birthday was approached again that evening, this time by Bruno. He was gentle. He spoke gingerly. He had gone out of his way the last weeks to treat Anna with exceptional compassion. "Don't you want to take a picture of Polly eating her cake? Come on, Anna. If you don't take a picture you will wish you had. You have pictures of the boys." He hadn't needed to remind her. Anna started crying and Bruno couldn't find a single word of consolation, though he tried many. He sighed as he stood and said to the wall that he was going upstairs to check on Victor. And then he did.

STEPHEN'S BIRTHDAY WAS THE first day of May. He'd turned forty-two the month after he left Switzerland. Anna had, on that day and this year on his birthday as well, gone into the city, to Neumarkt, and stationed herself at a table in the Kantorei where they had gone for drinks on the day that they met.

Both times she had gone with the sole intent to cry, though on neither occasion could she find the tears. In each instance, she started at the beginning and told herself the entire story. It had seemed an obligatory, if self-spiteful, ritual.

Was it really love? she'd ask herself. *Was it close to love? Did it live in love's neighborhood?*

Of course it was love. A version of love. With Polly Jean to prove it.

ANNA HAD SEEN DOKTOR Messerli only once since Charles's death. The Doktor spoke much slower than she usually did, and with softer intonations. Her sentences had intermissions. She asked the requisite questions: *How are you holding up, Anna? What are you doing to honor your son's memory? How are you interacting with your family? How are you taking care of yourself? Are you taking care of yourself?* She gave Anna another prescription for tranquilizers. Anna had never bothered to fill the first.

"Where do they go, the dead?"

Doktor Messerli answered honestly. "I don't know." They'd talked around this subject before.

"What do they do?"

"I don't know that either, Anna."

"Will I see him again?" Anna spoke with desperation.

"I hope so," the Doktor said. She meant it.

IN THE END, THERE was nothing to do about Polly Jean's party but have it. Ursula and Bruno insisted. Anna, limp as cotton cloth, didn't have the strength to fight them. They'd planned nothing extravagant—a supper with the family at Ursula's house. That was all.

Daniela would come from Mumpf and Mary would join them as well. Tim had a game and Max and Alexis would stay with the wife of a teammate. Max hadn't returned to Dietlikon since the accident. It was best. He didn't understand that dead meant forever.

Ursula made split-pea soup. Anna managed a few bites. This earned approving nods from Bruno and Mary, which Anna pretended not to notice. Ursula had also baked two white cakes, each covered in pale pink frosting: one for the family to enjoy, and a small one intended for Polly Jean alone. Polly Jean threw herself into its deconstruction, squealing with glee. There were crumbs in her hair and clumps of frosting in her eyelashes. Bruno took the photos. Polly Jean's laugh made everyone else laugh. Even Anna smiled, though it shamed her and she tried to stifle it. Mary put her arm around her and in a whisper told her that there was never any shame in joy. "If Charles were here, Anna, he'd be laughing too." Until that point every mention made of Charles had sent Anna spinning into sobs. But the tone of Mary's voice was yielding and her genuine belief that Charles, wherever he was, was fine and without a doubt happy and safe—*yes, Anna, in Heaven!*—pulled Anna away from the company of her despairs. Mary was sure. "Yes, Anna. I'm positive. Your son is well," she said. Mary had never given Anna any reason to distrust her. So in that moment, with her family around her, Anna tried to imagine Heaven, and Charles in it. *Where are you? What are you doing? Is this possible? Oh Schatz, my love! Can you see me? I miss you! I love you most of all!*

The attempt, to Anna's astonishment, succeeded. There

were no harps or halos. There wasn't a gate. In this Heaven there wasn't even God. And it wasn't so much a place as it was a dimension that existed just beyond the tangible three of the physical world and outside the immaterial chronology of the fourth. It was only a glimpse, and a quick flicker of a glimpse at that—but what she saw was a vicinity near to her own (nearer in fact than she would have expected) where time and physical form no longer mattered, if ever they mattered to begin with, and there, in that realm, was Charles. He was faceless and formless and yet altogether whole. The universal benevolence Doktor Messerli believed in cupped the soul of her son in its palm. The palm was warm. The warmth was real. This, she could accept. She could live with this.

Anna began to feel some of the hard, black fog lift from her shoulders and with Mary's permission, she embraced the feeling. *It won't be bad forever,* Anna soothed herself. *I don't need to feel bad forever.* She was hopeful but wary. A mood is a fickle thing. As quickly as it comes it can depart.

Polly Jean was a glorious mess. There was even cake in her ears. When enough became enough, Anna made a motion to pick her up and take her away, but Ursula intervened. "I'll bathe her. Stay with your guest."

Oh, Anna said, which she hoped translated to *Thank you.*

Victor ate two pieces of cake then ran off to watch television in Ursula's living room. He, too, seemed lighter. Bruno, Mary, and Daniela drank coffee and chatted. All interaction hedged against levity. Anna felt better, this was evident. Still, everyone remained cautious in his or her speech. No one wanted her disposition to slip.

The conversation began in earnest innocence. Mary had mentioned how much like Bruno Victor looked. "It's his eyes and nose. And the shape of his face. A Xerox, Bruno!" Mary laughed at this clever-only-to-herself remark. Anna nodded from the other side of her coffee cup as she sipped. Victor did look exactly like Bruno. *He acts just like him too. On his best days and his worst.* "Max and Tim look nothing alike. Well, maybe in the eyes. A little. Everyone says he favors my side of the family. But oh—listen to this. So my great-grandfather Alexander had two children . . ." Mary, who had already been talking in circles, launched into an even more circuitous story about Alexander's fraternal twin sister and what Alexis looked like as a baby. Anna wasn't listening. She was looping the memory of Charles's first birthday. It was a balmy mid-April day and the whole family and all the neighbors sat under the apple trees and watched as Charles took his first unaided steps. He toddled three feet and then collapsed on the grass in giggles. It was a good day.

Mary continued. Bruno listened closely, or pretended to. He smiled at the right pauses and made appropriate comments when the moments allowed and held an interested expression as Mary rattled on about babies and family resemblances. Mary had made no secret that she longed for a third child. When Anna asked why, Mary responded by admitting that having a baby would give her something to do. Anna laughed until she realized Mary wasn't kidding. At the time Anna had thought to herself she'd do better with a lover, they were less trouble.

". . . anyway, it was so strong a resemblance that people just assumed it was her baby! So"—Mary punctuated the end of her convolution by reaching for her coffee cup—"where'd that pitch-black hair and sweet little nose come from? She really doesn't look like either of you." Mary glanced at both Anna and Bruno. Neither spoke for a moment.

Anna froze. She'd never had to answer this question, though for a year now she'd rehearsed several responses. *That's what I looked like as a baby, my hair only lightened when I went to school. My mother's mother was Italian (or Spanish). Well, when both mother and father carry recessive genetic traits, there's a high probability that what's dormant in the parents will become dominant in the offspring. You see, the nineteenth-century Augustinian friar Gregor Mendel hybridized some pea plants . . .* These and more, Anna had practiced. But she hadn't practiced them enough because when she most needed them, none came to mind. *Jesus. I can't remember anything.* Anna bought time by shoveling a very large forkful of cake into her mouth. She avoided speaking aloud by pretending she couldn't.

As far as Anna knew Bruno had never had to answer the question either. But he answered it. Without hesitation, without hedging. "My father's uncle. Polly Jean looks like him. Her hair. Not her nose. His nose was much bigger." Bruno declared the size of his uncle's nose with the timing of a comic straight man.

"Which uncle?" Anna asked. She'd never heard this.

"Rolf." Bruno didn't have anything else to add. Anna tried to recall if she'd ever seen a picture.

Daniela piped in, "That's right, Rolf had the thick black hair when he was younger, *jo*?"

Anna couldn't tell whether Daniela was genuinely remembering a long-dead relative or if she was trying to somehow help—and if she was trying to help, was she coming to the aid of Anna or Bruno? "He had a big bristly black mustache, too. And," she started to laugh, "I remember that he used to curl it like a Bavarian!"

"And give you fifty rappen if you shined his boots when he came to visit," Ursula added from the kitchen. She'd changed Polly's clothes and set her to rest in the bedroom and was now starting on the dishes. *She's in on this too?* Anna took another bite of cake, an even bigger one, that she might have a moment of composure and talk herself down from that irrational ledge. *No one's in on anything. They're just talking. Eat your cake, Anna. You don't have to say a word. Eat your cake. You have your cake, now eat it, too.*

Bruno stood and took his empty coffee cup into the kitchen. "Yes. That's where she gets it. Rolf. Of course." The answer satisfied Mary, who changed the subject. Anna relaxed. But only a little.

TWO YEARS BEFORE MEETING Stephen, Anna was in the Dietlikon Coop. She'd made a list but left it at home and had spent the previous half hour struggling to recall what she'd written down. *What do we have? What do we lack?* She'd put salami in her basket, some rolls, a leek, a jar of stuffed pepperoncini, and five cans of tuna. She'd been inefficient, chasing the items as she recalled them, out of order and erratically. She felt like a pinball, being kicked and slung from one aisle to its counterpoint target. *Tilt* was only a matter of time. *I live in the grocery store,* Anna remembered thinking. *I'm the hired help, the domestic.* This was years before Anna's analysis, so Doktor Messerli wasn't around to challenge the authenticity of those statements and to suggest that if Anna felt repressed it was a sentiment of her own construction. *This is, after all, the life you have chosen for yourself,* she surely would have scolded. But Anna didn't have Doktor Messerli then. What she had were two young sons, a cranky husband, an aloof mother-in-law, and, on that particular day, a headache. Anna remembered they were out of sugar and turned the cart around and crossed into the baking aisle to fetch the sugar that both she and Bruno took in their coffee. Anna always bought it in cubes. She liked cubes. Their uniform architecture pleased her. *It's the shape. You always know where you stand with it.* She reached for the usual box but paused when her eyes fell on the one next to it. *Glückszucker,* the package read and instead of geometrically true squares, the portions were formed in the shapes of each of a deck of playing cards' four suits. Lucky sugar, it meant. Happy sugar. This brightened Anna. *How have I not noticed this before?* She imagined they were charms or talismans. Sweet, magic beans that had the power to conjure good fortune. It was a silly promise made by a substance only good for rotting your teeth. But that was the sugar Anna wanted. She took a box and set it with ceremony befitting the supernatural in her basket. *Now what?* she thought and then remembered that Bruno had asked for some cheese. She pushed toward the dairy case. *It has come to this? Such asinine indulgences?* She supposed it had.

As an ABBA song faded away (was it "Take a Chance on Me"? Anna didn't recall but thought that it would have been nice if it had been), the inimitable opening keyboard riff of Europe's "The Final Countdown" began. Coop markets loop playlists of familiar, dated songs between which they insert short advertisements for specials and rebate premiums. This season's promotion was a set of knives. Anna saved the stickers—*Merkli*—but rarely cashed them in. She tended to only remember them after they expired (a tendency that would play out in so many ways). These loudspeaker ads always ended with the grocery store's slogan: *Coop—für mich und dich.* For me and you. *For us.* Like the words a priest spoke over the bread and the wine quoting Christ: This is my body given for you. *But nothing is given away,* Anna thought. *Everything comes at a cost.* Everything always came at a cost. *We're headed for Venus!* the singer wailed, his voice hanging stupid and foolish in the air.

Stupid and foolish, Anna thought. *Like forcing meaning into sugar cubes.* Anna stood before a row of cheeses and butters and individually packaged desserts and juices that needed refrigeration and listened as the song screeched on. *I'm sure that we'll all miss her so!*

If I went away would I be missed? Anna looked into her basket. Each package was printed in three different languages, only one of which she understood and that was just barely. *Lucky sugar.* Her throat snapped closed. *Fuck.* It hit her. *This is where I'm spending the rest of my life. I'll never live anywhere else.* Anna held a block of Gruyère in one hand and a wedge of Appenzeller in the other. *Fuck.* It hit again. *This is where I'm gonna die.*

The song ended, another followed after it. A man in the orange jumpsuit of a Swiss rail worker passed in front of her without saying a word.

"Combustion won't happen without oxygen," Stephen said. "A fire is a living thing and it must breathe."

"Does fire have a soul?" Anna asked.

"I'm leaving in a week," Stephen replied.

DANIELA LEFT JUST BEFORE seven. Anna hadn't expected her to come and realized only as she was seeing her to the door how grateful she was that Daniela had made the effort. It's a convoluted trip and she'd only stayed a couple of hours. *I wouldn't have done it,* Anna thought, but then remembered that two months earlier, she had. *That was two months ago?* The thought caught her off guard. *That was just two months ago.* But Anna tried not to fixate on the past. Instead, she willed herself back into the present moment and forced herself into a suit of thankfulness. *People are being so kind to me. Have they always been this kind? I don't know why they are being so kind.* She did know why, of course. What she meant was *People are being so kind and I do not deserve it.*

Ursula brought a second carafe of coffee to the table then returned to the kitchen. Anna didn't have a read on this. Ursula's kindnesses were never overt and her friendliness and politesse were always tempered by her immediate situation, which in this case was the task of cleaning up. There was gratitude here, too, Anna supposed. She would try to thank her later. Tomorrow, maybe. Anna wasn't sure how. Mary made a move to help her but Bruno assured her that his mother could handle the dishes alone so Mary stayed put. Mary was picking at cake with her fingers and making light conversation with Bruno when Anna returned from seeing Daniela out.

Mary was trying out German sentences on him. She suffered through several. Bruno gently corrected her mistakes and coaxed her through the structures that were still confounding her. "Shoot! I can't!" But Bruno insisted she could and so they bumbled through perhaps a paragraph of painful niceties. Anna noticed that even with the extra month of classes, Mary's German was still less feasible than her own. And then Anna noted that it was shallow of her to notice that.

The chatter remained mostly superficial. Bruno praised Mary's progress and then, in a faux scold, forbade her from speaking English in his presence from that point forward. *From now on, German only! Nur Deutsch!* This made Mary blush. She waved him off and gave in and cut another slice of cake for herself. "I really shouldn't," she said, "but it tastes so good!" Anna hadn't eaten any cake beyond those bites she shoveled into her mouth in order to avoid having to answer Mary's questions. She wasn't sure she could stomach a whole piece. But Mary was right, it did taste good. Mary saw her eyeing the cake. "You want me to cut you a piece?" Anna didn't answer. "Okay, I'll cut you a piece." Mary put a slice on a plate and pushed it over to Anna. "Lots of icing because the icing is the best part!" Mary winked. Anna picked up a fork and took a hesitant taste. She took another. She'd never been someone who self-medicated with food. *No, that's what the sex was about.* If food were her drug of choice, she'd be the size of a house. *I need a lot of soothing.* In the moment, though, she could see the draw. The icing *was* the best part. You can hide a lot of sadness inside a pink sugar rosette.

Mary and Bruno talked about Tim. Bruno asked if Tim and Max had any interest in going to the transport museum in Lucerne. Bruno had promised Victor he would take him. As ambivalent as Bruno had always been toward Anna, he'd never been anything but attentive and paternal to his children.

His children, Anna thought. In the last month Bruno had done what any good father might and channeled his every spare effort into figuring out what would best distract Victor from his grief. No one wants to see his child suffer. But Bruno and Anna alike knew that there was nothing that could be done to prevent Victor's pain. At best, they could assuage it or mitigate it or curb it for a time. So going out for pizza and kicking the soccer ball around and visiting the train museum and attending every ZSC Lions game on the schedule and promising winter trips to Zermatt for skiing and planning summer vacations to the Bodensee for swimming and boating served only to take the boy's despair and put it on hold. But pain is an impatient customer. It wouldn't be long before it demanded attention.

"Oh, Max would love that. Are there trains or just airplanes or—what's there exactly?" Mary blathered. Either it was the extra piece of cake or the second cup of coffee or something else entirely, Anna didn't know. But she was rambling, and among the many things that made Anna nervous (in general and in that specific moment), Mary's jabber was one. Bruno affirmed that yes, the museum had trains in its collection. "Wonderful. Yes, I'm sure they'd want to go. You know Max. He loves the trains! Just like Charles." As soon as she said it, Mary wondered if she shouldn't have. Mary looked at Anna for affirmation. Was it really okay to talk about Charles? In the present tense?

"It's okay, Mary." Anna bowed her head and looked at her cake as if from it she could draw resolve and strength. "No, really. It is." She raised her head and nodded. "You're right. Wherever he is, I'm sure he still loves trains." The table observed a solemn moment of remembrance and then moved on to other talk.

Mary took charge of the conversation. She kept it breezy, so bright it felt frivolous. Five minutes passed and Bruno and Mary had moved from Max and Victor to Tim and the team to the Gilberts' plans to spend Christmas in Uster. "It's the first time we've spent it away from home!" Mary pined. Bruno took her to a slight but firm task.

"Where your family is. That's home." Mary accepted this minor dressing-down with a nod of understanding.

It was the night before Polly Jean's birthday and Anna lay awake in bed. She had been begging sleep to steal her for three hard hours. It hadn't. The slats on the shutters were open but the windows closed. There wasn't a moon. Clouds blocked out all starlight. The air was ominous.

Every day since Charles's death had ended with Anna in tears. She had learned to swallow them, awful as they were. They burned her throat. Nausea always ensued. She hadn't seen Charles dead on the ground, but that didn't stop her from imagining the scene. Every vision she had was worse than the previous. She saw the blood. She saw his hip, broken and skewed in an impossible direction. She saw a hole in the back of his head. She saw his vertebrae, she saw his brain. She shoved these images away but they came back harder, and the details of the scene grew more aggressive. She saw him in the oven that cremated him. She watched his skin turn black and burn away. She saw his dust.

Bruno? She nudged her husband, who'd been asleep since before Anna had come to bed herself. *Bruno?* He stirred but just as quickly settled. *Bruno, wake up. Put your hands on me. I want your hands.* She jostled him again. This time he didn't move at all. *Wake up, wake up.* Anna slid her hand under the blanket and up his arm, then down his chest, past his stomach to the waistband of his pajama bottoms. She ran her finger under the elastic. Bruno purred but didn't wake up. Anna let her hand travel on. She pulled his pajamas away from him, then down, then she drew back the comforter and lay her head between his legs and put her lips around his cock. It was soft. She sucked it like a baby does a nipple, a child his thumb. *Wake up, Bruno. Make love to me.* His cock grew marginally stiff, then stopped. It wasn't going to happen. She pulled his pants back up and fell back to her own side of the bed. When she closed her eyes she saw Charles close his own eyes that final time. She saw his very last breath.

She got up and threw on pants, a sweatshirt, shoes, and ran out of the house without locking the door. *My hill, my bench.* It was close to 2:00 A.M.

She was full-on bawling. *I've lost so much! So much!* Earlier that day she'd gone into the boys' room. Charles's clothes were still in the closet. She went in to grab the shirt he'd worn the day before he died (no one had washed it yet; Anna wouldn't let them). She brought it to her face, but the scent of him had faded. It was almost gone. She rifled through the rest of the closet, the dresser. Nothing smelled like him. It was like losing him once more. She would never see her boy again.

It was too much. At the top of the hill she yelled, she shook out her hands, she stomped her feet. *Goddammit!* She fell to her knees. She curled to a ball on the cold, rocky path. *Fix this! Fucking make it stop!* It was a prayer, maybe to fucking itself. *Wake up, Bruno,* she cried as if he could hear. *I need you to put your hands on me!*

Anna writhed and clutched at her skin through her sweatshirt, the ground was a pillow of stone. *Hands, I need hands.* In the moment, Bruno was useless. Archie and Karl were unreasonable possibilities. And Stephen was gone, gone for good. Anna slid her hands beneath her shirt and up to her chest. She grabbed her breasts hard enough to bruise them. She pinched her nipples. *That's it, Anna. Yes. Yes.* She had no one to rely on but herself. She put her right hand down the front of her jeans. She'd made herself wet. *That's it. That's it.* She slipped her middle finger in and rested her thumb on her clit. *Yes, yes.* In the shameless dark she tried to get herself off.

It was dire and wrong and even in the middle of a cloudy, starless night she felt one thousand eyes upon her. *From God no secrets are hid,* she thought. *He knows it all already.*

A dog barked. Anna bolted upright. *Oh, shit.* She scrambled to her feet and spun in all directions but she saw nothing. The dog barked again. *I have to get out of here.* Anna ran down the hill, yelling the entire way. *Fuck you, God. Fuck you, universe. I need hands! Hands!*

At home she could not bear the bedroom. *I have nowhere to go but down.* So she did. Down the basement stairs and around the corner to the root cellar. The floors were dirt and the walls smelled like rotten apples. She shrank into a corner and fell asleep on the ground. It was the farthest away she could get from the awful Eye of God.

FROM URSULA'S BEDROOM, POLLY Jean began to cry. Anna moved to stand but Ursula, queen of intervening that night, told everyone once more to stay put and came out from the kitchen and passed through the dining room on her way to get the baby. Bruno and Anna nodded in concert as she passed, an irrelevant display of marital unity. When Ursula returned just a moment later she carried a sniffling Polly in her arms. Again, in unison, both Anna and Bruno held out their arms to receive her. Bruno was closest. Ursula gave Polly Jean to him. Bruno sat the baby on his lap and turned her toward the table. The sniffling stopped when Polly saw the cake. She reached for it but Bruno said no and pushed it out of grabbing distance. Polly Jean whined and tried for it once more before giving up. She was too tired to fuss, even for cake. Bruno drew the baby closer to his body. Polly Jean yawned and sighed, then closed her eyes.

"I think she just wanted to be with the rest of us," Mary said. "She didn't want to be all by herself locked in that dumb old room!"

Anna watched her husband and her daughter. Her heart shattered. She hadn't wanted to be a mother. But she was a mother. A version of a mother. And Bruno was a father. But he wasn't Polly Jean's. But he was. Bruno kissed her head. *Look how much he loves her.* Had she noticed that before? Anna wasn't sure that she ever thought to notice. *Nobody wants to be locked up alone in a room.* But Anna did. She'd arranged her life in just that way. A secret serves no purpose but to isolate, Doktor Messerli had said. At the time Anna disagreed. But the Doktor was right.

Alone, alone.

Anna ate more cake and tried to swerve herself back to a center.

But every time the conversation shifted, so did Anna's equilibrium. And she had run out of cake on her plate when they came back around to the subject Anna had thought they'd dropped an hour earlier.

"You know, I honestly can't get over how unlike either of you Polly Jean looks. Did you bring the wrong baby home from the hospital?" Mary teased. She intended no ill will.

She smiled when she spoke. Mary almost always smiled when she spoke. She couldn't be cruel if she tried—she wouldn't know where to begin. Still, Anna's gut soured. The more Mary talked, the queasier Anna became. Bruno winced, but only Anna noticed it. "She's absolutely gorgeous, of course. Made of porcelain—and that raven hair!" Bruno drummed the table with his thumb. "What funny tricks genetics play!" Anna smiled weakly. Bruno didn't smile at all. But Bruno rarely smiles, Anna reasoned. There was no sense in reading into it now.

When Mary ran out of things to say, the dining room assumed a stiff, stifling pall. Mary took her plate in hand and ate the last bite of her second piece of cake. "So dang delicious!"

Ursula had returned to the table in the middle of Mary's prattle. She had nothing to add to the conversation but a blank-faced witness. Polly Jean twitched in her sleep like dogs do when they dream. Mary hummed to herself and licked the icing from her fork. Anna could hear the program Victor was watching in the other room. Anna looked to Mary, to Ursula, to Polly Jean and Bruno both, to the ceiling, and then to the floor, and then to her own hands, which she had begun unconsciously to wring. *The mistakes I've made, I can't unmake.* She'd had a simple evening's reprieve from tears. But they'd returned. They fell straight and fast from her eyes. Cold, slick round tears that were large enough to bounce on the table. Mary reached to stroke Anna on the shoulder but Anna dodged her touch.

Polly doesn't look like Bruno. Who cares? It had never

been an issue before. Why tonight? Anna couldn't think while being watched. She squeezed her eyes closed and searched the darkness for the answer. She couldn't find it.

But then she did.

It was a name she'd never heard before. But Bruno spoke it easily, immediately, plainly. Without hesitation. *Rolf.* It was a ready reply. As if he'd rehearsed it. As if he'd thought it through.

Jesus Christ, he's thought it through.

Anna stood quickly enough to dizzy herself. She stepped back from the table and stumbled over her own feet. Mary caught her.

"Oh, Anna. You don't have to go. It's okay to cry in front of us." Mary took her hand. "Do you want me to—"

"No." Anna cut her off. Whatever it was, she didn't want it. "I need . . . alone." She couldn't even form a full sentence. Bruno's stare was unreadable. "I'm sorry." The apology was compulsive and redundant. Anna backed out of the room, then left the house, then ran all the way back to Rosenweg.

22

ANNA STOOD BY THE STAIRS IN THE ENTRYWAY FOR SEVERAL seconds before she remembered how to remove her coat. When she finally recalled the process of letting her arms slip from their sleeves, she let the coat fall to the floor, not bothering to pick it up or hang it on its hook. Bruno hated that sort of carelessness. It sets a bad example for the boys, he'd say. *But he can't say that anymore,* Anna thought. *We only have one.* She stood in the entry a few seconds longer and then went into the kitchen in the hopes that she hadn't forgotten how to make tea.

She turned the radiator to its highest setting and then filled the kettle with water, put it on the stove, and then fished around in an open cabinet for a mug. *Yes.* Anna felt a little better. *I remember how to do this.* The tears had stopped but her face flushed with embarrassment. It shriveled her, breaking apart like that. *Should I go back to the party?* She decided against it. Surely they understood that her heart was bruised and tender and it pained when pressed on and was hideous to see. *Of course they do.* She made a silent wish that Bruno and

Polly Jean and Victor would stay at Ursula's a little while longer. She wanted to be alone with her devastation. Mary would understand, too, why Anna deserted them. *I'll call her tomorrow,* Anna thought, though she knew that Mary would likely telephone her first.

"Anna."

She hadn't heard Bruno come into the kitchen. She hadn't even heard him come into the house. His voice startled her; she dropped the mug. It broke into two large pieces and several smaller ones. "Jesus Christ, Bruno." Her heart throbbed a dozen times at once. "You scared me." Anna never had any great tolerance for surprises, and now, every ambush was mantled with an overlay of terror. She bent to pick the larger pieces up. The bending took the last of Anna's energy. "The kids?"

"Grosi's."

"Oh." Victor had spent more nights at Ursula's in the last month than he had the entire year before. Of course he had. Half of his own room belonged to a ghost. They hadn't taken out Charles's bed. They hadn't given away his clothes. They couldn't bring themselves to. Victor wasn't ready either. Mornings, when Bruno went to wake him, he would find Victor asleep atop Charles's mattress, his head upon Charles's pillow and his body underneath Charles's blankets and sheets. This was how Victor consoled himself. Bruno's plan was to swap the boys' bedroom with Polly Jean's, but he hadn't done it yet. It was a good idea, Anna agreed. Victor had nightmares in that room. He slept better at Ursula's. And he needed the sleep so deeply. And the nights he spent away from home relieved Anna from the trauma of watching him grieve. It was a selfish relief that Anna knew better than to share.

Anna turned to the trash bin with the pieces of mug in her

hand but stopped to wonder whether ceramic was recyclable. Then she wondered why she didn't know. Then she decided she didn't care and simply threw the pieces in the garbage can. "Mary leave?" Anna filled the air with words, dodging silence. Bruno came all the way into the kitchen and stood between Anna and the stove with his arms folded across his chest and gave a strangely civil nod. Anna was exasperated. "You're in my way."

Bruno didn't move. "How long?" The inquiry was blunt.

"For the tea? How long does it usually take? Two minutes?"

Bruno ticked his head once to the right, once to the left, then centered it again. "How long?" Bruno's speech was metered. Anna responded by not responding. "Who is it, Anna?"

"Who is what?"

The kitchen grew nervous. "I want to know his name."

Anna wasn't ready for this. "No, Bruno. Just . . . no." Anna had a headache. She closed her eyes and rubbed her temples with her hands and tried to figure out whose name Bruno wanted to know. There were several to choose from.

It's an otherworldly moment when the curtains behind which a lie has been hiding are pulled apart. When the slats on the blinds are forced open and a flash of truth explodes into the room. You can feel the crazing of the air. Light shatters every lie's glass. You have no choice but to confess.

"Yes. Now. Was it Archie?"

Anna did what she could to maintain herself. "This is getting old." Anna's voice sharpened. "I haven't—"

Bruno cut her off. His drill-bit stare bored through her. "You're lying to me. Who? Tell me a name. Now." Anna couldn't summon a reaction. For two years she'd been afraid of getting caught. And now he'd caught her. Sort of. *How much does he know?* She wasn't sure. *How does he know it?* She wasn't going to ask. *What happens now?* This, she would have to wait to find out. Anna separated herself from her situation by throwing down questions like sandbags and hiding behind them. *What's he going to say next? What should I say back to him? Are we breaking up? What will he do?*

What Bruno did next was repeat himself, but in a louder voice. He wasn't yelling, but he didn't need to. Even calm, Bruno's voice sustained an underlying boom. When angry, it shook with a tense, hateful rattle. He stopped to breathe after each word: *You. Are. Lying. Anna.* A corset of fear cinched her body into smallness. She didn't know what had tipped her hand.

Everyone has a tell.

"Stop it. You're scaring me." Anna took a step back. One step farther and she would have nowhere else to move. "Let's just please talk about this tomorrow. I feel sick." It was a plea Anna knew he wouldn't hear. Bruno stepped into the space where Anna had just been standing. And then he took another step, forcing Anna to the wall. He spoke directly into her face. "When did it start? How far back does it go? Is Victor a little bastard too?" Anna replied with silence. The sum of her efforts went into trying not to tremble.

Bruno grabbed for her hand but she pulled it away. They repeated that process until he caught it. He isolated the finger on which she wore her mother's ring and tried to wrench it off. Anna yelped. "What about Charles? Who's his fucking father?"

Stop please stop it please please stop! Anna tried but couldn't speak so she thought as loudly as she could. *You're hurting me, Bruno! Don't! Please don't!*

Bruno moved in close enough to kiss her. His hazel eyes were brown that night, his pupils so black they almost glowed. Anna's own eyes, flush with tears, asked *How?* and *Who else knows?* and, once more, *How?* Bruno offered little in the way of explanation. "You are a terrible liar and I know everything about you." Bruno pulled once again on the ring. It caught on Anna's knuckle. On the third attempt he yanked and twisted hard and then the ring was in his hand. Anna howled and tried a hopeless moment to pull free. She caught the comedy in her attempt. Bruno's strength and size had always overpowered her. This was partly why she fell in love with him. A version of love for him. A version of love for a version of him. Bruno held the ring very close to her face. Anna's eyes were infantile; they couldn't find a focus. The three pretty stones blurred into one. He shook the ring before her. "This is trash."

Telling the truth felt like the moment's worst plan. *You're wrong!* Anna cried. *What are you talking about?! Who's a bastard?! Polly's your daughter!* Such poorly chosen words. They pushed Bruno to his edge. He cut her off again. Bruno was Swiss. Bruno was self-contained. Bruno was cranky and gruff and distant and precise but he'd never, never been truly violent. In jealousy he could be bitter and cold. In anger he was rough. Rough, yes. He'd been rough before. In the kitchen Bruno was beyond anger. "Who is it? How many? Tell me their names." Anna shook her head: *No, no!*

It happened very fast. Bruno grabbed Anna by whole handfuls of her hair. She struggled but her effort was awkward. He pulled her toward him and then just as quickly shoved her away, then slammed her head against the kitchen's wall behind her. Once, twice, she struck the stone. Bruno yelled unintelligibly—he'd finally raised his voice. Anna couldn't understand a word. He was speaking Swiss and English simultaneously. He pulled her back toward him one final time, shook her, slapped her face, and then threw her to the floor as if she were something vile in his hands. As she fell, Anna caught her chin and cheek on the corner of the new dishwasher and hit the ground nose first. Bruno watched her fall, sniffing back tears. The kitchen was nothing but tears. Bruno muttered a curse that came out as a sob and wiped his nose on the back of his hand. As he left the kitchen, he tossed the ring at Anna's head. It landed near Anna's face with a cheery, casual *cling*.

Anna reached for her nose. It was bloody. Possibly broken. It hurt too much to palpate for the break. She moved her hands to the back of her head, which was also bleeding and the ache of it pounded, threatening the blindness of pain. She considered an attempt to stand but discarded it. She reached for her ring and tried to push it back onto her swollen, abraded finger. She couldn't get it past the knuckle so she let it drop back to the floor.

She didn't know how to get up. Her muscles had forgotten movement in the way that earlier her mind had forgotten the steps required to remove her coat. She resigned herself to the floor until both strength and a clear plan of action presented themselves. Two, three, five minutes passed. So Bruno knew. *Huh,* she thought. Then nothing more. The water roiled. The kettle whistled. She let it. With nothing else she could have done, Anna fell into a version of sleep on the kitchen floor.

* * *

Two weeks after Charles's death, Edith arrived in Dietlikon unannounced with a small pot of violets, a bottle of wine, and a box of chocolate candy. It was a shallow combination of gifts. *Like she's picking me up for a date,* Anna thought.

"You're not dressed? Anna! It's nearly one o'clock!" No, Anna wasn't dressed. It hurt her skin to wear clothes. It hurt her head to pick them out of the closet. It hurt her heart to move through the world of the living as if nothing had happened. As if nothing had fundamentally changed. Edith followed Anna into the living room and Anna returned to the same corner of the couch she'd spent two weeks attempting to hide inside of. She picked a blanket off the floor and pulled it up to her chin. It was stained. With what, Anna did not know. Edith played at being wounded. "Aren't you going to offer me something to drink?"

Anna pointed to the kitchen. "Help yourself." Edith set the chocolate and the flowers on the coffee table and took both the bottle of wine and her blasé attitude into the kitchen. Anna tried to be offended. Being offended would distract her. But Anna wasn't ready to be distracted yet. There were pains she still needed to feel.

Edith returned with a single glass of wine. "Oh, did you want one?" Anna shook her head no as Edith plopped down on the couch's opposite end and let out a protracted sigh. As if she'd just done something difficult. As if being in Anna's presence was almost too demanding to bear. She made the worst small talk. "I'm sorry I haven't been by." Anna told her it was fine. "The girls. I took them to Paris. We'd planned it months ago." Edith trailed off.

"I know," Anna said, her voice empty of affect.

Edith nipped at her wine. "So. I'm still seeing Niklas."

"Are you." It wasn't a question.

Edith cleared her throat. "Yes. Thrilling as ever." Anna returned an odd, inquiring series of blinks and wondered why if it was so thrilling did Edith speak of the affair so parenthetically. "The whole ruse of it, Anna. Ha! I feel like a spy! So scheming! I love it! And it's not just about the sex. It's not even mostly about the sex." Edith bit her bottom lip. "How about that?" The realization surprised her.

It hadn't been just about the sex with Anna either. "Where do you go?" Anna didn't really care. They were words to decorate the air. That was all.

"To fuck? I dunno. Lots of places. Many places. His apartment. A hotel. At the house—well, just once at the house—how forbidden! We had a weekend on the Bodensee three weeks ago."

"What did you tell Otto?"

"I told him I was going away with Pauline."

"Who's Pauline?"

"Nobody. She's imaginary. I invented her. But if it ever comes up—which it won't—I know Pauline from one of the clubs I lie about belonging to."

"Okay." Anna chewed on a fingernail. "How do I know her?"

"Silly Anna," Edith feigned exasperation. "You don't. She's one of *my* friends. You've just heard me talk about her. But only a little." Anna nodded an assent.

The room was almost entirely quiet but for the sound of wine being swallowed, the whisper of twill rubbing against twill as Edith crossed then uncrossed then recrossed her legs, and the rustle of the blanket under which Anna shivered.

"What do you think would happen if Otto caught you?"

"If he caught me?" Edith repeated Anna's question. "I haven't thought about it. I don't plan on getting caught."

"Edith?"

"Mmm-hmm." Edith telegraphed a waxing boredom.

"What would you do if one of the twins died?"

"Jesus, Anna. Are you serious?" Anna shrugged. Edith sipped her wine once more and put on a cheeky face. "Good thing I have a spare, I guess."

"Edith?"

"What is it now?"

"You really aren't a very good friend."

Edith looked into her wineglass. "I know," she said. It was an admission without scruple or reproach.

SHORTLY AFTER BEGINNING THEIR affair, Stephen attempted to end it. "You're surrendering to an attack of ethics now?" Anna asked. She was naked when she asked it.

Stephen hung his head and looked away from Anna as he buttoned his shirt, as if dressing himself was an act of contrition. "I'm just not sure this is a good idea."

Of course it's not, Anna thought, but said, "Of course it is!" Stephen squinted and tilted his head. He was waiting for an explication. She sighed. "Don't you like me?" She had wanted to say "love."

"Of course I like you." He said it plainly. The way someone would announce his fondness for a sandwich or a pair of shoes. *Yes, it tastes just fine. Most certainly they fit.* Any other woman might have understood this as a signal. Anna took it as a challenge.

"It's because I'm married?"

"Well, you are. It's adultery."

"Well then it's a good thing we're adults," Anna said. And then, "What's that have to do with anything?" It had everything to do with everything, but Anna underplayed it. She didn't care. Her marriage had stopped mattering. *Well, it's starting to not matter, that's enough.*

Anna found the loophole they were looking for. "I wouldn't worry about it. Technically you're not the adulterer. I am." Anna eyed Stephen with a deliberately threadbare gaze. She waited, but he didn't counter her argument. They sat together on the edge of his bed in a near reverential silence for almost a minute before Anna dressed and left.

On the train ride home, as Anna relived the day's lovemaking in her mind, she realized, in retrospect, that it had been more tentative than usual.

"IN GERMAN, AN ACTION that is done by one's own self to one's own self requires a reflexive verb. A reflexive verb is always accompanied by an accusative personal pronoun. To get dressed. To shave. To bathe. To clear your throat. To catch cold. To lie down. To feel either well or poorly. To fall in love. To behave. You are the object as well as the instigator. You do these things to yourself."

THE KETTLE HAD LONG since whistled itself empty when Bruno came back into the kitchen and took it off the burner. Anna opened her eyes and watched his boots shuffle around her head. Her own feet were hot in her shoes. They'd landed against the radiator when she fell. She didn't know how long she'd been asleep.

Anna tried to rearrange her feet and attempted to push herself up from the floor but she didn't have the muscle for it. She made a noise that couldn't be interpreted as words. Bruno stepped over her and moved to the sink. He turned on the water, then turned it off almost as quickly. Anna tried once more to rise. "Stop," he said. It was an aggravated command. He crossed over her two, three more times, moving with purpose. Anna didn't know what he was doing. She heard a drawer open and close and the faucet being turned on again, then off once more. Then Bruno knelt down by her head. Anna flinched against his approach. "Stop it," he repeated, and reached his hand toward her trembling face and laid a wet, cool cloth to the bruised side of it. "Hold this." Anna did as he told her. "Come on."

He put his hands under her arms and against her deadweight managed to turn her over and sit her up. She moaned as he leaned her against the same wall he'd thrown her into. "Does this hurt?" Bruno held her by the jaw and turned it toward better light and ran a finger along the ridge of her nose, which was still bleeding.

"Yes."

"It doesn't feel broken." It was a clinical statement. "Put your arms around my neck." Bruno took one of her arms and hooked it over his shoulder. Anna followed suit with the other one. "Stand up," he ordered, even as he was pulling her to her feet. He put an arm around her waist and held her as she steadied herself. The room jerked and Anna dropped the washcloth.

"Come on." Anna didn't have a choice but to follow him as he led her out of the kitchen and into the bathroom.

Bruno flipped down the toilet seat and positioned Anna on top of it. "Can you sit up?" Anna shook her head no, so Bruno angled her sideways and, as in the kitchen, leaned her against the wall. Anna would have laughed but for the ache in her ribs. *So much of me has been so frivolous,* Anna thought. *So very laughable. Ha, ha.* Anna was light-headed and loopy. She let her weight fall into the green tiled wall. She was suspicious of the architecture of the room but had no choice other than to trust it.

Bruno turned his back to her, put the stopper in the drain, and ran water into the tub. Anna asked again where the children were; Bruno had told her but she'd forgotten. Bruno didn't answer. Instead he swiveled back around to face her. He reached for Anna's left foot and removed her shoe and her sock and then set her foot back down. He repeated the process with the right foot. Then he helped her stand.

Her legs were jelly; she put her hands on his shoulders for support. Bruno unfastened her jeans, unzipped them, and pulled them down. "Step out." It was a tedious procedure but Anna did it without falling. Next came her panties. Anna wore a black thong with a satin bow. Under the circumstances, her underwear seemed obscene. Between the pain and her remorse, or a variable combination of the two, Anna started crying again. Her sweater was more difficult to remove. It caught on her nose as Bruno pulled it over her head. "Hush," he said again. It was not meant to console her. Anna wasn't wearing a bra. Bruno helped Anna into the tub with the same lack of ceremony with which he'd undressed her.

"Is it warm enough?"

"No." Anna reached to adjust the faucet but Bruno pushed her hand away and did it for her.

"Better?"

Anna nodded.

Bruno wet a washcloth and wrung it out and began to dab away the blood on Anna's face. He parted her hair. She was still bleeding where her head had hit the wall. "It'll be okay," Bruno said. He was looking at the floor when he said it. *He's hurt me more than he meant to,* Anna thought. She reached around to touch it but Bruno stopped her. "Lie down." He leaned Anna slowly back into the now-warm water before turning it off. He pushed her farther down. "We should wash your hair," Bruno said, reading her thoughts. The water around Anna's head turned pink. *It's like he's baptizing me. I'm washed in the blood.* Anna didn't know if she'd been baptized. She never asked her parents and they never said one way or the other so she assumed she hadn't been. Bruno and Anna had baptized all three of their children, but they'd done it simply out of custom and for the benefit of Ursula, who'd urged them to. Bruno sat Anna back up and gave her a perfunctory shampoo. He rinsed her hair with the handheld sprayer. Anna winced against the pressure of the water and the sting of the soap.

"You're fine," Bruno said as he took her face in his hand and, as in the kitchen, turned it back and forth to look at it in the bathroom's strong light. "You'll have a bruise." Anna blinked. Bruno reached behind himself for a towel and rolled it into a neck bolster and then he helped her lie back once again. He stood and looked down on her in the bath. Anna closed her eyes and fished the washcloth out of the water and put it over her face. The light was so bright that she imagined her every guilt was visible. "You'll be okay," Bruno said a final time as he left her alone in the bath, flipping the light switch as he pulled the door shut.

This was as close to an apology as Anna would get.

DOKTOR MESSERLI TRIED, ONCE, to explain Jung's concept of the shadow to Anna. "In the physical world a shadow is the dark shape that forms behind anything that light shines upon. A place where light—at present—isn't. In analysis we equate consciousness with light. Therefore, unconsciousness finds its parallel with darkness. Simply, the shadow is formed of what a person doesn't consciously know about herself. The self's unattended aspects. Places where consciousness—at present—isn't."

"The dark parts. The sinister parts." Anna bowed her head.

Doktor Messerli hemmed. "The unknown parts. The shadow isn't inherently negative. But yes, a negative shadow is very destructive. It will rarely be experienced as an intentional response or a rational force. It is an unconscious reflex. You don't control it. What stays in shadow controls you."

Doktor Messerli spoke with slow, dire counsel. "The result of not working toward consciousness is isolation. Instead of real relationships you'll have imagined ones. The less embodied you are in your conscious life, the blacker and denser your shadow will be. You have no wish to succumb to a negative shadow. And yet"—Doktor Messerli weighed the outcome of every statement that might possibly follow—"the effect of a compulsion is rarely positive. What conscious person would jump into a shark-infested sea? Who would eat glass? Who would shiver when she could so easily be warm? No conscious person would."

"So it's bad."

Doktor Messerli pulled back. "Not exactly. The shadow's potential to destroy is undeniable. Lightning might strike a house and set it ablaze. But harness the electricity and the same house can be illuminated with the turn of a switch. Consider a vaccine. Included in the serum is a small amount of the disease. Light needs the dark. It is the order of the universe. What would thaw in the spring if we didn't have a winter to endure? Consciousness is conditioned against its absence, Jung wrote. Amputate the serpent's tail and the power to heal lies within." Anna nodded. She tried to understand.

"All self-knowledge begins in the shadow's black rooms. Enter those rooms, Anna. Address the shadow face-to-face. Ask your questions. Listen to the answers. Respect the answers. The shadow will tell you everything. Why it is you hate. Who it is you love. How to heal. How to sit with sadness. How to grieve. How to live. How to die."

WHEN ANNA FIRST BEGAN to journal, her writing was intentionally rough. Doktor Messerli had challenged her to write like that, automatically and without judgment and self-editing. Anna was to let her thoughts flow unimpeded. In a rare instance of concession, Anna took the Doktor's advice and did as she counseled her. The resulting entries were hurried and overblown and her handwriting was illegible. But this was how it was done, she was told, and this is how she would try to do it. And it was good to have a place to let it all loose. The page was her sole confidant. *My soul confidant,* she thought. After

Charles's death, Anna's prose slowed and her already abstract logic grew more nebulous.

And what is a Swiss flag but a white cross swimming in a sea of red? I've no place to go but insane. Like trying to find your glasses without your glasses: impossible. Like a cell phone's incorrect predictive text: wrong, wrong, wrong. Like massaging a broken bone: it's done because it must be done. A blessing, a curse upon me. I merit every ache.

I want nothing more to do with my life.

An hour after leaving her alone in the bathroom, Bruno returned to help her out of the tub. The water had cooled. Anna had unrolled the towel underneath her head and used it to cover herself, out of shame and shivering alike. She had worked the whole dark hour on willing her mind to empty. She hadn't succeeded, but the attempt filled the time and distracted her from the pain.

She couldn't figure it out. *I know everything about you.* Anna doubted that was true but wasn't going to ask for specifics. As if he would have given them to her. That's how he always handled the boys. *You know what you did. Now go to your room.* The wondering was part of the punishment. How much did Bruno actually know? Anna was going to have to live without that answer.

Bruno was the only father Polly Jean had ever known. *And she's the only daughter he's ever had.* People parented children who were not their genetic offspring all the time. He loved her. Adored her. Was that so unusual? He would do anything for her. Would maintain every appearance for her. Would swallow his pain for her. For Victor and Charles.

For Anna.

Whom he loved. Truly, deeply loved.

Bruno helped her stand and then wrapped her in a towel and dried her off. She felt like a child. Bruno was neither tender nor rough. He toweled her down noncommittally. He'd brought a nightgown—Anna's favorite, she noted—into the bathroom with him and instructed her to lift her arms as he dressed her. He pointed past the bathroom's open door into the bedroom. "Can you walk by yourself? Lie down. I'll be in soon." Anna did as Bruno instructed her. She was the queen of compliance.

A few minutes later Anna heard the thin, airy siffle of the teakettle. *I was making tea and then . . .* She let the thought wander off. Another minute passed and Bruno was at Anna's bedside delivering the cup of tea she might have prepared two hours earlier. Bruno set it on the nightstand. Anna sat up weakly. "Here." Bruno offered an open palm. In it were three small pills.

"Three?" They were the pills Doktor Messerli had most recently prescribed. Anna had only taken a few, and no more than one at a time. But she took the pills from Bruno's hand, put them in her mouth, and washed them back with a sip of tea. "Bruno," Anna started.

He shook his head. "We're not going to talk about this tonight." And then he left the room and shut the door. Anna set the cup on the nightstand and let her body become the bed. *Help me, help me, help me,* she cried into her pillow. Her eyelids were swollen and sore. She repeated her plea until the pills began to soften her resolve to remain vigilant and her consciousness retreated into a lonely place inside that didn't have a name.

Then she fell asleep.

23

THE COLOR OF A FLAME WILL TELL YOU ITS TEMPERATURE. Yellow flames are coolest. The hottest flames are white. They are called dazzling flames. Red fire is not as hot as blue. The record for the hottest on-earth temperature is 3.6 billion degrees. It was reached in a lab. How is that possible? That's hotter than the center of the sun. Each year, two and a half million Americans report burn injuries. Suttee is the religious suicide of a Hindu widow. Self-immolation is a frequent form of protest. Every ancient culture had a fire god: Pele, Hephaestus, Vulcan, Hestia, Lucifer, Brigid, the Mesopotamian god Gibil, the Aboriginal goddess Bila, Prometheus. Domestic control of fire began 125,000 years ago. No modern country allows execution by burning. Smoldering is the slow, low, flameless form of combustion. God appeared to Moses in a bramble of fire. An intumescent substance swells when it's exposed to heat. Gretel pushed the witch into the oven where she died. Ash is the solid remains of fire. Incineration is the act of making the ash, and fire, if you'd care to be poetic about it, is ash's mother. Under rare conditions, fire will make a tornado of itself, a whirling vortex of flame. When struck against steel, a flint edge will produce sparks. The flame that tortures also purifies. Not all fires can be fought.

24

Anna snapped out of sleep. The trio of pills she'd taken the night before had all three worn off at once, and in the manner of slices of bread when a toaster's timer has run down, both eyes blinked open at the same time and Anna was awake.

The house was in a still and somber mood. The floorboards did not speak. The walls didn't breathe. The house on Rosenweg was made of quiet. This was unusual. Even with the windows closed, mornings were typically noisy with birdsong and cars and people walking up and down the street. But Anna heard nothing that day. The silence was sobering. She figured it for an aftereffect of the pills.

Her eyes found first their focus, and then the clock. It was just before seven. The bells would ring soon. *I will lie here until the bells ring.* Anna's head thumped. She would wait for the bells, then rise. *What day is it?* It was Friday. She would allow herself the indulgence of waiting on the bells.

When they came, Anna rose. She moved at an invalid's pace; each step made her wince. It took a full minute to shuffle into the bathroom. The absoluteness of the morning had been her imagination. Dietlikon was as busy as Dietlikon ever was. A man walking three sheepdogs passed by the house on his way up the hill. The postman was awake and at work. He zipped down Dorfstrasse on his yellow motorbike. He was a light-complexioned man in his upper twenties with a shaved head and a wide, silly mouth. For the first few months he'd worked this route, he'd been under the impression that Bruno and Anna were siblings, not spouses. In lumbering English he would flirt with her, ask where would she be that weekend, what she would be doing. Then, he would detail his own plans and end their interaction by mentioning how nice it would be if they happened to run into each other some evening out. Bruno eventually corrected him. *Why didn't you tell him I was your husband?* Bruno asked. *Why did you let him flirt with you?* Anna told him she hadn't realized he'd been flirting. Since then he'd kept a proper Swiss distance: ruthlessly polite but tediously reserved. He'd been their postman for five years. Anna learned his name once but she'd subsequently forgotten it and was too embarrassed to ask for it again.

Anna forced herself to look at her face. The area between her cheek and her nose had begun to purple; the socket of her eye—the entire eye, from beneath the lower lashes to above the brow—was a pale yellow green, awful as bile. Her finger was raw where Bruno had wrenched off the ring. Her arms and legs were sore but otherwise unharmed. Her face, though. She'd wear these bruises for a month.

This is my face, she thought. It was undeniable. That was she. She was that. It was the truest reflection she'd ever seen. Her perfect twin. Her doppelgänger.

Hello, Anna. Nice to meet you.

Bruno called her name from his office. When she didn't answer he came into the bathroom. He made a generous amount of noise as he approached in an effort not to spook her as he had the night before (but really, what more could be dropped, cracked, broken?). When he saw Anna's face in the mirror his own face fell. Anna had no reaction to this. Bruno patted her shoulder. "Get dressed. Come into the living room." His mouth was dry and his words scratched his lips as he spoke them.

"Okay," Anna said. Bruno returned to his office as Anna hobbled the several steps from bathroom to bedroom.

The day was gray. Pants would have been most practical, but Anna felt prettiest in skirts and rare was the occasion that dressing well didn't make her feel at least a little better. *Such frippery.* The question was not irrelevant. Is it wise to dose oneself with the medicine of foolish vanities? *Yes,* she thought. Then, *No,* when she rethought it. *A dress, a man, whatever. They cover you, you hide in them.* Then Anna shook all philosophies from her head and began to rifle through the Kleiderschrank. *I will take what comfort I can get.*

The blurry details of the night before began to sharpen at their edges and a picture came into focus. *Bruno beat me,* she thought plainly as if this were a fact she'd only just then realized. *He beat me badly.* Anna looked at herself in the bedroom mirror to see if anything in the last minute had changed. *Oh, Anna. You had this coming,* she thought. Anna knew there was something broken in her line of reasoning. No one ever has it coming, of course. *But . . .* she wasn't the textbook example of a battered wife. She hadn't been victimized into believing she deserved what she got. She decided it all on her own. In a violent, complicated world, Anna thought, it was a quick, lucid solution to a problem of have and lack. *I had this coming and I got what I deserved.* He'd never hit her before and he would never hit her again. Bruno wasn't a violent man. There was no pattern of abuse. *I brought this to myself. Myself, I provoked this.* Her face throbbed. She held on to these thoughts until she chose her clothes, setting the former to the side and picking up the latter. *There's only so much I can carry.* She dressed in a dark skirt, navy turtleneck, and gray tights. As she slipped on a pair of stylish flats she looked to the mirror yet again. Excepting the bruises, Anna looked pretty.

She was fastening her hair in an updo as she walked into the living room. She'd considered leaving it shaggy that she might better hide behind it. *What good would that do?* she decided in the end. *I've nothing left to conceal.* Bruno stared through the window at Hans and Margrith, who stood in front of their barn talking to the man with the sheepdogs, who had by then returned from his walk up the hill. Bruno turned around when Anna entered the room. He cleared his throat. "You look nice."

"Thank you." The mood was marked with politesse and grace. Both were nervous. Like blind dates at a prom. He had complimented her appearance and she thanked him. *Will he offer me a wrist corsage? Will we ride to the dance in a limousine?* But Bruno was not her date; he was her husband and she was his wife, and what Anna wanted most in that moment was to apologize, to explain, then to apologize again. For everything. And she did mean everything: every snide or damaged thought she'd had since the moment she stepped from the airplane into terminal E nine years ago. Every grudge she'd nursed while traipsing the hill behind their house in the middle of the night. Every lonesomeness, every terror. Every petty wound. Every social fear. Every desire. Everything, everything, everything. Every inevitability. Every mistake. The trouble with mistakes is that they rarely seem like mistakes when they are made. Sleep had set her right. She was prepared to name names. What use were secrets now? All had been knocked down. She stood in the rubble, ready to rebuild.

Bruno read this in her posture. "No." He interrupted before she even spoke. It was a sad, smooth no. "You have to leave."

Anna heard but didn't hear.

"You have to leave now." Bruno was calm and sad. His face was red, his expression complicated. He looked as if he'd cried all night. Anna turned her own face away. Next to the table was a small overnight bag that Anna only ever used when she'd be gone a day or two. She'd brought it to the hospital when the children were born. She hadn't gone anywhere since. It was zipped closed. Bruno had packed it.

"Oh."

Bruno took a step toward the bag and picked it up and handed it to his wife. It was light. *He doesn't want me gone for long. That's what this means.* For nine years Anna had fought against calling this house home. That morning the very last thing she wanted to do was to leave it. Irony of ironies. Neither Bruno nor Anna knew what to say next. Anna's window of apology had closed, and it seemed pointless to ask him to narrate his side of the story, from the general suspicions to the absolute facts. Anna broke the strained silence. "Are we . . . done?" "Done" wasn't really the right word. But it was the only one she could find.

Bruno answered truthfully. "I don't know." His voice was clothed in neutrality.

"The children?" Victor must have gone to school straight from Ursula's. But Polly Jean.

Bruno shook his head. "They don't need to see your face."

"Where will I go?"

Bruno sighed in a that's-for-you-to-decide way. It was a candid reaction. There was no flippancy here. The paradox of Bruno's frankness confused her. Everything about this moment was yielding and humane. This was the Bruno she'd wanted all along. But she had to betray him to get it.

"Oh," she said again but with less surety.

A second time Bruno cleared his throat. "Now, Anna." He moved toward her, put his hand on her shoulder, and guided her with slow ceremony to the door. He helped her with her coat and handed Anna her purse. And then he took her busted face cautiously in his hands and leaned into her and gave her a kiss. It was tender, meaningful, and it overbrimmed with grief. Anna didn't—somehow couldn't—kiss back. "Goodbye, Anna." His farewell landed with a heavy thud. A steel door closed behind it. He said he didn't know if they were done. But Anna knew. The kiss told her.

They were.

Bruno stepped back into the house and shut the door without locking it. He didn't look back.

GERMAN NOUNS ARE CAPITALIZED. WHY? *I don't know. They just are. Zürich is not the capital of Switzerland, Bern is. Bern and burn are near homophones. Capital also means money. Bruno works with money. You can't write Bruno without a capital B. The German alphabet has an extra letter called an Eszett. It looks like a capital B and sometimes it replaces a double s. In 1945 Germany's SS was banned, though this hardly has to do with grammar. Or does it? What, after all, is a grammar but a governing law? Order upon order, rule upon rule. Switzerland is so clean it even launders its money. Knock knock. Who's there? Alpine. Alpine who? When you're gone, Alpine for you. Said Wagner of Zürich's Grossmünster's towers: They look like peppermills. Wagner left Zürich when he fell in love with a woman who wasn't his wife. The Nazis loved Wagner. The Zürich Polizei wear their rifles like Gestapo. The standard issue Swiss Army rifle is a SIG SG 550. Dietlikon's standard, its coat of arms, is a six-point star on a banner of blue. The German word for star is der Stern. A star is stern, a moon is strict, the sky is serious business. Heaven is often unkind. You should never rely on the kindness of strangers. The kind-ness of strangers. They come in all sorts, like licorice. Das Kind. The German word for child.*

I miss them all. All of them. Every one.

ANNA STOOD IN THE street for a dumbfounded minute before walking away from the house and toward the *Bahnhof.* The neighbors had left, the postman had moved on, and Anna didn't know where to go. But all journeys begin at the train station. She arrived at the *Bahnhof* just past 7:45. She'd missed the S3 by two minutes. Six more minutes and she'd catch the S8. She'd been awake for less than an hour. This had all transpired in less time than it takes for a minute hand to circumnavigate the face of a clock.

What a funny thing time is. It's mutable. It speeds and it slows. It retreats and it attacks. But Swiss clocks boast the world's most unflinching precision. Incomparable accuracy. Exactness. Exactness is a form of truth. But nothing is exactly true. Truth, like time, is mutable. Both are *relative.* Both are *told*. When it's 7:45 A.M. in Zürich, it's 2:45 P.M. in Tokyo. Each city lives in its own hour. *Gleich und nicht gleich*. The same and yet not. The earth turns on an earth-sized axis. Everything oscillates. No one and nothing's exempt. The planet spins at an angled pitch. Therefore each day lasts as long as each day lasts. Hours are arbitrary. A minute may endure a thousand years. And an event can occur in an instant.

Anna rode to the Hauptbahnhof during morning rush. She stood near the doors and focused on looking through the window at the landscape. She kept her face angled to the ground. She didn't want to show it. Anna hadn't put on any makeup. The bruises weren't full blown, but if anyone cared to examine her, he'd find them. But the safest thing about a city is how inscrutable you become when you step into it.

She got off the train at platform 53 and walked almost a half kilometer down the Sihl before she realized she'd left both the small suitcase Bruno had packed for her and her purse on the train. She stuffed her hands into her coat pockets. All she had was her cell phone. *Now what?* Anna's purse and suitcase were now halfway to Pfäffikon. *Do I report this? Who to? Where?* Everything seemed so complicated. Day of all days. She couldn't think it through. But she tried and kept trying until something inside her shrugged *oh well,* whereupon she drew a deep, deliberate breath and kept walking south toward Löwenstrasse.

Anna wandered down Löwenstrasse without intent until she reached a tram stand. She took the last seat and when an elderly woman walked under the shelter, Anna didn't rise and offer her place. It didn't matter. A tram came and went and the elderly woman was gone as quickly as she had appeared. Anna took her Handy from her pocket and considered her legitimate options—there were so few. The obvious course of action was also the most correct and it presented itself first. *Mary. I'll call Mary.* Anna called. The phone rang but Mary didn't answer and Anna hung up before leaving a message. *I hate the telephone. I don't want to leave a message. What will I say?* Anna didn't have the luxury of neurosis that morning. She called again. Once more, the phone rang four times and then it went to voice mail. For the second time in a row, Anna did not leave a message. *Quit being an idiot!* she scolded herself. So rarely did Anna reach out for help that she wasn't sure how to do it. *Is that what I'm doing? Asking for help and failing?* She closed the phone and pressed it between her palms, as if the posture of prayer alone might make it ring. A minute later the phone trembled and an SMS came through. Anna avoided letting herself believe her prayer had anything to do with it. *Helping w/ Max's class—will call later. Hope you feel better. Am sorry you are sad. Am here for you. XO —M.*

But you aren't here for me, Anna thought. *You're there. And you aren't answering the phone.* Anna's thoughts had pity on her thoughts. She tried Mary a third and final time but the call went directly to voice mail. Mary had turned the phone off. Anna didn't leave a message. She hadn't figured out what to tell her in any case. She slipped the phone back into her pocket and stood up. An elderly woman—different from the one before—smiled thankfully and nodded as she slipped into Anna's chair. *She thinks I'm giving her my seat.* Anna wasn't but took credit for the good deed anyway.

Anna had wandered Zürich many times before. In the city she was alone with her sorrow in a different way than she was when she walked through the woods or sat on her bench. In the woods her sadness came to a sharp and undeniable point.

Every tree, every fallen log, every *Wanderweg* sign spoke aloud the same, sorry word: *alone, alone, alone.* In the city though, Anna's solitude was a blunt object, a rubber mallet. It drubbed on her. So when, in the clotted streets of downtown Zürich, loneliness attacked, she'd dissociate from it, slip into a fugue. *Where am I? How do I get home? I think I'm hungry. I've forgotten how to eat. What's my name?* At those times she distanced herself from herself and stood apart from her own volition in the most heinous of ways. A force (from within? from without? Anna could never tell) took charge and drove the bus of her where it willed. *Is this one of those days?* Anna asked herself. She didn't think it was. The wind blew some of her hair out of its barrette. She hadn't brought a hat. She pointed herself in the direction of the Bahnhofstrasse and walked with an unknown purpose, nothing but resignation and the ache of her face to compass her through the journey.

Anna's fondness for nice things notwithstanding, the conspicuous consumption of Zürich's Bahnhofstrasse had never wooed her. It was the too-muchness of it all. She couldn't see through it. But the day's gray climate made the shop windows shine. Everything invited her in. The designer eyeglasses showcased in the Fielmann window looked at her with a benevolent gaze, and the white, featureless mannequins in the Bally display appeared to be bowing with courtesy and grace. At the Beyer watch shop she leaned her forehead against the glass and (did she?) swooned over a 20,000 CHF vintage Cartier. Nine years in Switzerland and she'd never owned a nice watch. Anna let herself pine for a moment before moving on. She passed chocolate shops and toy stores. She passed the Dior and Burberry boutiques, the English-language bookstore, and several souvenir shops. She stopped at one and peered through the window. Postcards and T-shirts and glassware and maps and clocks and watches and Swiss Army knives. The knives pleased Anna. They were tools to implement, blades with uses. Of all the things she didn't love about the Swiss, their practical ingenuity wasn't one of them. Mary had said it about the handkerchiefs she'd given Anna for her birthday: *What good is a useful object if it can't be used?* The Swiss weren't just masters of accuracy, they were *Meisters* of use. This is why their clocks are categorical, their knives well whetted, their chocolate so toothsome, their banks so efficient. Anna was near Paradeplatz, home of the headquarters of UBS and Credit Suisse. It was inevitable; thinking of banks made her think of Bruno, but she wasn't ready to think very deeply on the subject of him yet. He'd known all along. All along he had known. Anna couldn't wrap her understanding around that so she didn't even try to. Instead, she let her focus shift from the knives in the window to the window itself. She saw her face in the glass and reflected on her reflection. She was otherworldly and misshapen. She could go anywhere she wanted. The going wasn't the problem. The problem was belonging where she went. This has been the issue from the beginning. It was near ten thirty A.M. She'd been aimlessly wandering for two hours. But she hadn't gone far at all.

Think, Anna, she implored herself. Mary wasn't available. Returning to Dietlikon wasn't an option. *Later, perhaps.* Anna clung to the possibility of later. If she couldn't go home, she couldn't call Ursula. Surely Bruno had told her everything by now or, if not everything, a version of events in which Anna still came off badly. She could call David and Daniela, but that was almost as embarrassing an option as facing Ursula. She opened up her phone and started scrolling through the names.

So many friends she did not have. All the distant relatives with whom she didn't keep in touch. School pals. Lovers.

Even as she was in the process of doing it, she knew that calling Edith wasn't a very good idea, and before Edith finished saying hello Anna felt an upswell of futility. *No way am I asking her for help. I'm not going to let her see me like this.*

"Oh. Sorry, Edith. I hit the wrong button." Anna covered.

"Ha! Well don't do it again!" Edith teased. "Make it up to me. Come into the city. I'm here already. You can buy me lunch."

Anna pretended to consider the possibility before declining. By instinct she looked over her shoulder. *Zürich's a big city, Anna. You won't run into her.*

"Suit yourself!" And with that Edith signed off. The conversation lasted less than half a minute.

You have to leave, Bruno had said. And Anna had left.

Anna crossed the bridge at Bürkliplatz and walked south along the bank of the Zürichsee. *I'll stay in the city today and then tonight, when he starts to miss me, I'll call. He'll want to make up. He'll feel bad. He feels bad already. I can go home and we can talk.* Bruno had been calm that morning, so calm. That was a worry Anna couldn't yet place. Going home was an option, but it was the last option on the list.

Anna was almost alone as she wandered down Seefeldquai. Most Züricher were at work, and tourism is thin during off-season. It was all right. She preferred it that way. The lake was gunmetal blue and unfriendly. Still, it soothed her. This was the Zürich she knew. The greater part of all comfort almost always lies in familiarity. A child's teddy bear. A favorite pair of shoes. In times of calamity we gravitate toward the things we know or know how to do. On the day of a funeral, it's the quotidian duty of bed making, dress ironing, dish doing that tethers a person to the physical moment and releases her temporarily from the territory of her pain. The comfort, therefore, was foremost the lake's gunmetal unfriendliness and secondly Anna's practice at being alone and wandering lonely paths. Were it otherwise, Anna would have felt worse.

She walked along the waterfront all the way to Zürichhorn, the small harbor where the Zürichsee begins to genuinely widen. She took a seat on the steps but they were cold even through her wool skirt so she stood up just as quickly. On clear days, the outline of the Alps separates the earth from the sky. *Eiger. Mönch. Jungfrau.* Indistinguishable but undeniable. And hidden in a mountain pass over the Schöllenen Gorge in Kanton Uri, the Teufelsbrücke, the Devil's Bridge. *Jungfrau.* Anna shook her head. *We plan and he laughs at our plans.* This is what the Doktor meant. All of this.

Anna turned around and walked back the way she came and with every step her stomach kinked and twisted. This was the misery she'd been trying to dodge all day. She supposed it was inevitable. A memory. Dozens of them. Times happy and terrible both. They came at her like diving birds. She couldn't fight them off. But even the terrible memories were happier than this. Anna felt helpless and very foolish. She walked past the Chinese Garden. In summer the rectangular thatch of land is crowded with families and sunbathers and picnickers. That day the field was empty except for a single young couple kissing near the gate, his hands under her jacket and her hands down the back of his jeans. A very old woman on a bicycle passed Anna on the left. She wore a dark skirt and thick tights and utilitarian shoes. She'd hidden her hair underneath a red and blue headscarf. She rang her bike bell as she passed. Anna was feebly amused. In the States, very old women didn't ride bikes lakeside on awful gray days. But Anna hadn't been to the States since she left them. Not even once. She'd had no one to visit and, like today, nowhere to go.

"There are two basic groups of German verbs," Roland said, "strong and weak. Weak verbs are regular verbs that follow typical rules. Strong verbs are irregular. They don't follow patterns. You deal with strong verbs on their own terms."

Like people, Anna thought. *The strong ones stand out. The weak ones are all the same.*

Anna's most recent appointment with Doktor Messerli would have been the day before, but she'd canceled. *I shouldn't have canceled. I need her. She's only ever tried to help me.* Yesterday was a century ago. *What would I have said to her?* They would have talked about Polly Jean's birthday and how sad Anna was and Anna would have asked whether Doktor Messerli thought the pain would ever go away. Doktor Messerli would have listened with compassion and responded as she so often did: *Vhat dooo yooo sink, Anna?* Anna checked the time on her Handy. It was a quarter after one. Doktor Messerli would be in her office. Anna could go there. She could tell her it was an emergency and the Doktor would see her. Of course she would. Wouldn't she? *Is this an emergency?* It wasn't a nonemergency, Anna was sure. It was already past lunchtime. Anna would have to figure something out. The Doktor would know what to do. *Yes, that's it. I'm going.* It was a reasonable, competent decision to have made.

Anna turned in several circles before she found her bearings and began the march toward Doktor Messerli's office. *Now, I must go now,* she thought, though she was already on her way. The closer Anna came to Trittligasse the faster she walked. A knot in her stomach tightened like a python around a pig. It was a caution Anna didn't heed. She walked faster. *Now. I must go. Now.* Panic began to replace the determination that had steered her from Utoquai to Rämistrasse. She ran the last quarter kilometer to Doktor Messerli's office, stopping only to peel herself off the ground after she tripped on the cobblestone steps at the west end of the street. She scraped her palms and ripped the knee of her stockings. She flashed back to that day in Mumpf, when she ruined her tights in the *Waldhütte* where she and Karl first fucked. *How did I become this?* She didn't need to speak it aloud. Every atom of Anna moaned. Her face throbbed and her soul reeled and she couldn't catch her breath.

By the time she reached Doktor Messerli's office, Anna was so manic that she wouldn't have been able to pass a sobriety test. She lurched. She could barely stand. She pressed the buzzer once and then decided once was not enough so she hit and hit and hit it as if she were clobbering a nail with the heel of a shoe even as she pulled her Handy from her pocket and attempted to reach the Doktor on the phone. It was beyond rude, Anna knew, the phoning and the buzzing alike. The Doktor was in a session. Appointments are sacrosanct, not to be interrupted. Anna knew she'd be pissed. But the day waned with every passing second and as Anna's options grew fewer, her worry simply grew. On the walk to Zürichhorn she had repeated it like a mantra: *I will be okay, I will be okay.* But by the time she fell on the cobblestone steps her cadence had stuttered and her incantation became *Will I be okay?* She had lost all talent for self-consolation. When the Doktor's phone went to voice mail, she went from frenetically poking the buzzer with her finger to maniacally pounding the door under the force of her fist. *Let me in, let me in, let me in, dammit.*

Eventually, Doktor Messerli opened the window and looked down. Anna was reckless and shaking, her whole body twitching like a muscle with an electrode attached to it. She couldn't see the Doktor's expression from three stories up, but her posture was angry and offended. Her glasses hung from her neck on a chain so she, in turn, wouldn't have been able to make out the wreck that was becoming Anna's face. As the day grew later it had started to swell. That might have made a difference. *If only she could see me!* Anna shouted an unintelligible plea. The Doktor cut her off, yelled back. Anna was to stop ringing the bell and leave immediately. The Doktor would phone her after her appointments at the end of the day. If Anna was in crisis then she needed to call 144 and have an ambulance take her to the hospital. Then Doktor Messerli closed the window with a mad, malicious slam. Anna didn't blame her. *But goddammit, I need help now.*

Anna's dread turned hard. Like a stone in her throat or a tumor. Aggressive and inoperable and terminal. The Doktor was firm in her counsel. *Dial 144. Wait for me to call you later. Either way? Leave. Now. Go.* The slammed window was the day's most definite answer.

Anna left the office.

IN THE DREAM *I am at a clinic with my mother. She is wearing a blue hat and her purse is filled with sandwiches. I can't help but laugh. This annoys her and she tells me so. When the doc-*

tor calls for us, he says I need an operation to fix my eye. I refuse to have it. My mother is angry. She threatens to force me into having the surgery by calling the police. I tell her to go ahead. She storms out of the office. I follow her but it's dark outside. I look for a while but give up and start for home, and in the darkness I lose my way. When I wake up I have forgotten that my mother is dead. It takes me almost half a minute to remember. When I do remember, I miss her terribly. More than I have in years, than I even have a right to miss her. I know it isn't, but all seems lost.

ANNA WALKED AWAY FROM Doktor Messerli's office in a stupor. The Doktor's rebuke had slapped Anna out of hysteria and into contrition, and almost immediately Anna felt like an ass.

She was halfway down Trittligasse when her Handy buzzed. It was Mary. Anna fumbled, opening the phone. "Anna. I am so sorry I couldn't talk earlier. I was in the classroom and—"

Anna interrupted. "It's okay." *It* is *okay,* she thought. *Mary will help me.* Anna spoke the next words painfully. "I need." She added no object. She was in need of many things. Help was only one of them.

"What do you need, Anna? Can I bring you anything? You're at home? Are you feeling better?" Anna tried to answer all the questions at once and the result was gibberish. Mary cut her short. "I'm having a hard time hearing you. I'm on the train. On the way to Dietlikon, actually. Tim's meeting me. We're going to that car lot by the Coca-Cola plant—you know where that is?" Anna did. It was just down the street from the train station. Until that point the Gilberts had been using a car-share service. But Mary, just the week before, managed to get her driver's license (*Can you believe it??? I know!!!* she said and said again to Anna) and with Tim so often gone and the Gilberts having now settled into a routine, they'd decided it was time to buy a car. "Can we drop over afterward? Are you at home?" she asked again. Anna tried to explain that she wasn't but the connection was weak and she didn't think Mary caught it. "Anna, I can barely hear you and we're about to go through a tunnel. We'll talk later. I am so glad you're feeling—"

The call was dropped before Mary could finish the sentence. Anna was left with Mary's good-intended but poorly timed wish: *I'm so glad you're feeling!* If only she knew. There was nothing in these feelings to be glad about. Mary had a driver's license. Mary was getting a car. Mary was volunteering at Max and Alexis's school. What else was Mary doing, having, being? When did this happen? Anna was jarred by Mary's progress. *Why her?* Anna searched for a pat response of logic or a Jungian truism that would situate (if not soothe) the sting of this defeat. *A defeat?* Anna self-reprimanded. *You really should be happy for your friend.* The poetic response to Anna's dilemma had to do with tribulation molding character the way that fire forges steel and how Anna—*Atta girl! Chin up!*—would pass through the flames, be purged of her flaws, and then she'd have earned her own grand and good reward. She, too, would learn to drive. She'd buy a car. She'd have a bank account! She'd be happy again. She'd be happy for once. But the regrettable truth came down to all and only this: Anna had already received her reward. Her reward was pain. And her character had already been forged. *I'm as good as I'm probably ever going to get.*

Anna wandered without aim for the next thirty minutes.

The interaction with Doktor Messerli had snapped Anna back from panic. But the outcome of her conversation with Mary served to kick her into the familiar fugue she'd walked away from on Bahnhofstrasse. *I'm running in circles. I'm back where I started.* That wasn't quite true. It wasn't a circle she ran in. It was a spiral. The near parallel arcs give an illusion of sameness. At each turn, though, she came closer to a center. Anna had moved through every quadrant of the emotional spectrum that day. There was no reason to believe that whatever had her in its hands was ready to let her loose. She harnessed her present calm and tried to clear what she could of her mind. She wanted to make lucid decisions while she could. And what she decided next was to go to Archie.

It was a decision that didn't require much forethought—she was already in the Niederdorf—but one that demanded a humility she might not have mustered but for the nearness of the shop and the ever-encroaching worry that come nightfall she'd have nowhere to go. Present need prioritized this possibility. Despite what had passed between them—perhaps even because of what had happened—she knew that he would absolutely take her in, at least for the night. They'd not spoken since the day at the zoo, and the last time she saw him was Charles's funeral. She'd go to Archie, he'd give her an icepack and a glass of Scotch and a place to sleep for the night. She did not dare to think beyond that. She looked up to the window of his apartment but it was closed. She'd deleted his number from her phone over a month ago so she couldn't call. *Who memorized phone numbers anymore?* Anna paced in front of the whiskey shop for ten minutes before finding the courage to go in. Even then, it wasn't courage that she rallied, but resignation.

A bell tinkled when she opened the door. A man who she presumed was Glenn stood at the counter. They'd never met. He was shorter than Archie and younger. But Anna could see the resemblance in Glenn's eyes and in his mussed, russet curls. He was going over an invoice, checking the list on his clipboard against a stack of boxes. Glenn looked up when Anna came in.

"Can I help you?" *Yes. Glenn will help me,* Anna thought. *He'll tell me where Archie is.*

Anna hadn't planned her words. She couldn't make a sentence. "Archie. Where?" Glenn narrowed his eyes and studied Anna's face. His stare was apprehensive.

"Ma'am, he's not here." His voice was even and polite.

Anna kept forgetting about her face. "Where's he?" Anna's own tone was crippled. She asked the question quickly and from an odd angle of inflection.

"Scotland. Comes back next week." Glenn looked her over. Her shoulders were hunched and the hand that held her phone trembled. Glenn's initial misgiving softened into concern for the strange woman in front of him. "Ma'am, is there something I can do for you? Are you okay, ma'am?"

Anna shook her head gently and chuckled. *This is pretty funny. So many failsafes, all of them failing.* No, there was nothing he could do.

"Sorry?" The laugh was up for interpretation.

"Nothing. I apologize for disturbing you." Anna stilted her speech to mask her disappointment, but that was all she had to say. Glenn called to her as she walked out the door, but Anna waved him off and kept walking. Outside the whiskey shop, Anna tightened the belt of her coat and wrung her hands. *Oh well. Oh well.*

It was colder than it had been before she went inside and yet she'd been in the shop for only a minute. The temperature was shifting as quickly as her mood. She laughed again. There was no other way to respond. Blackly funny, how her day was unfolding. How every avenue of escape was bricked up. How all of her choices were already ticked off an unseen list. Every option was bleak. *Now what?* She strained the ear of her heart to hear the answer. Nothing called back. Anna attempted to console herself. *There, there,* she coddled. *We'll figure this out. We will. We will!* In plural, she felt comfort. *Make it a game, Anna. Play along with this series of unfortunate coincidences.* Then again, in chorus, she reassured her selves: *There, there.* Anna sighed and headed south toward Stadelhofen.

Anna walked to Stadelhofen and then up the hill behind the train station and crossed through the small park behind the *Kantonsschule* and followed the s-curve of the street and turned left onto Promenadengasse and continued walking until she reached St. Andrew's Church, Zürich's English-speaking Anglican congregation. She'd been to this church before, three or four times in the early months of living in Switzerland when she was most lonely for company. But then Victor was born, and caring for an infant superseded her self-indulgent dolors. After that she met Edith and for a while hers was friendship enough. Anna circled the building until she came to the entrance. *Why not?* She'd walked in this direction without a conscious plan. But in she went. Anna wandered through the sanctuary and into the fellowship hall and down a corridor until she found an office she assumed belonged to the priest. The door was drawn but not closed. Anna pushed it open; she didn't bother to knock.

Medieval Christianity taught that there were eight, not

seven, deadly sins. The eighth sin was despair, and it was the only sin that could not be forgiven. For to despair is to deny the ultimate power and universal reign of God. Despair is complete disbelief, indulgent hopelessness, the repudiation of God's wisdom, his benevolence, his control. *Total depravity,* Anna thought. *Today's pain has always been mine. It's intended just for me.*

"I think I need help," Anna said. *Help.* It was the first time she'd said the word aloud that day. It didn't feel as good as she'd hoped and she wanted to retract it as soon as she said it.

The priest looked up from his desk with a start. "Oh!" He'd been typing an email and hadn't heard her come in. He scanned her face but couldn't place her as a congregant. He stood and held out his hand. Anna shook it limply. He gestured to an empty chair on the other side of his desk. He didn't blink at her bruises.

The priest was a short, very round older man with a tan face, a salt-and-pepper beard, and a Welsh accent. "Yes, of course. Let's talk." He smiled on her like a grandfather, though he couldn't have been more than fifteen years her senior. As in the whiskey shop, Anna hadn't planned what she was going to say. Each of the day's conversations had swerved in different directions. *I need to confess. I need him to take my confession.* She wanted to tell her story, her whole story, to someone. Bruno wouldn't hear it that morning. No one had ever heard it. *I'll tell the truth and he'll absolve me.* Anna took a hard breath and exhaled slowly, finding her courage. *I'll tell the truth. And all shall be well.*

But when she opened her mouth to speak, what tumbled out was a question.

"Do you believe in predestination?" They weren't the words she intended, but they weren't unfamiliar. She carried this uncertainty wherever she went.

"Do I? Or does the church?"

"You." She wanted to talk with a person.

The priest leaned back in his chair and considered his response. Anna's face gave him reason to take her seriously. He didn't ask her name. "Let's see . . ." He thought for a moment longer. "Okay, Miss." The priest rearranged himself in the desk chair and Anna smiled briefly when he addressed her as "Miss." "When you were a child, did you ever play with dominos? Did you set them in a line and topple them? Stack them? Push them over?"

"Yes."

"Of course. All that time spent putting them right, aligning them just so, and then with such a little push everything falls." Anna nodded. "Think of your life as a long line of dominos, yes? A chain of days and years. Every domino is a choice. This one is where you went to school. Here is the man you married. Here's the house you moved into. Here's the roast you cooked for Sunday supper . . ." The priest mimed setting up dominos with his hands. "Our lives are cause and effect. Even the smallest choices matter. One domino hits the other, and then the next and the next." The priest tapped the first invisible domino with his index finger and with that, the whole imaginary regiment pitched forward. Anna could almost hear the clink of bone-colored Bakelite as the array unzipped. "It's God who doles out the dominos. It is we who set them in line and tip them over. We have no control over the particular lot we're given. But we can choose how to arrange what we have. And we can choose to start over, when everything's been knocked down and broken. Do I believe in predestination? No. A foreordained eternity effectively puts me out of a job." He tittered and smiled at Anna, who tried to smile back.

It was a simple, sincere analogy built for a child. A kind truth spoken kindly, a kind man who spoke it. The tears she'd waited on all day finally welled in her eyes.

But as much as she longed to believe what the priest had said, she couldn't. Accidents that are fated to happen simply will. She'd wanted him to convince her otherwise. He'd come the closest of anyone.

The priest looked at her with sympathy. "Now," he continued, "can you tell me about the bruises?" Anna sniffed but didn't respond. He cleared his throat as he opened the bottom drawer of his desk and pulled out a file. He thumbed through the pages as he spoke. "I want to help you. But," he continued as he pulled a sheet of paper from the file, "I'm not sure that issues of doctrinal theology are among your most pressing concerns at the moment." His paternal voice was so soothing that it shattered her. "Perhaps it might be wisest if you consulted a professional." He passed the paper to Anna. It was a list of local English-speaking psychiatrists. Doktor Messerli's name was the fourth from the top. "Or, if you'd rather, I can call for you . . ."

Anna shook her head though without great conviction. *No, no, no.*

The priest was waiting on Anna to continue when a knock on the doorjamb caused both of them to turn and look. It was a tall, gaunt man with wide-set eyes. He looked over Anna's head without acknowledging her presence and began complaining to the priest about church music, organ repair, the choirmaster, the choir, and, in the end, the priest himself who hadn't answered an email of compelling urgency quickly enough. The man spoke impatiently; his voice was haughty and imperative.

The priest scowled at the man, who Anna assumed was the organist, who was tapping his foot and pulling a face of his own. The priest returned his gaze to Anna with continued sympathy. "I'm so sorry. Please. I'll only be a moment. Would you like some tea? I will bring you some tea." Anna blinked and the priest rose and left his office. She could hear him grousing at the organist as they walked down the hall, the click of their shoes on the floor growing less audible the farther away they walked.

Anna waited until she couldn't hear them anymore and then rose from the chair and left the office and slipped out of the church with the same sad ease she so often slipped out of her clothes.

So there it is. And there, just there, it was.

She walked back the way she came, past the high school, through the slim lip of city park above Stadelhofen, over the walkway, and down the swooping, skeletal staircase into the plaza in front of the train station, moving south toward the opera house and the lake.

She didn't even think twice once the idea occurred to her.

It was a number she'd never called. *What time was it?* It was just past three in Zürich. In Boston it was nine in the morning. She sat on the steps of the opera house. The phone rang twice before he answered.

"Stephen Nicodemus."

She hadn't rehearsed what she was going to say. There'd been no forethought to this call. It happened so quickly it was compulsive. She cleared her throat and pressed forward. "Stephen."

"Yes?"

"It's Anna."

"Anna?" She'd surprised him, that was clear. "Anna!" He repeated her name with brightness. Anna's heart lightened. "How are you?" His emphasis was on the "you."

"I'm . . ." She wasn't going to tell him how she was. She spoke through an imaginary smile. "I'm okay." There was relative truth in that. *Now or never, Anna. Say what you came to say.* "I've been thinking about you. I wanted to call and say hello. You know?" If he did, he didn't say so. "I miss you."

The dominos started to fall.

There was a crackle in the wireless connection. He was four thousand miles away and yet they were once again in the same room. The delay was empirical.

"I know. It was good." His voice was flat but earnest. Not cold, but matter-of-fact. *Good* was one of the last things Anna would have called it. Awful? Intense? Vexatious? Igneous? Lamentable? Productive? They had, after all, produced a child, though Stephen had no way of knowing that. But *good*? What was good about it?

"Yeah." Anna couldn't mask the letdown. She kept her words close. Their last conversation had been nothing but a chain of histrionics. The wind forced a hank of hair from its barrette as it had been doing all day. It flapped around her face.

Stephen sniffed. "Anna. I cared about you, you know that." He paused, not knowing what next to say. "You understand?" It was a question Anna heard as an imperative: *You. Understand.*

"Oh." Anna's mouth had been an open vowel all day long.

The conversation shifted. Anna willed it so. It was the quickest way out of the burning building, the least embarrassing, the one whereby she'd save the most face. She asked about his experiments, his work, what he was doing with himself. Stephen let it shift. He told her about his research. He also told her he'd gotten married and his wife was pregnant with a baby girl. It wasn't a cruel statement. Stephen didn't intend it to be and Anna didn't understand it as such. Still, a door closed.

It wasn't me. It was never me. It will never be me.

It hit her like a sledgehammer. The myth upon which the last two years were built. She was mistaken. As if she took the wrong bus. Or picked up someone else's drink at a party.

So there it was. It was there.

Stephen returned the questions. Anna said nothing but *Fine, fine, we're all very fine.* She wasn't going to tell him about Charles. What good would that do? She absolutely wasn't going to tell him about Polly Jean. Still, she spoke slowly in the way that she did on that first day and tried to draw the conversation out as far as it would stretch. She could hear him nodding and checking his watch over the phone. Even he knew he hadn't told her what she wanted to hear. "Anna, I need to go. I'm late for a class."

Okay, Stephen. It was an entirely deferential statement.

"But it's good to hear from you. I'm really pleased you called." And that was that.

That's that. She'd been wrong. A mistake that masqueraded as love. A self-deceit now almost two years old. It could walk and speak in full sentences. *Mine!* it hollered. It never learned to share. Anna had called Stephen. And now she knew.

He was polite, upbeat, and genuinely glad to hear from her. But he was as removed from their affair as the Atlantic Ocean is vast and two years are long. They were good for a season. But seasons change.

And now I know.

She rose from the steps and smoothed her skirt and looked around before deciding where next to go. She walked through Bellevueplatz, where in summer, the city of Zürich erected a Ferris wheel and where, during the World Cup, the city would install enormous screens and bleachers so that everyone could come together and cheer on the Swiss team. *Hopp Schwyz!* was the cheer. *Go Switzerland!* Anna walked to the middle of Quaibrücke, the bridge that spanned the Limmat from Bellevueplatz to Bürkliplatz. When she reached the middle of the bridge she turned south to face the Alps. She watched them for a minute, as if they might move. *Mountains, you mean nothing to me,* Anna thought, though she knew that wasn't true. They did mean something to her. But it wasn't anything good. *The Alps are the door I'm locked behind.* How tired she was of feeling like a prisoner. A swan paddled in circles in the water below her. His feathers were gray and matted and he was honking and snarling at his own wave-warped reflection. *Even the ugliest swan is still more beautiful than the loveliest crow on the fence,* Anna thought. And then she thought: *It is time to get off the fence.* And then with a lack of consequential concern, she took her cell phone from her pocket and tossed it in the cold, drab water. It was an impulsive act and the exact right thing to do. Anna felt lighter than she had in months. She clapped her hands back and forth in the manner of washing them clean and said to herself, *Well, that's done.*

A hook released from its eye. A door opened. An eerie, luminal shaft of light brightened the exact spot where Anna stood.

It was time to go.

"A VERB'S MOST BASIC form is its infinitive," Roland said. "It isn't finite. Its possibilities are not yet exploited. Someone, give an example of an infinitive verb . . ."

"Leben," Nancy said. *To live.*

"Versuchen," Mary said. *To try.*

"Küssen," Archie said. *To kiss.*

Every verb had a hundred likelihoods. Others were shouted out. *Fragen.* To ask. *Nehmen.* To take. *Lügen.* To lie. *Laufen.* To run. *Sein.* To be.

"Anna?" Roland looked to Anna for a word. She held a dozen in her mouth but settled on one. *Lieben.* The infinitive form of love.

For, Anna thought, *if love is not infinite or eternal? Then I want nothing of it.*

ANNA WALKED AT A casual, intentional pace. *It's time to think about the future,* she thought. *It is time to think about thinking about the future.* Anna entered the Hauptbahnhof at the concourse. On Wednesdays it became the site of an enormous farmers' market. Over fifty vendors set up stalls. Local growers, wineries, artisan cheesemakers, sausage sellers, crêpe makers, bakers—the list of merchants was long and varied. Anna tried to go every week. She bought organic olive oil and summer sausage made from highland cattle and as a usual treat she'd buy a cone of candied almonds or a *Schoggibanane*. At Christmastime, the hall was packed even more tightly with booths and stalls of seasonal foods and crafts all crushed around an enormous Christmas tree. That day the hall was empty and the stalls were gone. Everything echoed. A wind blew through. It made her cold.

And yet Anna lingered in the open emptiness comforted by the clipped, hollow complaint of her footfalls on the floor of the great, vacant room as she crossed it. She paused beneath the station's guardian angel, that strange one-ton sculpture made from god knows what that pended from the ceiling beams. *Christ, she's ugly,* Anna thought. It was installed ten years ago. Anna and the angel had lived in Switzerland for almost the same amount of time. She was pinheaded and faceless and clothed in a painted-on pushup bra and minidress. Her wings had holes in them. Her patterns were mismatched. And she was fat. Anna had read that the artist intended the angel's lusty, robust form to evoke an equally full-bodied femininity, an attitude native to women who don't give damns what others think. Modern art for modern women. Little wonder Anna couldn't stand her. Nor did she care for the installation on the other side of the room: twenty-five thousand tiny lights arranged in a tight, three-dimensional square and hanging from the ceiling. They pulsed in shifting patterns of color, design, and depth. The tiny lights dimmed, then beamed, then stalled, then strobed. The effect was hypnotic and omniscient. The way light sometimes was.

As in the night before. How the kitchen had never seemed starker underneath the overhead fluorescent bulbs. No room had ever been so bright as that, Anna decided. Nothing stayed in shadow. It was awful. The Doktor had warned this was the most usual side effect of coming into consciousness, and the Doktor had been right.

Anna watched the luminous box above her. It pinkened. It yellowed. It blanched. *Oh, Anna. A single lifetime and yet so many lies.* The lights turned blue. *I wonder which one's the worst?* Anna had never asked herself. But the answer was easy.

I've never been nearly as alone as I always say I am.

The truth was, there were people Anna could call. People she might reach out to. Her cousin Cindy, for example. As children they'd been as inseparable as sisters. Anna might have swapped her number for Stephen's in her Handy's contact list, but she didn't throw it away. It was at the house somewhere. She could find it. Nevertheless, Anna hadn't phoned her in years. And there was an aunt on the other side of the family with whom Anna had kept in moderate touch. Two years ago she passed through Zürich on a European tour and spent a weekend with the Benzes. Anna had almost forgotten that. *How did I almost forget that?* And the girls from the old neighborhood. They'd not spoken in almost two decades, but they grew up with one another and their families had been friends. An unexpected phone call to one of them would barely merit a blink. Even perhaps Anna's favorite teacher, the high school librarian who one day found Anna hiding in the stacks, Anna's rotten inner dejection attempting to consume her. She blotted Anna's tears and bought her a soda and said (Anna remembered this perfectly), *Honey, you don't ever need to feel as terrible as this,* which, in that moment, was enough. Anna had kept in touch with her through college. She came to Anna's parents' funeral. She attended Anna's wedding. It had been over a decade but she could call her, couldn't she? Of course she could. Anna could call any of these women.

But Anna's phone was at the bottom of the lake. Calling, in any case, is hardly the same as confiding in. In most ways it was easier for Anna to bear her own burden than to share it. The effort she'd need to explain it was greater than the weight of the woe she'd be confessing, she told herself. Walling herself off circumvented the risk of real closeness between two people and the eventual, unavoidable loss that always accompanies love. Liberating herself from the concern of others served a sinister purpose as well. There were fewer people to whom Anna was accountable. It's the easiest way to lie and not get caught: make yourself matter to no one.

The lights pulsed pink again, then white, whiter, whitest. Anna really was alone. She'd orchestrated it herself. But the lie of all lies was that her solitude had been inevitable. Obligatory. Foreordained. All other falsehoods were just arms of that same starfish.

The giant arrival board thwapped through a series of numbers as it updated itself. Anna looked at a station clock. In fifteen minutes she could catch a train to Dietlikon. Anna wasn't ready for that. She cut through the station to the other side.

Ten minutes after that, she crossed yet another of Zürich's seemingly endless supply of bridges and bore north. *All these goddamn bridges.* The Doktor would say they symbolized transition, a journey from one state of being into another.

Well, there it is, she said once more to herself. *What a funny thing to have believed in, love.*

But it wasn't love. It was a version of love. They are all versions of love. Ten minutes later she was at Nürenbergstrasse.

She didn't even toss Stephen's house a single glance. She was cured of that.

The last of the letters that Anna wrote but didn't send to Stephen had been short: *If it didn't mean everything, it meant nothing. If I didn't matter the most, I mattered the least.* She'd hoped it wasn't true when she wrote it. But now she knew it was. Still, she was glad she'd called, glad he'd answered. And glad that now she understood. *Yes,* Anna thought. *I understand. Heart's a muscle, not a bone. It doesn't really break.* But muscles can tear. She missed Charles with a desperation that had no name and would for as long as she lived. *The rest of my life.* And she regretted the fact of her misshapen marriage. All for what? Anna shrugged inside herself. Somehow it didn't matter. In the space of a day and in the shadow of the shell of the pretense of love Anna had reconciled herself to herself: *What's been done cannot be undone.* There was peace in that.

It was near four thirty. It had taken her an hour and a half to cross the city. She'd reach Wipkingen at about the same time as the train going toward Dietlikon.

Anna and Bruno's first fight on Swiss soil had occurred on that platform. It was a week after the move and Anna hadn't learned the trains. Bruno had asked her to meet him at Wipkingen station, but she missed the train they'd agreed she'd take. She took the next, but when she arrived Bruno was gone. She didn't have a phone. She didn't know how to get back home. So she did the only thing that could be done. She sat on a bench and wept.

When Bruno arrived an hour later—he'd gone back to Dietlikon when she hadn't shown up and returned to Wipkingen when he didn't find her there—he was furious. She tried to explain but he huffed and grunted and grabbed her by the arm and told her they were late—for what she could no longer remember—and led her out of the station wordlessly. How angry he was that day. How angry he was last night.

A heart doesn't subdivide unless it has to, she'd said glibly to Doktor Messerli once. The Doktor had no response.

What a day. Anna felt a present calm. As she neared the station she wondered how Bruno would explain her absence to Victor. *He'll tell him I'm on a trip, and then they'll go for pizza.* That was the most likely scenario. She began to miss Victor as dreadfully as she missed Charles. So many times she couldn't help but love him less. And now, finally, it shamed her. *Shame's the shadow of love*, she thought. And then she thought of Polly Jean and wondered if Stephen's other daughter would resemble her. She hadn't told him. She never would. Polly Jean would never know she had a sister.

It had been a day of revelations. Of missed connections. Of hurt feelings. Delusions. Despairs. Bad behaviors. Had she done anything that couldn't be taken back? *Oh yes. Yes, yes, yes.*

She thought about Switzerland. Where a smile will give you away as an American. Where what isn't taboo is de rigueur. Cold, efficient Switzerland. Where the women are comely and the men are well groomed and everyone wears a determined face. Switzerland. The roof of Europe. Glacier carved. Most beautiful where it is most uninhabitable. Switzerland with its twenty-six shipshape cantons. Industrious Switzerland. *Novartis. Rolex. Nestlé. Swatch.* So often was Zürich ranked as one of the world's best cities. She thought about that, then conceded that if she hadn't been so sad the last nine years she might have seen it. She wished upon Victor an attentive Swiss wife. She wished her daughter the freedom to leave, if she ever wanted to.

And then she thought again that failsafes sometimes fail. Unsinkable ships land on the ocean floor and rockets don't always survive reentry. Love is not a given. No one is promised a tomorrow. She had been wrong about every man she loved or said she loved. She'd been wrong about everything. She'd entered into her life in the middle of its story. She had confused herself with the actress who portrayed her.

And she thought about predestination. How the sum of her days added up to this. The plot of her life had already been published. Everything is foreordained. All is predetermined. *The things I do, I cannot help. Everything that will happen already has.* What had she learned about verbs? In the past and future tenses, the verb came at the end. And in the present it followed the subject. Wherever she went it tailed her. She dragged it behind like a sack of stones.

And she thought about Doktor Messerli, who, Anna was now sure, was wrong; the problem wasn't that her bucket was empty, the problem was that it was full. So full it overbrimmed. So full and so heavy. Anna wasn't strong enough to carry it. She'd have to pour it out. *I've severed the serpent, Doktor! Look what I have done!*

She thought about the woods behind her house. She thought about the hill. She thought about her bench. She thought about Karl and Archie, but her consideration was cursory. She thought about Mary. It had been less than twenty-four hours since last she'd seen her, but Anna wished she were there now. She'd never before had a girlfriend she was close enough to miss. She tried to think about Edith but didn't know what to think. She wondered what Ursula would say to the ladies in the *Frauenverein,* if anything at all. She thought about her mother and her father. So many terrible years since her father had loved her, since her mother had listened.

She thought about Bruno. Who she had loved and didn't love. But had loved. Who had loved her in return. *I was a good wife, mostly.*

And she thought about fire.

She reached the platform at Wipkingen station three minutes before the train. The day had depleted her. She was too tired to be anxious. This was new. But there was more. She had nothing left to worry about. What autonomy. It settled her. She stood at the center point of her own spiral and it was a fixed position. Anna was calm, guileless, and even-keeled. *Let this not become me,* she had prayed. But it had.

She looked to the station clock. Then, to the tracks. Then, to the tunnel. Then, she closed her eyes.

For the rest of the afternoon and well into the night, the city trains ran late.

acknowledgments

An ocean of appreciation to my first, best reader, Jessica Piazza, who wouldn't let me quit this. And to my other readers: Emily Atkinson, Lisa Billington, Janna Lusk, Laureen Maartens, Neil Ellis Orts—love and thanks. And love.

Merci vielmal to Stefan Deuchler, my chief source of all things Swiss.

Much gratitude to Gina Frangello for publishing a portion of this in *The Nervous Breakdown.*

A thousand thank-yous to the dozens of others who shepherded me through the process of writing and editing: to my colleagues in the UCR Low Residency MFA program, especially Tod Goldberg, hand-holder and ledge-talker-downer extraordinaire, and Mark Haskell Smith, my fiction spirit guide and go-to for advice; to Nick Hanna, the first person to tell me to keep writing this story; to Michelle Halsall, Diplomate Jungian Analyst and counsel-giver of the highest order; to Susana Gardner and Andrea Grant, whose ex-pat friendships saved my life; to Sivert Høyem and Madrugada, whose music I wrote this book to, and whose songs have become, in my artistic consciousness, Anna's songs; to Axel Essbaum, with whom I embarked upon the adventure of expatriation those many years ago; to Anna Tapsak, who let me grill her endlessly one evening about Swiss provincial life; and to Jill Baumgaertner, Reb Livingston, Cheryl Schneider, Jay Schulz, Louisa Spaventa, Becca Tyler, and Andrew Winer, whose friendships and encouragement I could never have managed without. Nor would I wish to.

Unflagging appreciation to Sergei Tsimberov, who facilitated the early stages of this experience and whose eagle-eye editing is in part responsible for the book you read today.

Immeasurable gratitude to my agent, Kathleen Anderson. There is no song that's fervent enough to sing out how treasured she is to me.

Colossal thanks as well to the National Endowment for the Arts. A portion of this book was written under funding of a literature fellowship. The financial support was a godsend. The creative endorsement was a grace.

Thanks of all thanks to my editor, David Ebershoff, who kept me on task and encouraged me despite my occasional frustrations and now-and-again moments of heavyheartedness. Thanks also to Denise Cronin and her entire, wonderful rights team. And to Caitlin McKenna for her comfort and assistance and to Beth Pearson for her wealth of patience. Thanks, in the end, to Random House. Everyone. How welcome you all have made me and Anna feel.

To the city of Dietlikon, which let me live inside of it for a little while—how lovely you are.

And to my husband, Alvin Peng. Who is my favorite everything.

And finally: I am not a psychoanalyst and therefore you mustn't take the words of Doktor Messerli as anything other than what they are intended to be: fiction. If you ever feel as terrible as Anna, please—I beg of you—seek help.

about the author

JILL ALEXANDER ESSBAUM is the author of several collections of poetry, including *Harlot, Necropolis,* and *The Devastation.* Her work has twice appeared in *The Best American Poetry,* as well as its sister anthology, *The Best American Erotic Poems: From 1800 to the Present.* A winner of the Bakeless Poetry Prize and recipient of two NEA literature fellowships, Essbaum is a member of the core faculty of the Low Residency MFA at the University of California, Riverside, where she teaches poetry. She lives and writes in Austin, Texas. This is her first novel.

HausfrauBook.com
@JAEssbaum

about the type

This book was set in Sabon, a typeface designed by the well-known German typographer Jan Tschichold (1902–74). Sabon's design is based upon the original letter forms of sixteenth-century French type designer Claude Garamond and was created specifically to be used for three sources: foundry type for hand composition, Linotype, and Monotype. Tschichold named his typeface for the famous Frankfurt typefounder Jacques Sabon (c. 1520–80).